Honeymoon Parish

Honeymoon Parish is available from Amazon as an e-book or a printed book.

D1737730

REVIEWS OF ROBERT HALE'S FIRST BOOK:

Jesus and His Friends

The first three reviews are from Central Presbyterian Church in Towson, Maryland.

"My favorite part is the personalization that puts me right into the Bible stories." Paul Bender

"Robert Hale invites us into the disciples' personalities and their experiences of Jesus with such humility and creativity that the lessons just sneak up on you. I found myself encouraged and challenged to think again."
Ian McFadden, Minister of Discipleship & Young Adults

"The reader will come to know these friends of Jesus through the author's authentic and thought-provoking peek into the minds of these extraordinary, and yet ordinary, followers of Christ. And that is hope for all of us." Eileen Pohlhaus

"This is a nice approach to Bible study: humanizing the apostles. Great job." Stuart McDonald, Roman Catholic, Newburgh, Indiana

■■■

"I've been enjoying reading and re-reading your book--it really makes the 'characters' come alive! It's also a great review of the backgrounds of the friends, and it's much more interesting than the textbooks on the subject."
Jo Ann Russell, former United Methodist missionary, Chanhassen, MN

Jesus and His Friends is available at Amazon as an e-book and a printed book. It is also available as an e-book from 13 other online bookstores.

Honeymoon Parish

by

Robert Hale

Robert Hale

Bud,
I hope you enjoy my novel.
It's great to get in contact
with the Lathrops.
Bob

Unless otherwise noted, all Scripture quotations are from the Revised Standard Version (RSV) of the Bible. All rights reserved under International and Pan-American conventions. Published in New York by Thomas Nelson & Sons and simultaneously in: Toronto, Canada by Thomas Nelson & Sons (Canada) Limited; and Edinburgh, Scotland by Thomas Nelson & Sons, Limited. Old Testament Section, Copyright 1952 and New Testament Section copyright 1946 both by Division of Christian Education of the National Council of the Churches of Christ in the United States of America.

Printed by CreateSpace, An Amazon.com Company

DEDICATED TO

My family, especially my wife Elaine.
Our most recent additions are great-granddaughter Georgia,
daughter of Christina and Adam,
great-granddaughter Evangeline,
daughter of Janine & Stephen Reter,
and grandson Steven's wife, Patrina.

To the United Methodist churches my wife and I
served in North Dakota:
Rolla and Dunseith, Harvey and Goodrich.
To our first church in Baltimore: St. Luke's United Methodist
and our current church: Central Presbyterian
and to all the churches and church members
we have met on the way,
especially our home church:
Wesley United Methodist in Grand Forks, ND

And to my two mentors in the faith:
Dave Knecht and Ralph Rowe,
good examples of what a pastor should be.

Preface

Thanks to Bruce Robinson and his wife, Lorraine Gordon, for scanning my typewritten novel, *Honeymoon Parish,* into the computer and for proofreading it. Thanks to both Lorraine and Bruce for all their help and encouragement.

Thanks to my wife Elaine for her laughter and constant encouragement.

Thanks to our daughter Beth for guiding me through the process of creating the book covers and sending the covers and the text of *Honeymoon Parish* to Amazon's CreateSpace and Kindle.

Thanks to the reviewers of *Jesus and His Friends* and *Honeymoon Parish* for their kind words of encouragement: Rev. John Schmidt, Rev. George Antonakos, Ian McFadden, Paul Bender, Eileen Pohlhaus, Dr. Barton Houseman, Megan Hula, Dr. Patricia Shearer, Rev. David Knecht, Stuart McDonald, Jo Ann Russell (former missionary), Rev. Keith Farnham, Beth L., Bruce Robinson, Larry & Stephanie Kraft, Todd Cunningham, Debi Brager, Janine Hale Reter, James (Tim) Bowling, and Keith Gordon. If I missed anyone, please let me know.

This book is not a theological treatise. It is basically a love story, interwoven among the funny experiences that happen in the ministry. I hope that you will enjoy the small town characters you meet.

I have bent the facts at times—remember this is a novel.

You won't find Webber, North Dakota, on a map. It is more a "state of mind." Nevertheless, Webber seems real to me. Come join me through the pages of *Honeymoon Parish.* I'll take you up to the café to meet the Coffee Gang. A free link of kielbasa (polish sausage) to all who come. Ya sure you betcha.

Robert Hale

P.S. *Honeymoon Parish* and my first book, *Jesus and His Friends,* are available from Amazon.com in two formats: as an electronic book and as a book printed on paper.

"... turn the other cheek..." Matthew 5:39 (Beck's version)

1 Sem-Antics

It was spring, and the classroom windows were open, letting in a drowsy breeze from Lake Michigan. Spring was bringing changes to Garrett Seminary, an island in the middle of Northwestern University's campus. For one thing, the legions of Northwestern girls were now parading by in their summer uniforms: light dresses, shorts, and even swimsuits. I leaned farther toward the window. What a contrast to the religious (but plain) girls in the seminary!

"David Rowe ... David Rowe!"

I spun around to see the president's dragon conferring with Professor McDonald in front of the blackboard.

"David," said the professor, "President Smith would like to see you right away."

Hastily gathering up my books, I followed the dragon out of the classroom. "Why does the president want to see me?"

She pursed her lips and uttered her favorite maxim: "All in due time."

Surely he wouldn't drag me out of class for the library book I had lost or my parking fine. No, it was probably about my fellowship.

We got on the elevator and rode up to the president's ivory office in the tower.

"Just go right in."

I hung back. The sight of the venerable patriarch bent over his desk filled me with awe. I was reluctant to enter the Holy of Holies, to be so close to this man who was so close to becoming a bishop.

"David."

I looked at the dragon with unbelieving eyes. She was actually smiling. "It's all right. He's already crucified his student for the day."

"Thanks," I said gratefully, and then tiptoed in and sank slowly into the soft leather chair.

The president hadn't looked up when I had entered, and he was continuing to write. I became more and more nervous.

"Sir, I'm sorry about that book I lost - I'll be glad to pay for it."

He looked up and shook his imposing white head.

"Is it about my parking fine?"

"No, Brother Rowe, this is not about one of your misdemeanors. No, this is a problem which may affect the destiny of this school. The trustees -"

"Yes?"

"The trustees have been hearing stories about drunken Garrett students."

"Really?"

"Not our students, of course. It's those students from the seminary across the street. They have no scruples about drinking. They go down to Chicago, imbibe alcoholic spirits freely, and request the taxi driver to 'take them to Garrett.' After he dumps them on our campus, they weave their way across the street to their seminary. Unfortunately, the trustees have heard a garbled version of it and are coming next Tuesday to investigate. And that's the danger - then they'll probably see our students running half-naked to the showers." He leaned toward me. "You're president of the student body. I want you to stop it."

"But I don't even live in the dorm."

"I've taken care of that, Brother Rowe. I've arranged for you to move in with a mature older student." He stood up, towering over me impressively. "I will not have our students endanger the future of this institution with their senseless antics."

But he was probably more worried about us torpedoing his chances of becoming a bishop.

I couldn't help but wonder if there were any drunken Garrett students who took a taxi to the other seminary....

* * *

Carrying my suitcase and some books, I crossed the grassy quadrangle to Wesley Hall, entered it, and knocked at the door of room 101. The door swung open to reveal a smile clad only in a towel. So this was the "mature older student"! He was about my height, 5 foot 9, but possibly fifty pounds heavier.

"Ron Wright?" I asked, and he nodded. "I'm Dave Rowe."

"Aha, the spy! Well, you caught me on the way to the shower."

"You better not - the trustees are coming next Tuesday."

"Then it's safe today." He pushed past me, clopped down the stairs, and streaked across the quadrangle toward the showers in Asbury Hall.

So much for me as a deterrent.

After Ron came back from the showers and got dressed, he took me around the dorm and introduced me as the "resident spy." I knew a lot of them already through student government, Ping-Pong, and classes. Some, like Ron, I hadn't seen often because they were the weekend pastors, disappearing from Friday noon until 4:00 p.m. Monday, the end of the long Garrett weekend.

"I can hardly wait until I graduate," Ron said. "I've served churches all through college and seminary. Soon I'll be out of school and down to only one job."

"You're ahead of me, Ron. I've never served a church."

"Well, it's no picnic - going to school and trying to raise a family on student pastor wages."

"You have a family?"

"Yep, prettiest little wife you ever did see and five healthy youngsters."

"Then you're way ahead of me. I don't even have a girl friend."

Ron smiled. "I'd like to take you out to see my family this weekend, but I have to stay in and crack the books."

The next day, Saturday, we studied from breakfast on. About mid-afternoon Ron threw down his pen and slammed his book shut. I jerked out of my reverie.

"We need a break. Come on."

I followed Ron next door, where he inserted a credit card and opened the door. "Just look at that - every room identical. Don't you suppose Ralph and Jim get tired of the same old thing? Let's rearrange their room for them."

Looking back, I wonder why I so readily went along with Ron's pranks. I see now that he had the makings of a great moral leader - he could make anything seem moral.

"Here, give me a hand with this chest of drawers."

Swept along by his enthusiasm, I began pushing, but the chest weighed a ton. I crouched and shoved it with my shoulder.

"Good boy," cried Ron. "A little farther, a little farther - there, that's it!"

When I straightened up I found myself in the closet. "Hey, what's this?"

"Just a little creative rearranging."

"Count me out."

"Now, David, look on this as a scientific experiment. Do you think it would be theoretically possible to get the entire contents of this room into this closet?"

"Put that way…." I turned and looked at the pairs of desks, chairs, chests, beds, and lamps. "I would say that it would be possible - providing everything was dismantled - but we don't have any tools."

"Follow me, doctor." Ron went across the hall to Professor McDonald's room and pulled out his trusty credit card.

"But should we be going into his room?"

"Oh, he said I could borrow his tools anytime."

After we walked into the professor's room, I stood there admiring his worship center on a small table. "That's very nice."

"Pretty plain, if you ask me - the old cross-Bible-candle routine. What it needs is something to liven it up. Hmmm, I've got just the thing. Wait right here."

Ron left me alone, feeling like a nervous interloper. "What if the professor comes back?"

"Don't worry." Ron reappeared and walked up to the worship center. He replaced the Bible with another book.

"*God's Little Acre*! Ron, you can't do that."

"Why not? Isn't it just a book about stewardship of the land?" Ron opened up the bottom desk drawer and took out some tools. "Come, Dr. Accessory, we have an experiment, to complete in the lab."

I followed him reluctantly, but after I had started unscrewing the furniture, I got caught up in the "experiment." And I was right - everything did fit into the closet.

"Now, wasn't that a good break?"

I had to admit that I didn't feel the least bit drowsy. We went back to our studies with renewed devotion. Every now and then Ron would start chuckling. "I can hardly wait till Ralph and Jim come back. Can you imagine the expression on their faces?"

I was afraid I could.

His anticipation and my dread kept us alert through the long weekend of studying until early Monday afternoon when, once again, Ron slammed his book shut.

"How about some Ping-Pong?"

"Sounds good."

We went over to the recreation room and got into a hot series. A moist wind, making it almost impossible for sweat to evaporate, blew off Lake Michigan. The sweat was able to rise to the surface, but it had no place to go - the air was supersaturated with humidity. After seven or nine games we swam back to our room. I worked my soggy clothes off and laid them out to dry.

"Grab a towel and let's head for the showers," Ron said, tucking a towel around his waist.

"But the trustees are coming!"

"Not till tomorrow."

Ron was already out the door, so I followed him, right across the grassy quadrangle to the bliss of the showers. Then we toweled down and started back across the quadrangle, clad only in our wet towels.

When we were about halfway across, a group of dark-suited gentlemen led by President Smith entered the quadrangle.

The trustees! A day early!

Ron quickly reached over, whipped off my towel, covered his face, and ran toward the dorm. When he grabbed my towel, his fell to the grass. I picked it up, torn for a moment between modesty and anonymity. Then I followed suit – actually, without suit.

It was difficult running blind across the grass in sandals, so I kicked them off. Fortunately, there were no trees and only one bicycle, which I leaped over. Fortunately, too, I had zeroed in on the door. I went up the steps behind Ron and into our room. As Ron was closing the door, I saw Professor McDonald standing in front of his desecrated altar. He glanced up in surprise at our bareness. Ron slammed and locked the door. As we hurriedly began to dress, we heard the noise of a group coming up the stairs.

"I think they went this way!" exclaimed President Smith. "If we hurry, we can catch them. Oh, Professor McDonald, did you see two students run by here?"

"What did they look like? How were they dressed?"

"Dressed – uh - well, they weren't."

"Hmmm, they must have gone to the second or third floor."

When the knock came, I was putting on my shoes, and Ron was still struggling into his trousers.

"David, Ronald," the president called out.

We heard Professor McDonald say, "I think the boys are deep in prayer." And we were.

"Thank goodness there's some religion left in the seminary," said the president. He knocked again. By then I had my shoes on, and Ron had slipped into his slippers on his way to the door.

"I'm sorry to break in on your devotions like this. I don't suppose you saw or heard anyone come in." President Smith turned to the trustees. "Gentlemen, these boys represent the student body at its best. Both are honor students. David Rowe is student president and doing a little undercover work for me. Ronald Wright is not only carrying a full academic load but is also serving a church on weekends. These are the true representatives of Garrett."

We hung our heads in embarrassment, which was probably misconstrued as modesty. The trustees shook our hands and beamed until President Smith gathered them up and took them away.

Professor McDonald appeared in the doorway, his blue eyes twinkling above his white beard. "Well, it looks as if the old seminary is going to remain open the next hundred years - both because of and in spite of you fellows. Hmmm, you're both wringing wet - I think you could use a shower!"

After he closed the door, Ron said, "He's an O.K. guy. I wish I hadn't laid *God's Little Acre* on him."

A few moments later there was a knock, and Professor McDonald came back into the room. "Just returning your book, Ron. Your name is on the flyleaf."

"Sorry, professor. Thanks for covering for us."

"Covering...yes, that's exactly what you needed."

Just then we heard footsteps coming up the stairs. Ralph and Jim had returned from their churches in Wisconsin. With a feeling of doom, we saw them go by our door. We had sown *God's Little Acre*, and now we were going to reap it. I waited for the sound of the key in their door.

"Empty! It's all gone!"

"Hey, Ron! Come here!"

Ron reluctantly got up from the bed and went next door, while Professor McDonald and I followed.

Ralph's voice echoed around the empty room. "Our furniture's gone. Ron, did you hear anything this weekend?"

"Well, David and I weren't here all the time. And when we were here, we were pretty busy."

"Very busy," said Professor McDonald.

"Will you guys help us look for it?" Jim took off his suit coat and opened up the closet door, disclosing the crammed closet. "What? Our furniture!"

"It's not lost, after all." I turned to Ralph.

"Rejoice!" said Ron. "There is more joy in heaven over one set of furniture that has been found than over ninety-nine sets that were never lost. Isn't that the way it goes, Dave?"

"Something like that."

Ralph looked at the jammed closet. "It'll take us hours to put it all back together!"

"Don't worry," said Professor McDonald. "I'm sure that Ron and David wouldn't mind helping you, would you, boys?"

"Not at all."

"The least we can do," I added.

"Besides," said the professor, "they need a break from their long hours of study and prayer."

The next day we had a guest speaker in chapel - a lean and likeable pastor from North Dakota, who spoke with deep feeling about the Great Plains: "How would you like to breathe clean air? How would you like to see a landscape uncluttered by the hand of man? How would you like to meet real people, uncut gems right from the Creator's hand?"

After I got back to the dorm, Professor McDonald brought the chapel speaker over to our room.

"These are the two I was telling you about: Ron Wright, the prime mover, and Dave Rowe, his assistant. Boys, meet Harold Hutton, a district superintendent (D.S.) from North Dakota."

Reverend Hutton smiled as he shook our hands. "I understand you fellows believe that cleanliness is next to godliness."

I went red, and Ron turned a couple of shades pinker.

"Yes," said Professor McDonald, "they were certainly as clean as a whistle yesterday."

Hutton's eyes twinkled. "Well, at least you boys can't be accused of being stuffed shirts."

"Or of putting up false fronts," McDonald added.

"And they have learned that most difficult spiritual lesson of all: how to turn the other cheek." Hutton, noting our embarrassment, turned his attention to Professor McDonald. "Sam, you're the scholar. Wasn't there some mention in the Bible of a man running away naked?"

"You're right, Harold." Instantly, Professor McDonald was back in the classroom. "The incident occurred when Jesus was arrested in the Garden of Gethsemane. The soldiers grabbed ahold of a young man - probably St. Mark himself - who was wearing only a linen cloth, but he slipped out of their clutches and left his covering behind." (Mark 14:51-52)

"Well, the trustees must have been as frightening as the soldiers." Hutton chuckled. "So, in a way, you two were just being biblical." Reverend Hutton threw back his head and laughed till the tears came. "I wished I could have seen President Smith and the trustees pursuing you into the dorm."

Professor McDonald joined in the laughter. "And it's amazing to think that a first century streaker went on to write a Gospel!"

"And didn't Mark also run up a pretty good track record as a missionary?"

"Yes, Harold, after one or two false starts, he finished the race as a valued helper of both Peter and Paul." (II Timothy 4:11, I Peter 5:13)

"From bare beginnings...." Hutton wiped his eyes, and then put his hands on our shoulders. "And now that I've found you two potential St. Marks, why don't you come over to North Dakota and help us?"

"A journey of a thousand miles begins with a full tank." Secretary of Transportation Evel Knievel

2 Warm Reception

"But it's so far to North Dakota," mother lamented, holding onto my arm as I sat in the car ready to depart on June 15 to my first church. "Why are you leaving all the comforts of Chicago, its great museums, its opera house, its - "

"Its pollution, its noise, its dirt. Besides we haven't gone to a museum or opera that I can remember."

"Yes, but it's nice to know that they're there." The gritty Chicago wind swirled her blue hair around the top of her faded housedress. "I wish you'd get a church in the suburbs and work your way up to becoming a bishop close to home."

Ah, mothers. "Well, it's time for me to go if I'm going to make Aunt Eleanor's by nightfall." I started the engine of my $50.00 clunker.

My father, the atypical college professor, crept out of the sanctuary of the apartment building. "Did you check the oil?" He was dressed in his summer uniform, the light plaid bathrobe and the old gray hat. Thank goodness the oven mitts, which he used as winter gloves, were in moth balls till fall.

"Dad, I just got an oil change."

"That's even more dangerous - sometimes they don't put any oil in. I knew a man once who -"

"Who burned up his engine, right?" I grinned. I had heard all the old horror stories. Shutting off the engine, I turned to dad. "I don't suppose you'd check the oil for me." Dad started backing toward the apartment, driven back by his twin fears of dirt and work. I smiled as I got out, lifted up the hood, and pulled out the dipstick. "At least let me wipe this on the bottom of your robe."

"No, no!" cried father, disappearing into the entryway.

"Mom, do you have any Kleenex?" She reached into the pocket of her red apron and pulled out a piece. I wiped the stick, stuck it back in, and pulled it out. "There, dad, its right to the top." He gave me the high sign from the entryway.

After I closed the hood and got back into the car, dad began calling out the old school-morning ritual: "Do you have your hat, your gloves, your earmuffs, your galoshes, your bus ticket?"

There was no end to the list. His voice sounded sad. I suppose it was hard enough to lose a son but probably even harder to lose a good ritual.

Mother reached in and touched my shoulder. Dad, now safely behind glass, waved from the entryway. She and I chorused good-bye at the same instant - and I was off. I waved at them, the apartment building that had been my home for nearly twenty-four years, and the elevated train that was rumbling overhead.

Twenty-four years in a box on Chicago's Northside was hardly the recommended training for a pioneer, but I was going to chance it.

And now I was leaving Chicago behind. My car was full of books and clothes, but the only thing I really valued was my cat Sylvester. In some ways I thought of him as more dog than cat. Every night in Chicago he had gone with me for a walk - without a leash - and heaven help the new cat or dog that mistakenly tried to defend its territory. Sylvester was a strong Methodist - he believed the world was his parish, and he quickly converted other animals to his point of view.

"Well, Sylvester, let's hope I made the right decision." Sylvester, at least, saw nothing wrong with the decision and was sleeping in a confident, comfortable ball on the front seat.

My only regret was that Ron couldn't sell his family on moving to North Dakota. Even though he kept leading me astray, I still liked him and hoped our paths would cross again someday.

As we crossed the border into Wisconsin, a sudden rain cascaded over my old car and washed away some of the soot and grime of the city. Then the sun came out, highlighting the lush green hills. Those conical hills and the dairies seemed to go well together. Sylvester and I rolled happily through Wisconsin and made pit stops every hundred miles or so to feed a quart of oil to my twenty-year-old engine and a saucer of milk to Sylvester. And whenever Sylvester would scratch the door, I would pull over quickly.

Crossing the state line into Minnesota with its forests and 10,000 lakes, I found myself enjoying the scenery even more. Still, I wondered if anyone had actually counted the lakes - perhaps there were only 9,999.

Though I adored Aunt Eleanor, I decided - out of my new sense of freedom - to by-pass her big home in Rochester. Sylvester and I spent the night in a roadside park and took turns swatting mosquitoes.

The next day we went around Minneapolis/St. Paul and drove and drove and drove across Minnesota, angling ever northwest. At a Minnesota information center, we asked for a North Dakota map, but they were out of them. However, we got handwritten directions to Fairmount, ND, located in the extreme southeast corner of ND. Soon after that we crossed the North Dakota border. Without waiting for a scratch at the door, I turned off the road onto an approach to a field.

"Come on, Sylvester. Come on and try North Dakota." Sylvester struggled sleepily to his feet, arched his striped back, and leisurely dismounted from the car. He had already adapted to western ways.

All around us stretched fields of waving green without obstruction - a horizon to horizon view. It was my first taste of infinity. I waded into a field of new wheat - the wind made it ripple like waves in a sea of grass. No wonder the pioneers needed schooners to cross this vast inland sea. And such a green, an emerald green, a newly-minted green. The colors out here were clean and sharp. Everything had been soot-tinged in Chicago.

Up from the ditch flew a blackbird with red and yellow chevrons on its wings. Instantly Sylvester became the primordial hunter. A larger bird flew up from the field, my eyes catching a flash of brown spots and a white ring around its neck. Sylvester went wild, running through the fields, flushing birds, and leaping high into the air. Soon the sky was filled with birds, stacked up and waiting to land, just like at O'Hare Field in Chicago.

A truck rumbled up and stopped. An old, capped head peered out. He had a beautifully lined and etched face, not like the faceless throngs of Chicago. "Havin' car trouble, young fella?"

"No, just stopped to take a look at your state."

"Where you from?"

"Chicago."

"I bin there onct, back in …" He removed his cap and thought a minute. "Back in aught 30. Where you headed?"

"Webber."

"I bin there onct, back in aught 31. Well, maybe it was aught 32."

"How do I get there?"

"Lemme git a map outa my truck." When he came back he spread a North Dakota map on my trunk. "Welcome to North Dakota." (I was to discover later that the state was often called Nort' Dakota or Nord Dakota. The Scandinavian accent slipped into everyone's speech – no matter what country they came from originally.) He continued, "Here's where you are now – just over the border on highway 11. Go about 10 miles and you'll bump into I-29. Go north on it. You'll pass Fargo, our biggest city. Keep going on 29 to the Forks."

"The forks?"

"Ya, Grand Forks. There you'll run into highway 2. Take that west for about three hours till you see a big billboard about Webber. Follow what it says."

"Thanks."

"Sure you don't need no help?"

"Yes, I'm sure. The car runs fine as long as I add a quart of oil every two hours." As he drove off, I called Sylvester by whistling a few bars of "Chicago."

Once again we started rolling across the prairie, passing Fargo, Grand Forks, and a lot of smaller towns until I spotted a big billboard: "WEBBER, turn left at next intersection." Soon I was seeing other signs for Webber: Red Owl Grocery, Olson's Hardware, First State Bank, Webber Dairy, and, nicest of all, The Churches of Webber Welcome You. We zoomed by before I could read the entire list. I caught just a glimpse of Catholic and Lutheran, but I hoped there was a Methodist Church there, too.

What would I find in Webber? Would they be "God's Frozen People," as my mother had called them, or rough frontiersmen, as my father feared? The people - would they accept a stranger? Would I find the right one for me? No, that would be too much to expect. I hadn't discovered anyone in Chicago's millions - how could I hope to do so in a town of 2,392 people? Well, I would soon find out, for ahead of me lay Webber, its three grain elevators a startling contrast to Chicago's bristling skyline. It gave me a strange feeling to think that I was going to be living in a town that contained fewer people than my Chicago neighborhood, probably fewer than the apartments in my block. Would they welcome a stranger into their midst?

No sooner had a prayer for a warm reception escaped from my lips than a cloud of steam escaped from my radiator. What a way to enter my first parish - in a car that was spewing forth like a Stanley Steamer. How embarrassing! I slowed down and looked for a gas station. There was a Mobil at the end of Main Street, just a few blocks ahead. Two ladies coming out of the Red Owl store pointed toward my steaming car. A group of kids started running behind. Even a fat man sitting in front of Olson's Hardware, lowered his newspaper and gazed after me. But this wasn't my idea of a warm reception.

I pulled into the Mobil station, followed by the gang of kids, the two ladies from the Red Owl, and the fat man. They stood around, sometimes shifting from one foot to the other, but not saying anything. I felt so embarrassed. We all waited for some service. Finally the man went over to the door and called in. "Hey, Ben, come on out here. There's a stranger here with some radiator trouble."

In the fullness of time, a slight old-timer came to the door and took a leisurely look. "Thanks, Fred." Then he went back into the station and got a hose. After he opened up the hood and unscrewed the radiator cap, he stuck the hose into the radiator and started filling it with water.

"Hey, Ben," said Fred. "The water's runnin' out on the driveway!"

Ben pulled out the hose and looked under the hood. "I see the problem now. That little hose at the bottom of the radiator is cracked." He went back into the station, shut off the water, and came back with a replacement hose for the radiator. It was only three or four inches long. "I'll fit this on and you can be on your way."

"I'm not going anywhere. This is my destination - I'm the new Methodist preacher."

A smile lit up Ben's weather-beaten face. "I should have known it was you, Rev'rend Rowe. I was setting there at Conference when your name was read. I'm Ben Graves, chairman of our Official Board." He reached over a scrawny hand that turned out to be all steel cable and vise-grip pliers. I hastily pulled away my mangled hand and massaged it behind my back. And to think I'd have to shake hands with a congregation of these westerners every Sunday!

"Soon's I git this on we'll take a look at the church and parsonage." I watched him reach in and work next to the steaming radiator and hot engine. Every now and then he would pull back and wave his hand in pain, but he kept on.

"Why don't you wait till it cools down, Mr. Graves? I'm in no rush."

"That's alright, Rev'rend. Almost done."

It was then I realized that my new title had only two syllables. Later I would be surprised by some people uttering just one syllable, Rev.

Ben straightened up and wiped his hands on an oily rag. "That should hold you, Rev'rend."

"Mr. Graves, please call me David."

"You can call me Ben, but it ain't fittin' for me to call you David, Rev'rend."

I followed him back into the station, anxious to learn the size of the bill. The station was good-sized and filled with several rows of counters with auto and truck supplies and work clothes. It even had enough space for a new Ford on display. Ben went up to a counter and started punching the keys of the prototype of adding machines. Finally, he pulled the squeaky lever and tore off the tape. I held my breath.

"That'll be $1.53 with the tax."

I could hardly believe my ears. Maybe I would be able to survive on my salary of $3800.00 a year.

"Hey, Sven," Ben called out to a pair of feet sticking out from under an old Chevy, "watch the pumps for awhile. I'm goin' over to the church with the new Rev'rend."

Ben opened the door to my car. "Well, now, I see you gotta passenger. Cat, do you mind if I join you?" Sylvester slept on, unmindful that his rear quarters were being slid across the seat. "Now, Rev'rend, go back down Main Street, and I'll tell you where to turn."

We went past two blocks of buildings, including the fire station and the hotel. "That's the best hotel in town. Of course, that's the only hotel in town." Ben chuckled. "Now turn left, just after the dairy." My old car swept majestically past two milk trucks. "Now slow up. There she is."

To my left was a beautiful new brick church. I could hardly believe my luck.

"Nope, not that one - the one on the other corner."

I glanced over at a small white frame church. It looked like a million others. My first appointment was a disappointment.

I got reluctantly out of the car and walked toward the church, when suddenly my attention was caught by an outdoor bulletin board which proclaimed: WEBBER UNITED METHODIST CHURCH, REV. DAVID ROWE, PASTOR. I stood in front of it, the realization of a dream that had started in high school and stayed with me through four years of college and three years of seminary. Even if it wasn't a mighty cathedral, it was still My First Church.

"Um, sorry to bother you, Rev'rend, but would you like to see the inside?"

"What? Oh, yes. Come on, Sylvester." We all started up the church steps. When Ben opened the door, a delightful odor of cedar surrounded us. It was too much for Sylvester, however. He turned tail and ran back to the only home he knew, the old car.

Ben and I walked into the church. "It smells just like mother's cedar chest."

Ben laughed. "It always takes newcomers by su'prise. It is cedar. See, the wainscoting and even the altar and pulpit is cedar."

I gazed around my little church. The colors of the cedar and its rich resinous aroma blended with the brass altar ware and the rainbow light from the stained glass windows in a delightful harmony of the senses.

"Ben, this is really lovely."

"Thought you'd like it." Ben looked very pleased. "I had a hand in fixin' it up about eight years ago."

"It's even better than I had imagined."

"Rev rend, did you ever hear how this church got started?"

"No, Ben."

He lowered himself onto a dark oak pew. "It was started by Brother Berdahl, the walking circuit rider. Brother Berdahl was too poor to own a horse, so he usta walk all over this territory and he usta say, 'When I raise a smell to heaven, the Lord calls down: "Time to stop and wash your socks and start another church."' So, you see, the cedar not only adds to the beauty, it also -"

"Covers up any lingering smell from his socks."

"You're quick on the uptake, Rev'rend." A grin flashed like lightning in his tanned face.

Ben led me through the rest of the church. At the back of the sanctuary were three large sliding doors, which could be opened up for an overflow crowd. According to Ben, the last such crowd had been in for the mayor's funeral twenty years ago. Behind the doors was a Sunday school room with colorful pictures, a model of the Jewish Temple in the midst of other handicrafts, and a small worship center. Someone had poured a lot of time and love into this room.

"My wife Birdie teaches the first and second graders here," Ben said proudly. Then he directed me into the entryway and down a narrow flight of stairs to the basement.

We came out into a large dining room, which was paneled in knotty pine. "I think I recognize some more of your handiwork, Ben."

"Oh, I did swing the hammer a few times."

The basement also had a kitchen, a furnace room with a monster furnace, and a rest room. "We're a little crowded. We have to use all the rooms for Sunday school, except for the bathroom, of course. Well, that's it. Would you like to see the parsonage?"

"Sure."

Ben led me out the side door and around the front of the church over to a large white frame house almost as large as the church. I turned and whistled for Sylvester, who shot out of the car window and raced down the sidewalk right to my feet.

"That's quite a cat you got there."

"Shh, he thinks he's a dog."

"O.K., Rev'rend and Rover, let's go inside. Uffda!" (I was to hear that Norwegian word often in my stay at Webber. Uffda, I found out later, was an all-purpose interjection.) "There's one thing I better tell you first. Just turn around kinda casual-like. You see that house across the street? Now turn back. That's Mrs. Larson's." I thought I saw someone peeping through the curtains. "You'll find that she keeps a weather eye on the parsonage. If she bugs you too much, lemme know and I'll talk to her. She's really a purty nice ol' lady but her nosiness may've driven the former pastor off the deep end."

Ben pushed open the unlocked door - people never locked their doors in Webber - and we entered the parsonage, our footsteps scuffing across an old rug and worn linoleum as we made our way into the kitchen.

"The floor seems sort of shaky, Ben."

"Don't worry about the parsonage floors, Rev'rend - they're as sound as a dollar."

I glanced over at Ben. Surprising - I thought I was quite a bit taller than he was, but now we seemed to be eye-to-eye. In fact, he seemed to be getting taller by the second - until he went clear out of sight. I fell into blackness, my feet striking small, shifting objects. Gravel? No, coal, and soft coal at that. Thank goodness - anthracite might have killed me! I recalled a guy who was thrown out of heaven and landed on a coal pile. Was this part of my warm reception?

"Rev'rend, you alright?"

I looked up and saw Sylvester and Ben peering down at me through the hole in the floor. Sylvester was giving his worried meow, wondering where his meal ticket had gone.

"I'm O.K., Ben. I seemed to have landed in the coalbin."

"Be right down, Rev'rend." I heard quick footsteps on the basement stairs and then a light flashed on. The door to the coalbin swung open, and I saw Ben's worried face. Sylvester leaped up to the top of the boards which blocked the lower part of the doorway, laid a tentative paw on the loose coal, and decided to return to the security of the concrete floor.

I clambered over the shifting terrain and tried to squeeze out of the opening above the boards. Ben helped me out. He was quite strong for his age and height. I noted that I was once again quite a bit taller than Ben.

"Ben, I thought you said the floor was as sound as a dollar."

He took off his gray cap and scratched his gray head. "Well, I guess the dollar's shakier than I thought. I'm really sorry, Rev'rend. Are you hurt?"

"Not a bit. The coal broke my fall."

"Thank the Lord!" Ben said before sticking his head into the coalbin. "Uh-huh, I see the trouble - that last load of coal musta knocked the support out from under the floor joist. Rev'rend, I'm gonna go git some help to put the support back."

"I'll be glad to give you a hand, Ben."

"Sure you don't mind - it's dirty work."

"Not at all. Besides, I'm already dirty."

"That you are."

Ben rounded up a couple of old shovels and we crawled into the coalbin. He was right - it was a messy job. We had to shovel the coal away in order to stand the floor jack on solid cement. Then Ben turned the jack down a little, and we started to raise it up under the break in the joist.

"Wait a minute, Rev'rend. First I gotta put this metal collar around that break."

Ben fit a U-shaped piece of metal around one of the broken ends of the joist. Together we raised the jack under it until the collar slipped around the other broken end, and the joist was once again parallel to the floor.

"That'll do for now, but I'll git a crew down here to make a permanent fix and patch the kitchen floor. Now I'm gonna give the rest of the floor a check before we go back up. Otherwise both of us could come down purty fast."

I wandered around the basement while Ben checked the floor – actually the basement ceiling. Sylvester loved to explore - was as curious as a cat. Knocking down cobwebs, we made our way around the big coal furnace which dominated the basement. I took an informal inventory of the clutter: three bald tires, a set of galvanized washtubs next to a wringer-type washing machine, a bunch of old tools, some dusty Mason jars, a worn broom, a hot water heater, two broken chairs, four clotheslines (one broken), and some other junk.

Every now and then we heard Ben tapping the ceiling and muttering. Finally he came over to us. "That's the only bad spot, Rev'rend. The rest of the ceiling looks O.K. to me, but I'll check it again when we fix it. Meanwhile, better stay away from the hole."

We went upstairs to the empty first floor and by-passed the hole in the kitchen floor. Ben pointed out the study, just off the dining room. Then he led me back through the living room and up the steps to the second floor, where he showed me the bathroom and all the bedrooms.

"You got plenty of room for your family." His voice echoed through the empty rooms "When'll they be along?"

"Ben, I'll have to get married first."

"Well, ain't that the way - a single preacher assigned to a parsonage with five bedrooms! Then when you do git a family, the bishop will prob'ly put you in a matchbox. That's the system, Rev'rend. That's the system."

I absorbed his sagebrush counsel - then thought back to my tour of the church. "Ben, you said that you're short of Sunday school space. Why don't you use the parsonage? I won't need all these rooms."

"Good idea, Rev'rend. Say, when'll your movin' truck be comin'?"

"Fooled you again, Ben. My car contains all I own."

"Well, now, I better pass the word that you'll be needin' a few things. Meanwhile, why dontcha stay up to my place till you git some furniture?"

"Thanks, Ben, but Sylvester and I can camp out here. I've got an air mattress and a sleeping bag."

"Suit yourself . . . but lemme give you a hand movin' in. Then you can come up to my place for supper."

"Thank you, Ben. The D.S. was right."

"What about, Rev'rend?"

"That Dakotans are 'uncut gems right from the Creator's hand.'"

"He was prob'ly tryin' to say that we got rough edges."

"Honeymoon Period: the period between the appointment and the disappointment." (from Bishop Shears' *Dictionary of Liturgical Terms*)

3 Honeymoon Period

"So nice of you to come and take potluck with us, Rev'ren'." Mrs. Graves beamed at me out of her pleasantly pink face.

I looked at the table laden with our leftovers: roast beef, baked potatoes, peas, creamed corn, homemade rolls, gravy, and pie. "I would hardly call that potluck."

She glowed. "Another slice of mincemeat pie, Rev'ren'?"

"Well, maybe just a sliver."

Ben snorted. "Do you realize how much rum Birdie puts into her mincemeat? If you keep this up, Rev'rend, you'll have to tear up your temperance pledge."

"Don't report me to the bishop, Ben." I leaned back with a sigh of contentment. "This is a welcome change from truck stops."

"Here's your pie, and I'll pack a lunch for you and some scraps for your 'dog.' Do you have sumpthin' to eat off of?"

"No, ma'am."

"Well, then I'll fix you up with the fixings."

Thus began my honeymoon, which lasted until my wedding. I walked away from the orgy with a quart of country cream, a picnic basket of leftovers, and a box filled with kitchen utensils, dishes, and silverware.

Sylvester scolded me for being out so late, but he relented when he smelled the roast beef. I dug through the box and pulled out a dish. "I christen this Sylvester's dish." Into it went a meaty bone. Sylvester accepted the peace offering eagerly.

"Now, Sylvester, I'm going to leave the back door open for you. Good night." The ungrateful creature never even looked up from his bone.

I turned out the kitchen light, walked across the dining room, cut through my strange diagonal front hallway, and bounded up the circular stairway and into the master bedroom. This was distinguished from the other four by the presence of my sleeping bag and my stereo.

Lights were burning across the street at Mrs. Larson's; I could see her still at her post. She might be "The Eye That Never Sleeps," but I wasn't. I was tired out from the long trip, the excitement of coming to

Webber, and the big meal at Ben and Birdie's. Making a quick job of it, I was soon stretched out on top of my sleeping bag, on top of my air mattress, on top of the bare floor.

For awhile I thought of the friendly trucker, my warm reception, and Ben and Birdie's hospitality ... but I couldn't go to sleep. It was too quiet. I was used to the elevated train going by my bedroom window every few minutes. Finally I got up and put a demonstration record on my stereo. The soothing sounds of Niagara Falls, a jet take off, and an express train soon put me to sleep. I don't know what Mrs. Larson thought - if her ears were as good as her eyes.

The next morning when I went down to the kitchen, there were three cats gnawing on the bone. Sylvester was lying near the back door and watching his guests. "Sylvester, what's come over you? Are you becoming a pacifist in your old age? No, I guess you just miss your friends. Well, that'll teach me to leave the door open. Go on, cats. Scram!" The three visitors departed, and I closed the door. "We can't feed the whole neighborhood, Sylvester."

I went over to the counter and started looking through the picnic basket. "You know, a piece of mincemeat pie looks awfully good. That should give me my Minimum Daily Requirement of sugar." I cut a slice and carried it into the empty front room. Whew, the room was hot and stuffy. I was surprised that North Dakota got so hot. Going to the front window, I tried to raise it, but blocking the way of any fresh air was a storm window. A storm window in June! I'd soon rectify that.

I set my piece of pie on the newel post and went outside. Getting as close to the window as the window box would allow, I tried turning the four butterfly catches that held on the storm window but they were painted fast. This called for the heavy artillery. I went to the Buick, opened the trunk, and hunted through my tool chest for a hammer. Thus armed, I went back to the window and soon loosened the unwilling catches, but the window still resisted my attempts to remove it. As I was going back to the trunk to get two screwdrivers, whom should I meet flying across the street but Mrs. Larson?

"Don't take it off."

"The Eye That Never Sleeps" had now turned into "The Nose That Never Stops Prying." I felt a wave of anger. "Why not? It's summer, you know." She couldn't answer because she was still puffing from her sprint. "I'm hot, and I want to get some cross-ventilation," I said crossly.

As I worked at the window edges with the screwdrivers, I noticed her lurking at the limits of my vision. Finally, she gave up and went home. Good. Now I could get some work done.

I had a busy morning taking off all the blue-edged storm windows and replacing them with screens. Then I went back inside and opened up all the windows. I rescued my pie from the newel post and sat on the floor right under the front window. The breeze felt good, but the pie tasted even better.

A car went whizzing by, crunching on the gravel. So did another. And then the sandstorm came right through the window, half into my eyes and the other half into my pie. And I had thought that F.D.R. had ended the Dust Bowl.

Setting the pie down, I went into action, first slamming all the inner windows shut. Then I compromised with myself - I put storm windows only on the living room and my bedroom windows.

When I came back inside, I dumped what was left of the pie into the garbage and went and stood near the telephone. Should I call Mrs. Larson or not? Well, no use having false pride. I picked up the phone and asked the operator to ring Mrs. Larson.

"Which one?"

"Er, the one that lives across from the Methodist parsonage."

"That's Hannah Larson, Rev'rend, and welcome to Webber."

"Thank you, operator."

"The name's Tillie, Tillie Engstrom. Anything I can do, just call."

"Why, thank you, Mrs. Engstrom."

"Miss."

"I'm sorry, Miss Engstrom. Could you tell me how to get a phone book?"

"Tell you what, Rev'rend. I'll bring you one when I get off of work. Now I'll ring Hannah for you. Bye."

"Good-bye."

"Hello, hello?" Mrs. Larson came on the line. "Who said 'good-bye'?"

"He was sayin' good-bye to me," said Tillie, "not to you."

"Well, git off the line, Tillie. If there's anything' I can't stand, it's a snoop. Hello, anyone there?"

"Yes, it's me, David Rowe. I'm sorry I snapped at you, Mrs. Larson. You were right - the dust was terrible."

"That's alright, Rev'ren'. You young folks has got to learn things for yourselfs. Say, why don'tcha come over for a little lunch?"

"That's awfully kind of you."

"In fact," said a familiar voice, "that's the first kind thing she ever done."

"Get off of the line this minute, Tillie Engstrom, or I'll tell your boss."

"You just told him - he's listenin', too."

After I heard the sound of a phone crashing into its cradle, I hung up, also. I wondered what the Russian who invented the phone would have thought of that conversation.

I went upstairs, took off my sweaty clothes, washed, and put on a flowered shirt and some blue slacks. Sylvester followed me across the street. Mrs. Larson, of course, opened the door before we knocked.

"You keep that cat away from my song birds. I'm still a purty good shot with a BB gun." Her exterior was rough, but I had a suspicion that inside she was melted butter, just like my gramma.

"And I'll bet you're a dead-eye. All you have to do is point the gun at him, and he'll take off."

"Humph, why don'tcha come out to the kitchen?" We walked out into a large old-fashioned kitchen with a wood-burning stove. "I could use some muscle. Ain't made a big meal since Elmer died - that'll be nineteen years next March."

"I'm sorry to hear that."

She gave me a quick look. "I guess you really mean that."

"Yes, it must be lonely for you."

"You're right there, Rev'ren'. There's not much to do except look out the winder. What else can a body do when they's eighty-five and in good health?"

"And have good vision."

She laughed. "Oh, the Lord has blessed me with good eyes alright. I don't miss much that goes on within eyeshot. Say, what was that infernal racket I heard last night?"

I reddened. "I couldn't sleep, so I. ..."

"Ya, ya?"

"I put on a loud record."

"And that helped you sleep?" Her hands stopped putting flour into a brown bag, and she looked up.

"Well, you see, back in Chicago the elevated train goes right by our apartment, so I'm used to noise all night long."

"I hope you git used to the quiet here in Webber, so we both can git some sleep."

"I hope so."

"Now I need you to stir this cake." She handed me an egg beater. "Then you can whip some cream, and after lunch I'll git out the ice cream churn."

"It's going to be hard work eating at your house."

"Don't worry, Rev'ren' - it'll keep you slender." She put some pieces of chicken in a bag, shook them around in the flour, and put them on to fry. They sizzled in the big pan.

"It's so nice to have a man to talk to, specially a big handsome man."

"Until you said that, I thought you had good vision."

"And modest, too. That's unusual in a preacher. Most of 'em got such big egos that it's hard for 'em to git through the door of the church. Now you take the preacher that just left - he was downright stuck-up - wouldn't say two words to me on the street and never come over here."

I looked up from the chocolate cake I was stirring. "Is that enough?"

"No, better mix it some more." She turned the pieces of chicken over with a big fork and glanced back at me. "I can see with half an eye that you ain't even thirty yet - even with that gray hair."

"No, ma'am. I'm only twenty-four."

"A child! When I was twenty-four, things was different then … horses and carriages and sleighs in the winter … all tied to hitchin' posts in front of the church. None of them short skirts, neither. A lady never even showed her ankle - and that was quite a trick gettin' down from them wagons."

I was thinking that there was nothing theologically wrong with a good ankle.

"All corseted and straight-laced and proper we was…"

I didn't tell her that my great-great-grandmother had campaigned successfully against the wasp-waisted corset through the pages of *Godey's Lady's Book*. Her liberation of women had not gone unnoticed.

"There - that's enough mixin'. Now pour it into this pan. You can lick the bowl. I remember my boys always loved to lick the bowl." She grabbed the pan and stuck it into the oven.

"Where are your boys now?"

"They was both killed in the War."

"World War II?"

"No, the First War."

"You really are alone then." I put a chocolaty hand on her bony shoulder. She pulled a crumpled handkerchief out of her apron pocket and turned away. The kitchen was quiet except for the sizzling of the chicken and an occasional snap from the wood-burning stove.

Suddenly she came to. "My goodness, the chicken'll burn!" She moved quickly, shifted the pan to a cooler part of the stove, and turned the crisp pieces over. "Now we'll keep that warm while I heat up some veggies for you. What do you like, Rev'ren'?"

"Do you have any creamed corn or beets?"

"Think I do. Lemme take a look in the pantry." She walked past me. "You don't even dress lika parson. That's a right purty shirt." In a few moments she came back. "You're in luck, got 'em both."

"Here, let me open them for you." I took the cans from her.

"Oh, it's nice to have a man around the house."

She gave me a look that would have been coquettish if she hadn't looked like Billy Goat Gruff.

"Are you married, Rev'ren'?"

"No," I said, concentrating on turning the can opener.

"Well, I predict you soon will be."

"Umm." I didn't think so.

"Your parents livin'?"

"Yes, they live in Chicago." I almost had the first can open.

"What's your paw do?"

"Dad teaches Latin and Greek at Northwestern University. Here's the corn."

"Fine." She took it, poured it into an old bent saucepan, and put it on the stove.

"Got any brothers and sisters?"

"Just an older brother." I started on the can of beets. "He's way up there in the Internal Revenue Service. He makes a lot of money, and he'll probably take a big bite out of what little I earn."

"That's only scriptural, Rev'ren'. 'For to him who has will more be given; and from him who has not, even what he has will be taken away.'" (Mark 4:25)

She was alert, and I was getting to like her very much. "Well, here are the beets."

She grabbed the can from me and dumped it into another old saucepan. We waited till the beets and corn were ready. "O.K., let's go into the dinin' room." She carried in the pans and set them down on trivets on the dining room table. Everything else seemed to be there already, so we sat down.

"Rev'ren', will you please say grace?"

"Certainly ... O God, I thank you for my new church and for the wonderful people in it like Mrs. Larson. Bless this food that we will share together. Amen."

"Thanks, Rev'ren'." She gulped. "Help yourself to some chicken and the veggies you picked. Reach into that basket for some bread - I apologize for it. Made it yesterday, but I hope it ain't too dried out."

I helped myself and started munching. "Um, good homemade bread."

"Thanks, Rev'ren'. This your first church?"

"Yes, it seems as if I've been in school all my life."

She began nibbling a wing. "All a person usta need was The Call – schooling didn't matter. Oh, we had some real dummies then. Why, I can remember a boy from up north of town. One day he gits up at prayer meetin' and prays, 'Thank You, Lord, for makin' me ignerant. If You can do it, make me more igneranter.'" Her eyes twinkled. "His prayers was answered."

"You've got a good memory."

"And enough imagination to fill in the cracks." She took a spoonful of corn. "I think maybe this seminary business makes sense - specially when we gotta set and listen to a preacher Sunday after Sunday. I hate hearin' every thought they ever had about sixty times."

"Seminary was a good experience, and the best part was clinical training."

"What's that? Sounds awful medical."

I smiled. "Yes. In fact, it was conducted in a hospital. We learned how to understand illness and health, both physical and mental."

"Did it teach you how to git along with old bats like me?"

I got up from the table and kissed her wrinkled brow.

She spun away and dabbed at her eyes with her apron. "My Land of Goshen, you didn't learn that out of no book. I don't know yet whether you got The Call, but you sure got A Way With Women."

Unfortunately, I thought, only those under six and over sixty. Women my age terrified me. "Thank you, mother."

"Uffda, there you go again - I'm old enough to be your grandmother, and you know it. Maybe even your great-grandmother." She held her apron up to her face. "Rev'ren', I seen you settin' on the floor. Why don'tcha take that chair over there?"

I looked at the graceful polished wood of a Hepplewhite and the lovely needlepoint seat she must have made. "Why that's a priceless antique--like you."

"Eyewash!" But she went for her apron again. "Away with you, Rev'ren'."

I smiled as I walked over and picked up the chair. "Thanks for the meal and this lovely old chair - and don't forget your cake in the oven."

"My cake!" She jumped up and scooted into the kitchen. I heard the sound of the oven door dropping open. "Thank goodness, it ain't burnt." I walked to the kitchen door and saw her pull a straw out of the broom and stick it into the cake. "Double lucky, it's done. Why dont'cha stay for some cake and ice cream?"

"Thanks, Hannah, but I'm too full. Let me take a rain check."

"O.K., Rev'ren', you know your capacity, but I can't eat this cake all by myself. I'll frost it and bring most of it over to you."

She walked me to the door. "Rev'ren', I ain't sayin' I'll stop watchin' the parsonage, but I'll tell you this - my lips is sealed."

I smiled at her as I carried the chair out the door.

"And if you can think of something for an old battle axe to do, lemme know."

"I will, gramma dear."

The last I saw of her she was making another dive for her apron.

I crossed the gravel street and went into the parsonage. "Sylvester, I'm home." He came out of the kitchen. "Look what we got, our first piece of furniture." Sylvester gave it a thorough sniffing before I whisked it out from under his nose. "This goes upstairs, kit."

When I got upstairs, I put the chair right in front of the window and moved the curtain back. I didn't want Hannah to get eyestrain. I sat in the chair and waved at her. She started guiltily but soon recovered and waved back. Better to be under surveillance by a friend than an enemy.

The phone pulled me out of my new chair. As I ran down the steps, I met Sylvester coming up. He flattened himself against the outside, which left the narrow inside steps for me. Somehow I kept my balance. Next time, I resolved to walk. No phone is worth a broken neck.

"Hello."

"Hello, Reverend Rowe. This is Mrs. Grundy. Could you come over to my house for supper?"

Food again! "Why, I suppose so, but don't go to any trouble. I just had a big lunch at Mrs. Larson's."

"You don't mean Hannah Larson's?"

"Ya, ya, he does," said the familiar and ever-present voice.

"Good afternoon, Tillie," said Mrs. Grundy.

"Hello again, Miss Engstrom. I trust you've had an interesting day."

"Business bin perking up ever since you hit town, Rev'rend."

"Now, Tillie, remember 'silence is golden.'"

"Ya, ya, Teacher." Tillie sounded like a little girl as she temporarily left the airways.

"Sometimes I regret that I taught that child to talk," Mrs. Grundy sighed. "Reverend, please come over any time after five o'clock. I'll fix a Spartan repast."

"What's your address, Mrs. Grundy?"

"Oh, we don't have house numbers in Webber, but I'll tell you how to get here: Walk out of your house, turn right, go to the corner, cross the street, turn right again, and walk along until you find a house that's squeegycattywampus. Good-bye, Reverend."

"Wait, Mrs. Grundy ..." But I was talking to a dead line - without even Tillie on the other end. How could I find a house that was 'squeegy something'?

Five o'clock found me trying to follow the mysterious directions (sort of a treasure hunt for my next meal), and then I saw a house that looked, that looked, well, 'squeegy'. The house was all odd angles, with the top wider than the bottom. I followed the path that led up to the front, but it ended at a window, rather than a door. Looking for a door, I made a complete circuit of the house. No doors. A face peered out of a window. Then the window swung open.

"Come on in, Reverend."

"Your house - I've never seen a place like it. It fits your description."

She laughed. "Squeegycattywampus. Yes, it's The House That Jack Built all right. My late husband Jack used to say, 'Why build a house that looks like everyone else's?' So he didn't."

"No, he certainly didn't." Mrs. Grundy was almost as remarkable looking as the house. She looked like the Great Earth Mother, big and round and loving. I knew that she must be a good cook. You've never seen a good cook that was skinny, have you? Well, Mrs. Grundy looked like a very good cook.

I stepped through the window into a museum. The walls and mantel were covered with the pictures and plaques and school papers she had saved over the years. "May I take a look around?" I asked.

"Yes, Reverend. Go right ahead while I finish making the meal." She waddled out to the kitchen. Maybe the greatest cook I had ever seen!

I began wandering around the room and looking at the plaques and pictures: first graduate of Webber High School, first woman graduate of Dakota Wesleyan University, and many pictures of the classes she had taught in Webber from the one-room school up to the new consolidated school. What especially caught my eye was her retirement ceremony. There she was in a large cap and gown standing at the podium and, according to the *Webber Wolfcall*, "… surrounded by a constellation of former pupils including Governor Gunderson, Justice Rolvaag, Senator Langer, and scores of luminaries from the worlds of commerce, letters and the professions."

"Congratulations, Mrs. Grundy." I raised my voice so she could hear in the kitchen. "You certainly had a marvelous career in teaching."

"Forty-three wonderful years."

I went to her bookcase, drawn by the leather edition of the *Harvard Classics*. I opened up the first volume. There, written in a vigorous hand, was the following: "Dear Teacher, I remember how you used to scrimp to buy books - wasn't the book budget for the entire year $10.00? Here at last are great books for a great teacher. I would not be governor if I had not first been your fortunate pupil. Deepest affection and highest regard, Sigurd (Sig) Gunderson (the bad boy in the back row)."

"That's quite a gift from the governor."

"Thank you, Reverend. Feel free to borrow them anytime. There's no public library in Webber, you know."

No library in Webber - an idea began to grow in my brain.

And then I noticed a slender volume just below the Classics, *The Other Wise Man* by Henry van Dyke. When Mrs. Grundy cruised slowly through the door like the largest ship capable of going through the Panama Canal, she saw me reading the little book.

"I used to win declamation prizes with the story of *The Other Wise Man.*"

Another idea hit me. "How about giving that at our Christmas Eve service?"

"Why, thank you, Reverend. I'll try, though I haven't done it for years. The snack is ready now, if you'll follow me."

She had a wider turning circle than my eighteen-foot car.

As I followed her, I felt like a high school quarterback behind the entire Notre Dame line. She beckoned me to make a wide end run, so I swept around her right flank to see the 'snack' or 'Spartan repast,' as she had earlier called it. The dining room table was spread with a feast like Thanksgiving dinner. I wondered what she would call a large meal.

"Will you please carve the turkey, Reverend?"

"Why, uh, I'll try." And try is what I did, both to cut and eat. I should have cut and run.

During the meal she told me a lot about Webber's history. At one point Mrs. Grundy set down the turkey leg she had eaten to the bone. "I don't suppose you've heard the story of Elizabeth Harding yet."

"No, I haven't," I mumbled through a mouthful of sweet potatoes.

"Elizabeth Harding was a lady-in-waiting to Queen Victoria. She was a very proper English girl leading a sheltered life at court until Buffalo Bill's Wild West Show came to London. Queen Victoria was still in mourning for her deceased husband, Prince Albert and forbade any of the court to attend 'the American spectacle,' as she called it. But you know young girls. Elizabeth and a few others sneaked away to the show. They were fascinated by the marksmanship of Buffalo Bill and the mock battle with the Indians, but the person that impressed Elizabeth the most was a tough young broncobuster from North Dakota. Dressed in buckskins, he was a thrilling contrast to the stuffed shirts Elizabeth had always known - may I pass you more of anything, Reverend?"

"Maybe less." I clutched my distended stomach.

"Just picture that broncobuster dropping onto the back of a keg of dynamite that exploded into kicks and hops and stiff-legged jumps. That horse was a real matchmaker, for it deposited the young Dakotan right in

Elizabeth's lap. The horse accomplished in five seconds what would have taken an Act of Parliament and a three-year English courtship."

"Well said."

She smiled. "The broncobuster seemed to find Elizabeth's lap a much softer place than the back of the rampaging horse, and he was in no hurry to dismount. Finally he drawled, 'Howdy, ma'am, my handle's Dakota Brown. What's yourn?'

"Elizabeth didn't reply. I don't know whether it was the language barrier, the cultural shock of meeting an American face-to-face, or something as simple as having the air knocked out of her. Or you might even say that Cupid, disguised with war paint and feathers, had shot an arrow through her defenses.

"Elizabeth never missed a show during Buffalo Bill's stay in London. Her young hero outrode himself under her adoring eyes, sticking closer to the horse than a saddle burr. Between performances, he stuck even closer to her. When the Wild West Show returned to America, Elizabeth came with it as Mrs. Dakota Brown. Her husband left the show in New York. The newlyweds rode across the country on the train to Devils Lake and then by open sleigh through a blizzard to Webber. Quite a change from Buckingham Palace to a sod house!"

"I'll say, but did the marriage last?"

"Almost fifty-two years. Mother died in '35 and father in '37.

"No wonder you're such a remarkable lady."

"Just a plain old country schoolteacher."

"Who happens to have taught the governor, a senator or two, and a couple of dozen members of Who's Who."

"Yes, teaching had its rewards, but not in money. Do you know how much we were paid back in the Depression?"

"A thousand a year?"

"Fourteen dollars a month, and that was only for the nine school months."

"How did you live?"

"All of us were in the same boat." A dark shadow crossed her placid features. "We … managed."

And in those brave words I saw poverty, hunger, freezing, and starving. No wonder she had gone hog wild.

"Thank you, Mrs. Grundy, for the greatest eating experience of my life and for your delightful stories. I can hardly wait until Christmas so I can hear you tell the story of *The Other Wise Man*. Now I better be getting back to the parsonage. Sylvester has been cooped up for five hours."

"My goodness, it's almost ten o'clock. You're a good listener, Reverend."

"You're easy to listen to."

"Come back anytime that you want either food or stories. But first let me pack you a lunch for tomorrow." She got up from the table and went out into the kitchen. Returning with a wooden box full of jars, she went to work filling them with cranberry sauce, turkey, mashed potatoes, escalloped corn, sweet potatoes, lima beans, and gravy. I figured it would last Sylvester and me about a week, providing we had no other invitations. Maybe we could feed all the cats in the neighborhood.

When I got home, I didn't wait for Sylvester to start scolding. I lowered the box into sniffing range. That emptied his mind of "cat-tankerousness." Still, first needs first. Sylvester had to go outside before having his Thanksgiving dinner.

The phone rang. "Rev'rend, this's Ben. Been trying to git you all day."

"Sorry, Ben - I've been over at Mrs. Larson's and Mrs. Grundy's."

"Not Hannah Larson's?"

"Yes."

"She ain't had no one in her house since her husband died 'bout twenty years ago. Rev'rend, you're a marvel! And I'm glad you got to meet Mrs. Grundy - she's the closest thing we got to a saint around here."

"She is a dear old soul but, to tell you the truth, I preferred Hannah Larson." After I said it, I hoped Tillie wasn't listening in.

"Now that's right su'prisin'. Maybe I'm gonna have to drop by and see her - now that she appears to be receivin' company. Rev'rend, tell you why I called. I'd like to take you up and down Main Street tomorrow and interduce you to the store owners and such like. How'd you like to do that?"

After a moment's hesitation I agreed, although all I really wanted to do was to lie down for about six months and digest Mrs. Grundy's "snack."

There is manna; there is ambrosia; and then there is Polish sausage."
(Found on the wall of a Roman tomb)

4 I Hit Main Street

Sleep works miracles. I had gone to bed, arms aching from my tussle with the storm windows and Mrs. Larson's cake batter, stomach aching from everything but the cake. I awoke after eight full hours … with aching arms and aching stomach. Remarkable.

I padded into the bathroom. In my creed, a bath is always worth an hour's sleep. The tub filled while I rubbed my beard off with an electric shaver. I reminded my mirror image, old Eagle Beak, that shaving was invented as a masochistic rite by the priests of Isis and Osiris, way down in Egypt land. Then I took the plunge and lay back in the warm water. I believe in hydrotherapy.

I supposed I should wear something ministerial as long as I was going to be on display. No flowered shirt today. I put on my navy suit because it was my only suit. Had my shirt collar shrunk? I could hardly button it. I even detected a little hangover the belt. No food for me.

I surveyed myself in the full length mirror on the back of the closet door. I did look ministerial with my navy suit topped by my prematurely gray hair, but inside I felt nervous about meeting so many people, people I would be living with and working with for years.

Ben's car pulled up. I waved through the window at Ben and Mrs. Larson, too. Then I hurried downstairs. "Come on, Sylvester. Better go outside." We went out to meet Ben.

"Good mornin', Rev'rend. You're lookin' mighty sharp, but now I feel embarrassed to be in these greasy duds."

"You look fine, Ben. I wouldn't know you any other way. Am I too dressed up?"

"Maybe for an ordinary mortal, but not for a preacher."

"That's good - it's my only suit."

"Is your dog comin'?"

"Come on, Sylvester." But at that moment his attention was claimed by a feline visitor coming around the back of the house. Sylvester sauntered over to the visitor. "It looks like Sylvester has other plans."

"O.K." Ben chuckled. "I guess he's decided to be a cat for a while. Well, we might as well walk up town, 'less you wanna wait for the elevated train."

"Not during this century."

We walked past our church and crossed the street. Ben noticed me admiring the Lutheran Church. "Quite a spread, ain't it?"

"Yes, it is. The Lutheran pastor must feel like 'the king of the hill.'"

Ben gave me an odd look. "Well, you'll prob'ly meet him sooner or later."

We continued past a couple of little houses. Ben pointed to the one closer to Main Street. "The Olsons live there. They're members, and their son runs the Hardware. Might as well start with his store."

We crossed Main Street and stopped to chat with the sheriff at his post in the captain's chair in front of Olson's Hardware. "Fred, this here's the new Methodist preacher, David Rowe."

He stuck out a huge ham that engulfed my hand. "I seen him comin' the other day in fire and brimstone, ya, ya, fire and brimstone. Hee, hee, hee."

"It takes sumpthin' like the Second Comin' to git Fred outta his chair."

"Ya, ya, and I'll tell you my philosophy of law enforcement, Rev'rend. It's *laissez faire*. I'm lazy but I'm fair."

Ben slapped Fred on the back. "'And he's so good at it we've made him both chief of police and sheriff."

"Glad to meet you, Sheriff - and Police Chief."

"Welcome to Webber, Rev'rend."

"Thanks."

"We'll see you, Fred." Ben took my upper arm and led me into Olson's Hardware. A countless number of saws, hammers, rolls of wire, sacks of feed, bins of nails, and other items that would be discovered only by some future archeologist crowded the place. They certainly wouldn't be found by the forgetful young man who ran the store.

A customer came up to him just before we did. "George, where's the Elmer's Glue?"

George looked up from the western he was reading. "Beat's me. If you find it, lemme know." His head disappeared back into his book.

"Um, George," said Ben, "if you can spare a minute I'd like you to meet someone."

George held up his hand. "Just a second - they almost made it back to the hideout ..."

I was learning how to run a town and how to run a store.

Finally George set the book down on the counter. "What is it, Ben?"

"George, meet Dave Rowe. He's come to be our preacher."

George and I shook hands. "Where you from, Rev'rend?"

"Chicago."

"So, you've come all the way from Chicago out here to the Land of Ice and Snow. Tell you what, Rev'rend, if you can find a snow shovel, take it home with you. You'll need it." Inasmuch as he popped his nose back into his book, I figured that the conversation was over.

"You're in luck, Rev'rend," said Ben. "I know where things are better than George does. His Pa did, but he don't. Follow me."

Ben led me down a dark aisle and out to a shed in the back. After rummaging around in a pile of, assorted shovels, rakes, hoes, and fence post diggers, he pulled out a snow shovel. "Here, Rev'rend."

I took hold of the shovel and followed Ben back through the store.

"Thanks for the shovel, George."

"Ummm."

"Say, George, would you have any space for a library?"

"A liberry? Nope, I ain't got enough space now. If you find a place, lay in plenty of westerns."

"O.K., George. Good-bye."

"Ummm."

Carrying my snow shovel, I walked out of the dark and cluttered hardware store into the brilliant June sunshine.

Fred gave me a surprised look. "So you're startin' to git ready for winter already."

"A person's gotta plan ahead," said Ben. "Can't be like the grasshopper, always settin' in the sun and enjoyin' hisself. Come on, Rev'rend, us ants hasta git movin'."

Fred shook his head as he watched us walk down the street.

"Let's go over to Penney's. We gotta bunch of Methodists over there."

We passed the Red Owl and the Post Office. "We can bowl over a lotta ducks with one washtub. We'll catch 'em at kaffeeklatch." We crossed the street to Penney's. "It's the newest store in town, only eight years old."

When I walked in, carrying my blue snow shovel, clerks and customers turned to look at me, and the manager came running up. "May I help you?"

Ben came out from behind me. "Ken, shake hands with Rev'rend Rowe, our new pastor. You heard about a new broom. Well, Rev'rend's a new shovel."

I shifted the shovel to my left hand and shook hands with Ken. "Pleased to meet you."

"Welcome to Webber, Rev'rend. I see you're thinking about winter already. Can't start too soon, no sir. Just follow me and I'll fix you up with the warmest coat you ever seen." We walked through the brightly-lit aisles, 200 light years ahead of the hardware store. "Just lay that shovel down, Rev'rend, and' slip your arms into this. There now, how does that feel?"

I caught sight of an Eskimo in a triple mirror. No, it was myself, weighted down with an ankle-length, fleece-lined, fur-collared strait jacket. "It's very warm," I gasped.

"No blizzard can cut through this coat. When you wear it, you'll t'ink it's summertime."

"You're right, it feels like summertime."

"Ha, ha. This ain't no test. Just take it on home and be sure and tell me next winter if I sold you a bill of goods or not."

"Oh, Ben, is that the new minister?" A lady was calling down from the balcony.

"Ya, ya, Carol."

"Well, bring him up then. Us girls wanna see him."

I struggled up the stairs inside my heavy gray coat, the equivalent to scaling the Himalayas wrapped up in a shag rug.

The "girls," ranging in age from forty-five to sixty-five, were giggling at me bundled up in my coat. They flocked around me. "Oh, Rev'ren', you're not gonna brave the chill June sunshine without a hat." Someone slapped a fur hat on my head. "There, don't he look just like a Russian Cossack?"

"You'll freeze without gloves."

"And a scarf."

"And fur-lined boots."

Before I knew it, I was pushed and pulled and made to sit while they dressed me for the trek to the pole.

"Now you're ready for summer in Nort' Dakota." There was more giggling as I clumped my way down the stairs.

"Ben, I feel ridiculous. Let's get out of here."

"Come now, Rev'rend, they're just havin' a little fun. Just keep it on a little longer, and you'll make a big hit on Main Street."

Down the hot sidewalk I walked, stiff-legged like the Abominable Snowman come to raid a mountain village.

"Let's slip into Kowalski's Grocery for a minute. She's everybody's gramma, but she likes the old Polish word better. It's Busia."

The minute Busia Kowalski saw me she screamed and ducked behind the counter.

"What's the matter, Busia?" Ben called.

Her head emerged above the counter. "Oh, for one minute I t'ink he Russian Cossack."

"No, Busia, this's the new Methodist pastor."

"Oh, excuse me, Father. You must come from very hot place. Are you gittin' so cold here in Webber already? Have just the thing for you" She reached under the counter, pulled out a round object, and tied it around my neck. "Always wear nutmeg, and you never come down with the grippe."

"Thank you, er, Busia" I muttered from the depths of the furs.

"And I got somethin' else for you, Father." She walked over to a refrigerated unit and brought out a grease-stained package. "Here is last of kielbasa. I save it for special day and now you've come, Father."

"That's really very nice of you."

She opened up the package to reveal a mound of sausage. "Don't let anyone take kielbasa, except gypsies, of course."

"Gypsies?"

"Ya, it's their right to steal, don'tcha know. Before Our Blessed Savior was nailed to cross, gypsies steal nail. Soldiers one nail short - have to nail both feet with one nail - much better for Blessed Savior."

"I see," I said, but I really didn't.

"Ever since, gypsies have God-given right to steal, so if gypsies want kielbasa, give them kielbasa."

"Yes, I will, Busia."

"Good-bye, Father."

"Good-bye."

When we got outside, I handed Ben the greasy package. "Here, you better hold the sausage. A little more grease won't hurt you."

"True enough."

"Ben, did you understand about the gypsy business?"

"No, but Busia believes it."

"Ben, I've got to get out of these winter clothes."

"Just hang on, Rev'rend. We're almost to the cafe. All you gotta do is git across the street. If you can stand it just a few more minutes, you'll make quite an impression on the Coffee Gang."

I tried to think cool thoughts - Niagara Falls pouring tons of cooling water on my smoking hide, but the torrent was reduced to the trickle of my own sweat. Somehow I made it across the street.

When Ben threw open the door to the cafe, dozens of conversations stopped. Coffee cups halted midway to astonished mouths. Cafe farmers pushed their chairs back to get a better look. Children cried.

Like a circus barker, Ben pointed toward me: "I want you all to meet up with the new Methodist preacher, Rev'rend David Rowe. You'll excuse his appearance, folks, but his blood's a little thin from burnin' the midnight oil at seminary. He ain't adapted to the Far North yet."

Grins became contagious, and the old-timers found their tongues: "Uffda, I see you're ready for winter, Rev'rend."

"Just wait'll July when the snow starts fallin'."

"We're gonna have a record winter this year - forty feet of snow and forty below."

I started pulling off my furs. "That sounds good to me. I'd like to jump into a snowbank right now." After I had removed my coat, hat, gloves, boots, scarf, and nutmeg, I started on my suit, stripping off my coat and tie.

"Please, Rev'rend, not in front of the ladies," Ben said, taking my elbow and leading me back to the big table at the rear. "Rev'rend, I want you to meet the Coffee Gang. If you ever see 'em all in church at the same time, it might go up in smoke. Here's where they can be found 'most any day at 10:00 and 3:00 and sometimes in between."

I looked around at them - and they had faces, not the closed and shuttered faces of Chicagoans, but open, warm, smiling faces. I couldn't help smiling in return.

Ben pointed a permanently grease-stained finger at a short, white-coated man on my left. "Rev'rend, meet Mad Ole, the barber - he'll shave you with an ax, if you're crazy enough to let him. Next to him is Carl Lysne, the banker." Carl looked like a mortician on vacation, for underneath his somber face he was dressed in a red plaid shirt. "And next is Alf Langdon - what do you do, Alf?" This was greeted by appreciative laughter.

Alf grabbed his suspenders and leaned back in his chair. "I set around and wait for their houses to burn down."

"Alf claims to be fire chief," said Mad Ole, "but he's really a fire bug."

"And next is Curt Winter - he farms a few acres west of town when he ain't gettin' plowed."

"Don't believe him, Rev'rend. The strongest stuff I ever drink is this cafe coffee." He raised his cup toward me.

Carl Lysne turned his Lincolnesque face to me. "Curt farms a few t'ousand acres, Rev'rend, but he does it all on borrowed money."

"Whatcha mean, Carl? How could I do anything on the pennies you lend me?"

"Well, you could pay for your own coffee for once."

"I can't help it if I'm lucky at the dice."

Carl swept the dice cup off the table and hid it underneath. "You don't hafta tell the Rev'rend everything, do you?"

"Oops, sorry."

"Where're the other guys?" asked Ben.

"Frank had to take a run over to Minot," Alf addressed Ben, before slipping an aside to me. "Frank's the manager of the Red Owl. And Fred's a little late this mornin'."

Just then the light streaming in the front window was eclipsed by a huge shadow.

"Speaking' of the devil, there he is. Mad Ole got up. "You can have your chair back, Fred."

"Thanks, Ole." Fred lowered his four hundredweight into the oversized chair. He was puffing and sweating from the exertion of walking the half block from Olson's. When he spotted the grease-stained package in front of Ben, he quivered to attention. "Is that B.K.P.S.?"

"Ya, ya," said Ben, "it's Busia Kowalski's Polish Sausage alright, but it belongs to the Rev'rend."

Fred gave me a hungry look. "I'd give anything for some of Busia's sausage. Bin tryin' to buy it off of her for months."

"Me, too," said Curt. "I offered her a free pig if she'd just make half the sausage for me."

Carl pointed at the greasy package. "Rev'rend, you'll find that Busia's Polish sausage is the acne of culinary achievement."

"Don't get so highfalutin', Carl," chided Mad Ole. "What Carl's trying to say is that nothin' tastes better."

"However you say it, all of us love it." Ben joined the other endorsers of the product. All of them looked at me.

"Well, I'm sorry, but Busia said not to let anyone else have the sausage - except for the gypsies, of course."

A groan went up from the Coffee Gang.

"Listen, Rev'rend," said Fred, "I'm gonna tell you a little-known fact about my family. My ma was childless till the day the gypsies come to town. I was actually found in a basket on the front steps."

"Actually it was a piano crate." Ben poked the sheriff in the tummy.

"My folks raised me as their own child, but I always knew I had gypsy blood." The sheriff looked at me solemnly and hungrily.

"And he's supposed to be the guardian of the law." Mad Ole shook his head.

"The thought of Polish sausage sizzlin' in the pan is enough to corrupt the most honest man," Carl declared.

They looked so imploringly at me that I said, "Are you suggesting that there's a little bit of gypsy in every man?" They nodded hopefully. "Then I have to let you have them."

Ben called out to the waitress, "Quick, Gladys, put this sausage on and don't burn it - it's Busia Kowalski's Polish Sausage."

"Really!" She picked up the stained package and carried it reverently out to the kitchen.

"Rev'rend, you just became a charter member of the Coffee Gang," Ben said. "Right, fellas?"

"Amen," said Carl in his sepulchral voice.

"Amen, amen," the others joined in.

"This place's gittin' to sound lika prayer meetin'," Mad Ole complained.

"Rev'rend," Alf asked, "where did you pick up those winter duds?"

"Dave just walked by some clothing' stores and sucked 'em out lika vacuum," Ben explained. "Better watch your wallets, gentlemen."

Everyone clutched at his hip pocket.

"Tell me about the winters," I said. "Just how cold does it get?"

Mad Ole turned to me, his uncombed hair looking like he had horns. "I remember back in '36 - most unusual year. It hit 121 above in the summer and 60 below in the winter. That's Fahrenheit, of course."

"Wow, that must have been about the greatest temperature range in the world!"

"I dunno. I t'ink it gits a little colder in Russia."

"Curt," said Carl, "tell Rev'rend 'bout the time you was cultivatin' corn."

All eyes swung to Curt. He rolled his roly-poliness around in the chair. "Well, one July I was out cultivatin' corn with my horse-drawn cultivator, and the sweat was pourin' down me like rain. Well, it got so hot that the corn popped right on the cob. The horses, thinking it was a blizzard, froze to death."[1]

The gang looked at me expectantly.

"Froze to death, did they? O.K., from now on I'm going to be a little careful about swallowing what you guys tell me."

The only thing that stopped their laughing was the coming of the sausage. Gladys set a platter in the middle of the table. Hands shot out. By the time I got my fork in gear the platter was empty.

"Alright, you pigs," Ben scolded the gang, "share some with the Rev'rend. It's his, you know. Now each one give the Rev'rend a couple of links. Fred, you better take six off that mountain you got."

"Aw, gee, Ben."

I spoke up. "That's all right, fellows. I ate too much yesterday. Just one link will do for me."

They looked relieved - especially Fred - when Ben gave me one of his. I speared it in the approved Coffee Gang manner and lifted the whole thing up to my mouth. One bite informed me that this was, indeed, sausage par excellence. The Coffee Gang was silent except for the smacking of lips and an occasional sigh.

Suddenly I remembered my project. "Do any of you have space for a library?"

"What do you have in mind, Rev'rend?" asked Carl.

"I was thinking of just one room, preferably on Main Street."

There was some head shaking till Alf spoke up. "Tell you what, Rev'rend; let's go over to the fire hall after I finish this sausage. I t'ink I got sumpthin' that'll do."

At last all the links were missing. The guys leaned back with sighs of contentment - in Fred's case, discontentment. He had overeaten as usual.

"Let's go, Rev'rend." Alf stood up and wiped the back of his hand across his mouth.

As I rose, Carl said, "Come back anytime, Rev'rend, and if there's anything' we can do, let us know."

"Thanks, men. I'll see you later."

Someone leaned in the door of the cafe. "Hey, Ole, wanna cut my hair?"

"Comin'." Ole jumped up and hurried out of the cafe.

Alf and I crossed the street and walked to the fire hall, a large white building two doors down from Busia Kowalski's. Lying in the open doorway in front of Webber's only fire truck was a Dalmatian. The dog lifted its head and wagged its tail, but seemed unable to rise. Alf leaned down and rubbed the old dog's head. "Old Flame is almost twenty-two. He don't chase the fire engine no more, but he likes to be near it."

Then Alf led me around the fire engine to a flight of narrow steps. "Up at the top there's a room you can have. If you want it, we'll throw the junk away."

I climbed up the steps - they seemed sound enough - and went into the room. It was long and narrow and filled with old boots and hoses and other fireman's gear. I closed my eyes and saw a steady stream of townspeople trooping past Old Flame and up the narrow steps to a room full of books, books for all ages. The thirst for knowledge and curiosity would bring them. I turned around and called down to the now small-appearing man in front of the fire engine. "I'll take it."

When I came back down, Alf asked, "Who you gonna git to run the liberry? Or are you gonna do it your own self?"

"Well, Alf, I haven't asked them yet, but I was thinking of Mrs. Larson and Mrs. Grundy."

"Which Mrs. Larson?"

"Hannah."

"Uffda, Rev'rend. I'm sure that Hannah won't do it, and Mrs. Grundy can't do it. She could never make it up those stairs."

"Well, let's take one problem at a time, Alf. First I have to ask them. If they'll do it, I'm counting on you to solve the stairs problem."

"I dunno, Reverend."

"Remember the sausage."

"O.K., Rev'rend, I owe you one."

I started out for Hannah Larson's. (I had found that the fastest way in a small town was not to phone or drive but walk.) Hannah answered the door before I had a chance to knock.

"You again. Between you and that pesky cat, I can't git a thing done." I looked over at Sylvester snoozing comfortably on the sofa. "And he eats a lot, too."

"And I suppose he just reached up and turned the doorknob and walked right in."

"Well...."

"Don't be embarrassed to be caught in a good deed. I know you have a kind heart."

She made a dive for her apron, but found she didn't have one on. "Here." I reached in my pocket and pulled out some Kleenex. She grabbed one with a quick, bird-like motion and dabbed at her eyes.

"I promise I won't tell a soul about how good and kind you are."

"You're a rapscallion, Rev'ren'. What brings you here today - food or furniture?"

I laughed. "Neither. I've got a job for you."

"What?"

"How would you like to work in a library?"

"The school's already got a paid liberrian."

"No, not there. I want to start a community library right on Main Street - in the fire hall."

"I don't know the first thing 'bout liberries - never went beyond the eighth grade."

"But I know someone who does."

"Who?"

"Mrs. Grundy."

"I suspect she does, but her and I don't git along too well. Fact is, we had words many years ago. I don't remember what they was about now, but we ain't speaking."

"Well, I'm sure that two intelligent and mature women can rise above that."

"You don't take no for an answer, do you, Rev'ren'?"

"No."

"Well, I'm willin' if she's willin'."

"Good Old Dragon - I knew you would."

"Dragon! I'm goin' after my broom, and if you ain't outa here in two seconds, I'll ..."

I left laughing.

Next I went to the squeegycattywampus house. This time I knew the right window to enter.

"Welcome back, Reverend. Are you hungry?"

"No thanks, Mrs. Grundy. I came for something else. I'd like to start a library in Webber, but unfortunately I don't know the first thing about cataloging books and setting it up. I figured that if anyone knew, you would."

"Why, yes, I did start the school library. I'd be glad to help. Do you have anyone else lined up?"

"Actually only Hannah Larson."

"Now that's strange. Do you realize that she and I split over having a school library?"

"You know, Mrs. Grundy, Hannah has forgotten the reason."

"Does she know that you planned to ask me?"

"Yes."

"Well, I can forget the old argument, too." She glanced up at her many plaques and honors. "Poor Hannah just hasn't had enough recognition in her life."

"Which we will give her."

Mrs. Grundy looked perceptively at me. "There's a lot of wisdom behind that youthful face of yours. Yes, we will give her recognition. Just where is this library of ours supposed to be?"

"In the old fire hall - there's a room upstairs."

"Sorry to disappoint you, Reverend, but I could never climb those stairs."

"Don't worry, Mrs. Grundy. I think Alf Langdon can surmount that obstacle."

Mrs. Grundy bent over - a major operation - and rubbed her shin.

"What's the matter?"

"Whenever I hear that boy's name I think of how he kicked me."

"He kicked you!"

"Yes, many years ago when I had him in school. His family had just moved from Pierre, South Dakota. Well, you know how children are. The Webber boys wouldn't accept Alfred into the Coffee Gang until he proved himself."

"The Coffee Gang?"

"Of course, they had a different name for it back then: the Buccaneers or Pirates or some such."

"What did Alf have to do to get into the Gang?"

"He had to fight Freddie Schwarz."

"The sheriff?"

"Yes, those boys fought before school and during recess and after school. They were pretty evenly matched. Freddie was heavier, but Alfred had a longer reach. The gang reserved its judgment, hoping for a clear decision either way, so the fighting went on day after day. I spent a lot of time bandaging cuts and caring for bloody noses. Each of them spent most of the fourth grade lying down and holding a handkerchief to his nose. I tried to keep them from fighting, but the school bell was the signal for them to rise up and start another round."

"Who won?"

"Neither - it was always a draw. Then after Alfred found that he wasn't getting into the gang through combat, he shifted to grades. Oh, Alfred was a good student, bright, courteous, inventive. He was always taking apart clocks and motors and inventing some Rube Goldberg contraption. Our school had the first - maybe the only - automatic flag raiser."

"So the gang accepted him for his good grades."

"Goodness, no! No one who got above C was welcomed into the gang."

"How did he get in then?"

"Through deportment. He kicked me to get an F in deportment." She leaned down and rubbed her shin, and the tears ran down her soft old face. Then she struggled erect, like an ancient elephant. "I kept him after school that day. After all the children had left, he ran up and threw his arms around me and cried in my arms. He told me that I was his 'first love' - I was young and slender then - but he just had to do it to get into the gang."

"I see." I turned toward the window and wiped away my own tears.

"That's one of the reasons I'm no good on stairs."

"He owes it to you then."

"Yes, I think - if it's at all possible - that Alfred will come through."

As I left, she was bending over and rubbing her shin again.

"What could I tell the aged saints that they hadn't already heard a hundred times?" David Rowe

5 Getting Ready For My Screen Test

When I got back to the parsonage, the thought of Sunday came to me, and I remembered what my preaching professor (Walter Matthau's double) had said "The problem with Sunday is that it comes once a week. A lot of TV performers have found out that once a week is too often - and they even have a stable of writers. But a preacher is expected to write his own material and come up with a good show every week."

I stared at my bare desk and mused about his words .,.. If only a preacher could be relieved of the weekly shows and be allowed to do a couple of specials a year ... but I guess that would be too much of a break with tradition. It's a little unfair - a clergyman is the only creator who is expected to come up with a masterpiece every time. If a Michelangelo or a da Vinci hacks out a good work every decade or two, that's all right, but a minister has to do it Sunday after Sunday.

My eyes flicked over to the calendar from Graves' Service. And to top everything off, this was going to be my first Sunday, the first time I was going to face the assembled members. I was afraid I was going to fall flat on my face. What could I tell the aged saints that they hadn't already heard a hundred times? And probably better?

There was a knock on the door. I came out of my reverie and went through the hallway. As I opened the door, I glanced at a short, white-haired man wearing a white apron. His rugged face was wreathed in smiles. "Welcome to Webber, Brother Rowe." With that, he clasped me to his aproned front and kissed me on the cheek. "It's good to have another Man of God here in this modern-day Sodom. You wouldn't believe the sinnin' that goes on here." His somber words were in strange contrast to his twinkling eyes and beatific smile. "Why, do you know there're actually church members who play cards and go to movies and even dance!"

"Really?"

"I tell you they're on a roller coaster to Hell."

"How about roller coasters? Are, they evil, too?"

His smile brightened two degrees. "The prime construction of the Devil hisself."

"Pardon me, but what is your name?"

"Forgive me, Brother Rowe. I'm Brother Katzen from the Four-Square Gospel Tabernacle." He glanced down at his apron. "Like the Apostle Paul, I gotta work to add to what my little church can give me. There's just small flock of the faithful who come up to my standards."

"Where do you work - other than at the Tabernacle?"

"At the Red Owl. It gives me a chance to do alot of witnessin', but that's not why I come. I wanted to git to you before you was contaminated by the other clergy and sinful laymen in this town."

"And what's the good word, Brother Katzen?"

His smile doubled in brightness, and his voice trebled in volume. "Hell! Give 'em Hell. That's the only way to burn the sin and depravity outa 'em. Shake 'em over the burnin' coal fields of Hell." His voice subsided and tears rolled down past his perpetual grin. "I'll give you my personal testimony: I love Jesus so much, 'cause if I didn't, I'd burn forever."

That was too much of a mind-bender for me. I shook my head to get my thoughts back in order. "Well, thank you, Brother Katzen, for your, er, kind words."

"You're most welcome. And anytime you git up to the Red Owl, I'll be glad to give you more tips on handlin' those varmits."

I wondered if there was another chain grocery store in town. Or maybe I could order by phone. Maybe I could learn to live off herbs and roots.

Brother Katzen turned to go. "I gotta git back to the store. There're many other souls hungerin' and thirstin' for the Word."

Also for steaks, chops, and Hi-C - if they could ever get past Brother Katzen. I had some parting words for him: "When you rake someone over the coals, keep smiling."

He turned the full brilliance of his paradoxical smile on me. "Never fear, brother."

I guess my remark was unnecessary. Nothing would get him to stop smiling. I stood in the doorway watching him walking fast, with flapping apron, toward Main Street and the Red Owl.

The phone rang. With a shake of my head, I turned away and went into the dining room. "Hello?"

"Rev'rend, me and the Missus would like you to c'mon over for supper."

"Why, thank you, but I'm going to have to log some study time, or I'll be speechless for Sunday."

"Speechless, eh? Well, this's Eldon Chance, the treasurer. Then why don'tcha preach on my favorite text? Gotta pencil handy? O.K., here's how it goes: 'you're cursed with a curse, for you're robbin' me; the whole nation of you. Bring the full tithes into the storehouse, that there may be food in my house ...' (Malachi 3:9-10) There's more to it than that, but that gives you the flavor of it. It's rich sermon material - just what those skinflints need."

"Well, thanks, for your suggestion, Brother Chance."

"You're welcome, Rev'rend. See you Sunday, if not before."

"Yes, see you Sunday."

I replaced the phone in its wall cradle. Well, now I had two red-hot suggestions: Hell and tithing. I wondered how many more I would get before the week was out. And now I was getting a little scared. Did I have a congregation of "depraved varmits" and "skinflints"? Then I thought of Ben and Birdie, Hannah Larson, Mrs. Grundy, the Coffee Gang, and all the others. They were the warmest and best people I had ever met. I decided to rely on my judgment of the people rather than Brother Katzen's or Eldon Chance's, but whoever was right, it would be good to start with communion. I wanted to stress unity and sharing. In that case, I had better alert the communion steward. I picked up the phone again.

"Tillie, you don't happen to know who the communion steward is, do you?"

"No, Rev'ren'."

"Then please ring Ben for me."

"Ya, ya."

"Hello? Graves' Service."

"Ben, this is Dave." As an afterthought, I added, "From Grave Service."

"Well, it sounds like we catch people both comin' and goin'."

I laughed. "You're right, Ben."

"Hey, Rev'rend, you walked outa the cafe without your winter duds."

"No wonder I felt chilly on the way home."

He chuckled. "Rev'rend, you're O.K. The gang thinks so, too."

"Does that entitle me to learn the gang handshake and the secret knock?"

"Uffda, all that stuff was lost years ago - the only thing left is the old gang itself. Say, how's that liberry business goin'?"

"Just great, Ben! We've got a room upstairs in the old fire hall, and Mrs. Grundy and Mrs. Larson will spearhead the project."

"That's wonderful, Dave - you don't mind if I call you Dave?"

"Not at all. In fact, now that I'm a member of the Coffee Gang, I expect you to call me Dave."

"Thanks, Rev'rend."

"Say, Ben, who is the communion steward? I thought it would be a good idea to have a communion service on my first Sunday."

"Good idea, Rev - er, Dave. The communion steward is Ol' Mrs. Morgan. She lives in a yeller house over by the hospital."

"Do you have her phone number handy?"

"Ya, it's 12-J."

"Another thing - I could use a list of church officers."

"Don'tcha have one in the study?"

"No, Ben. There's nothing in the study. Even the book shelves have been ripped off the walls."

"That's one for the books, alright. You see, the last preacher had sorta sticky fingers. When he left, he took the light bulbs, curtain rods, shades, fridge, and stove. We hadda replace all that. I didn't notice that he'd stripped the study, too."

"Yes."

"Dave, I'll bring you a list of the officers along with your winter duds. And if you need anything' else, just ask."

"Thanks, Ben. Good-bye. Tillie, would you ring 12-J."

"Sure enough, Rev'ren'. There's bin mysterious goings on ever since you hit town. A guy dressed for winter was seen goin' down Main Street, and the Coffee Gang got aholt of B.K.P.S., thought to be extinct, and there's been alotta calls about a liberry."

"You don't say." I smiled to myself. "Tillie, if you would like to work in the new library, call Mrs. Larson or Mrs. Grundy."

"I would. I git tired of settin' here and listenin' to other people do things. I'd likta do somethin' for a change."

"But it must be interesting to listen to all the conversations that go on in Webber."

"Rev'ren', you got no idea of the kind of drivel that pours through these wires, talk that starts nowheres and winds up nowheres. It's just like what Father Murphy says 'bout confession: 'People think it's excitin', but it's borin'.'"

"But you do keep listening?"

"Ya, sure, even the unluckiest prospector comes up with a nugget sometimes."

"O.K., Tillie. Would you please ring Mrs. Morgan? You may listen in - it should be pretty innocent."

"Then I won't bother. Say, Rev'ren', Mrs. Morgan's purty harda hearing. You'll hafta yell."

"Thanks, Tillie. Bye."

"Bye, Rev'ren'."

The phone rang about a dozen times before a high-pitched old voice answered.

"Hello, Mrs. Morgan, this is David Rowe, your new pastor."

"No, this's Mister Morgan. Hang on. I'll go git her."

During the wait I planned how to fix up the study. I'd fill in the holes in the walls and make book shelves out of bricks and boards. My pastor back home had cut pieces of fiber board to put between the bricks. That leveled the uneven bricks and looked like mortar.

"Hello, Rev'rend Road," a deep voice blasted through the earpiece.

I jumped and held the phone away from my ear. "Hello, Mrs. Morgan, this is Reverend Rowe, not Road."

"Sorry, Reverend Rowenotroad. I'm sorta harda hearin'."

"Not Rowenotroad - just Rowe."

"Sorry, Reverend Justrowe."

I gave up. "Mrs. Morgan, would you prepare communion for next Sunday?"

"What?"

"COMMUNION! WOULD YOU PLEASE PREPARE COMMUNION NEXT SUNDAY?"

"Oh, communion. Why, I suppose so, if I can git Rex stirrin' that early. Tell you what, Rev'rend Justrowe, remind me Saturday."

"Yes," I said despairingly.

"Rev'rend, would you do me a favor and preach on the begats - you know, 'Abraham begat Isaac, and Isaac begat Jacob,' and so on. I often wondered: How'd they do it? Was there Virgin Births all the way back? I never heard a sermon on the begats."

"Thanks for the suggestion, Mrs. Morgan." My pastoral psychology professor would probably conclude that she had an unhealthy interest in begatting. It was unlikely that she would ever hear a sermon on the begats. "I'll remind you on Saturday about the communion. Good-bye."

Well, I had only three days left until Sunday. I had to find something. If only I could come up with a new idea that they'd never heard before, but I suppose that they had heard it all many times. No wonder people were bored in church. The repetition. And if I were bored to start with.... My three suggestions so far almost put me to sleep just trying to remember them. What were they anyhow? Let's see… Brother Katzen wanted hellfire, and the treasurer wanted tithing, and Mrs. Morgan wanted begatting. I yawned. Wait! I had it. I bet they never heard what I wanted to say. That was it! After all, my preaching professor had said many times: "Preach on your passion." And that was definitely my passion.

"Now this was much better, for coming toward me was a beautiful vision." David Rowe

6 My First Sunday

The long-awaited, yet dreaded, day came.

I arrived early and strode down the aisle to lay my sermon notes and props on the cedar pulpit. The needle fit nicely along the lip at the edge, but I had to put the piece of kindling inside. As I turned on the pulpit light, something gnawed at the back of my mind, something not kosher. I glanced back at the altar - there was no communion ware. Well, maybe Mrs. Morgan was downstairs in the kitchen cutting the bread and pouring the Methodist wine (Welch's Grape Juice) into the tiny glasses.

I hurried down the narrow basement steps to the kitchen. No one there; no sign of communion. I grabbed the phone. "Tillie, ring Mrs. Morgan right away!"

She caught the urgency in my voice and didn't linger to chat. "Ya, ya, Rev'rend!"

The phone kept ringing and ringing. Maybe they had gone out of town; maybe they were ill. I glanced at my watch - 10:47. I could hear people arriving upstairs for the service.

"Hello," came the deep voice of Mrs. Morgan.

"Mrs. Morgan, can you get the communion set up in the next thirteen minutes?"

"Communion? We havin' communion today?"

"Yes, Mrs. Morgan," I said, for the third time

"I knew there was some reason we shouldn't have slept in. Rex and I couldn't possibly make it now. If only you'd called sooner …"

"But, Mrs. Morgan, I called you yesterday and Wednesday."

"Sorry, Rev'ren' Justrowe. Maybe next time you'll call us early on Sunday mornin'."

"O.K., O.K. Good-bye, Mrs. Morgan." There went my idea of a communion service.

I heard someone coming down the basement stairs. "Rev'rend, you down there?"

"Yes, Ben."

Ben tugged at the collar of his starched shirt. "Well, the folks's asking about you."

"Oh, Ben, Mrs. Morgan forgot about setting up the communion."

Ben frowned. "She's gittin' more and more forgetful. Now, Dave, don't worry 'bout a thing. I'll git it set up. You just go ahead and start the service."

"But what if –"

"Don't worry. One way or the other I'll git it ready."

I went back upstairs to the entryway and saw Mrs. Larson coming up the outside steps. "Oh, there you be, Rev'ren'. I just went over to the parsonage to see if you was there. Everything O.K.?"

"Not really, Hannah. Mrs. Morgan forgot to prepare the communion."

"Can I help?"

"Ben said he'd take care of it, but he might appreciate a hand." Mrs. Larson disappeared down the basement steps.

"Hello, Rev'rend." Two men were coming up the front steps. One I recognized as Carl Lysne, the banker and member of the Coffee Gang. The other was a small dapper man in a cutaway coat and pin-striped trousers. Carl shook my hand warmly. "Rev'rend, this's Doc Hodgson. He and the editor got the inside scoop on most of the folks in Webber."

"Nice to meet you, Dr. Hodgson," I said.

"Forgive me for not shaking hands - germs, you know. But, I assure you, my welcome is no less warm. Welcome to Webber, Reverend Rowe."

As they passed into the sanctuary, I noticed an old man standing at the foot of the steps. Maybe he needed some help getting up the high and uneven stone steps. I walked down to him past some other folks and offered him my arm.

He broke into a cackle of laughter. "No, Rev'rend, I don't need no help to git up. Hee, hee, hee. Stand aside, Rev'rend." The slight old man turned and hobbled away from the steps. Then he turned around, waved me out of the way, and started a fast shuffle toward the steps. Surely he was not going to try to jump - at his age. I reached out to grab him, but powerful arms pulled me back just as the old man launched himself into the air and sailed up over the five stone steps and halfway across the landing. He landed unsteadily, turned, and bowed to the cluster of people at the bottom of the steps.

"Amazing!" I looked at the big man who had grabbed me.

"Not hardly. You shudda seen Fodder when he was younger - he could yump over three draft horses."

The old leaper tottered down the steps just as Mrs. Grundy hove into view. "Good morning, Reverend. Good morning, Mr. Johnson." She took the arm of the old leaper and went slowly up the stairs, while she leaned heavily on him for support. They were unequally yoked: a stick and a boulder - there must have been tensile steel in the old man.

Ben, followed by another man, came flying down the steps. "Dave, this's Frank, the only other member of the Coffee Gang you ain't met yet. He's gonna open up the Red Owl for the bread and juice. Be back soon's we can." And they were off down the street.

When I went inside, I met Hannah in the entryway. "Some more bad news, Rev'ren'. The pianist ain't here yet. Sometimes she don't show up at all."

I looked at my watch - 11:06. I had better go forward.

With shaky legs, I walked the last mile down the church aisle. From the pulpit, I looked at the curious and expectant faces. Clearing my throat, I began the call to worship: "Who shall ascend the hill of the Lord? And who shall stand in his holy place?" (Psalm 24:3)

Certainly not this improbable creature coming down the aisle and wearing a turban covered with pink sequins, which sent a million reflections spinning around the walls just like the mirrored globe in a dance hall. It was the eleventh hour pianist, Miss Osgood, and she was peering around nearsightedly as she shimmered her way toward the piano.

"Good mornin', Sophie," someone called to her.

She spun blindly toward the voice. "Who's that, dear?"

"Your sister," came the reply.

"Oh, good morning, Gertrude." Miss Osgood turned and stumbled up the steps, sending a blinding dazzle my way. I closed my eyes and unbelievingly heard the tinny dancehall music from the Stardust Ballroom in Chicago, where some of us seminary students would occasionally go on a "field trip".

Suddenly the music stopped. I opened my eyes and realized that I was in church. Glancing over at the pianist, I saw that she was making an awkward movement with her foot on the pedals, trying to take the piano out of dancehall mode. A roar of laughter went up from the youth section. Miss Osgood's face now matched her pink turban. She jumped up, knocking the hymnal off the music rack, and flounced out of the church.

I had lost the pianist and still didn't have the communion.

Again I started the call to worship: "Who shall ascend the hill of the Lord?"

Now this was much better, for coming toward me was a beautiful vision. (I knew she was a vision - most religious girls are a sight.) Was God sending an angel to save me from further embarrassment? Was I going to be taken up to heaven without even finishing my first Sunday service?

The angel went over to the piano, picked up the hymnal, and began to play. I sank down in the pulpit chair and occasionally stole glimpses of my angel during the prelude. Her slender back was to me, but every now and then her head would turn slightly to disclose a perfect ivory profile beyond the brown hair. She finished the piece and turned around and smiled at me. A smile looked as if it were nearly a full-time resident of those lovely lips. I smiled back. I was content just to look at her face, though there was nothing wrong with the rest of her anatomy. Her face made me think of lace and cameos. If the eyes are the mirror of the soul, she obviously had a beautiful soul.

Gradually I became aware of a scuffling of feet and a murmuring of voices. I glanced up, amazed to see that my angel and I weren't alone. And I was supposed to be doing something. I jumped up and looked at the order of service I had so carefully prepared. "Ah, let's turn to hymn number 387, 'Break Thou the Bread of Life.'" I took a carbon copy of the order of service over to my angel. She was busy turning the pages of the hymnal, so I set it on the music rack. She played the hymn with a sure hand - actually two sure hands - and led out in a lovely clear soprano. I joined in with my baritone. For awhile it seemed as if we were singing a duet, but then more and more voices joined in. By the last verse, the congregation sounded pretty good.

"I want to thank you for the warm welcome you've given me. It was a little scary leaving my parents' home in Chicago and coming all the way out here to 'The Land of Snow and Ice,' as George Olson put it."

I glanced over at George. He was holding a western partly hidden behind his hymnal.

"In Chicago, people can live side by side for years without getting acquainted, but I have found that there are no strangers here in Webber. I've met some wonderful people already: Ben and Birdie, Hannah Larson, Mrs. Grundy, George Olson, and the folks at Penney's, who clothed me for winter."

There was a general laugh. They must have heard about the off-season Eskimo. Ken, the manager of Penney's, wiped his eyes.

"And I appreciate meeting Busia Kowalski and the Coffee Gang, a group of modern-day gypsies."

More laughter. They must have heard about that episode, too.

"I look forward to meeting the rest of you." I looked around the crowded church, filled with open, friendly faces. "This week I've received a number of sermon suggestions. I hope you won't mind if I use only Ben's: 'Keep it short.'" The people seemed to appreciate that. "I know how it is. My pastor always preached thirty minutes, whether he had a regular service or a long communion, but I belong to the school of thought that believes there are no souls saved after twelve noon."

The old leaper turned to his son. "What did he say?"

"NO SOULS SAVED AFTER TWELVE NOON."

The old man nodded his head vigorously.

"Today I'm going to talk about something that's close to my heart and something which I hope is new to you - the humor of Christ."

Hannah Larson winked, Mrs. Grundy smiled even more broadly, and most of the congregation seemed to lean forward.

"I think it's too bad that we picture Christ as a sobersides and the disciples as plaster saints who would crack if they smiled. If I read the New Testament correctly, Jesus and the disciples had the rough comradeship of a football team, an army patrol, or the Coffee Gang."

Carl Lysne, who had started to look glassy-eyed, pricked up his ears.

"Why do I think so? Well, for one thing, Jesus had nicknames for some of the disciples. He named the wavering Simon 'Peter' (John 1:42), or in modern terms, 'Rocky,' like Rocky Marciano. I think Jesus did that to remind Simon to be a rock, not a weathervane, turning whichever way the wind blew. Jesus named James and John the 'sons of thunder.' (Mark 3:16-17) I think Jesus called them that after James and John wanted to burn up a Samaritan village which had refused them hospitality. (Luke 9: 51-56) Does that sound like the disciples were plaster saints? Not to me. It sounds as if Jesus was kidding those disciples about their shortcomings and calling them to be at their best."

Carl nodded his head. Hannah smacked her fist into her hand. "Amen, Brother!"

I had warmed to my subject, losing myself in the close interaction of speaker and audience, of preacher and congregation. I reached down and picked up the needle. "Jesus said: 'It is easier for a camel to go through the eye of a needle than for a rich man to enter the Kingdom of God.' (Matthew 19:24) That's biblical humor. Imagine a camel trying to go through the eye of this small needle. First he worms his right front foot through the tiny hole, and then his left. Now he pokes his protruding lower lip through, followed by the rest of his huge sad head. The long neck is easy, but now he is stuck fast at his hump. He wriggles and struggles and maybe spits in your eye. Finally, with a mighty heave, he humps his way through."

I walked around to the side of the pulpit. "Is that funny? Perhaps not up to the Coffee Gang standards of salt in the sugar bowl or of fleecing the new minister out of his sausage, but it was number one on the laugh-meter that year."

Laughter spread through the congregation, rich and warm and infectious. Carl slapped Doc Hodgson on the back and nearly drove the little doctor against the back of the next pew. Hannah shouted in glee, "That's telling 'em, Rev'ren'."

"I have one more example before I rest my case in defense of biblical humor." I bent down and pulled out the piece of kindling. I now had everyone's attention as they wondered what their new preacher would do next. I lifted the kindling up in front of my right eye. "Christ told about a man who had a log in his eye - and we're all like that man at times. (Matthew 7:3-5) Now, even though I have a log in my eye, my vision is so good that I can see a speck in Mrs. Grundy's eye."

The congregation laughed at the ridiculous accusation against their saint.

"Now you'd think that I'd want to get this big log out of my own eye, but, no, I'm bothered about that speck in Mrs. Grundy's eye. In fact, I just have to remove it right away."

They laughed as I walked down from the platform and reached toward Mrs. Grundy's eyes. Flick, flick. "There, now I feel better." I glanced up at Carl. "Ah, two specks." I reached over the back of the old oak pew. Flick, flick. "And you, Doctor, you don't mind a little eye surgery, do you?" Flick, flick. "There, now I give you a clean bill of health."

As I passed from person to person, removing imaginary specks, the laughter grew and grew, melting the last of the reserve between us. When I came to George Olson, I said, "Hmm, I don't see any specks, but I notice that your eyes are bloodshot - probably from too much Bible reading." He sheepishly hid the western inside his suit coat. My angel flashed me a smile of such great brilliance that I was nearly blinded. Fortunately I had the log to protect my right eye.

I walked back to the pulpit. "Now you Methodists are all cleaned up and ready to be models for the community. I just hope that no one looks at your preacher."

And then I saw Ben and the Red Owl Manager race through the front door and heard them go clattering down the basement stairs. The first team had failed - the Lord was sending in the substitutes.

I took a deep breath and made the leap of faith. "Let's start the communion ritual on page 523 of our hymnal." During the flurry of page turning, I prayed that the second team could pull it off in time. What if I got to the point where I was supposed to serve the bread and (Welch) wine and there was nothing there? Could there be such a thing as a 'spiritual' communion - without elements? I could just hear myself saying: Let us imagine that we are eating imaginary bread and grape juice which represent real bread and wine which represent … No, that wouldn't do. Neither could I stop to say, Sorry, folks, but we're temporarily out of stock. Get your rain checks at the door.

All this was my unspoken litany as we were plodding inexorably through the ritual toward the moment when - the door at the rear of the sanctuary creaked open and a stack of communion trays along with some bread plates slid in. I walked over, trying to convey the impression that this was the way they did it in Chicago. Though the second team had gotten more juice on the trays than in the little glasses, they had done the job.

After I gave the invitation, the ushers started directing people forward to kneel at the communion rail. I was doing all right with the first group of a dozen or so, which included Mrs. Grundy and Mrs. Larson. Mrs. Grundy, of course, had to stand. As I handed out the bread, I said the words that I had carefully memorized: "This is my body which is given for you." Then, when I handed out the glasses of juice, I said: "This is my blood which was shed for you." (I Corinthians 11:23-25) I dismissed the first table with a blessing.

The ushers directed some more people forward. This group included Carl Lysne and Doctor Hodgson. As I was working my way down the second group of gray and white and bald heads, I came to the dark brown head of my angel. If only she hadn't looked up as I was saying, "This is my body," I might not have said, "which was shed for you." Lord, can I take it back? Body shed for you! Oh, no. I had a terrible picture of a huge snake wriggling out of its skin. She must have had a similar picture, for she quickly bent her head. I saw her slender shoulders shaking as I crawled down the rest of the line.

It is hard to fall in front of a congregation. It is harder still to fall in front of an angel. I was so shaken that I spilled the pseudo-wine on an innocent by-kneeler.

Being so close to a beautiful girl/angel played more tricks with my mind. As I was giving the prayer to dismiss the second group, I suddenly remembered an announcement I had forgotten to make earlier: "May the Lord go with you ... down the side aisles."[2] Again my cheeks flamed. Just when I was trying to impress my congregation - especially the visiting angel. What if she reported everything back to God, and He revoked my ordination?

Finally the moment came that millions have prayed for, both laity and clergy: the benediction. Now all I had to do was run the gauntlet of the handshaking. Unfortunately, one-way communication was now over, and talk-back time was here. I went to the entryway, prepared to hear the worst.

Hannah was the first one out. She threw her arms around my neck and kissed me on the cheek. "I never thought I'd live to hear a *new* sermon. and thanks for overlooking' all the logs in my eyes."

"What logs?" I said, returning her hug.

"Now, Rev'ren', you could go to the Hot Place for sayin' things like that."

At least I had one friend.

Carl Lysne came out next, followed by the doctor, but Carl stepped aside and allowed the doctor to go ahead of him. Doctor Hodgson reached out his small, well-kept hand. "I'm going to violate my own rule and shake your hand, Reverend. That was a delightful change of pace, especially from the ramblings of your predecessor. He used to start his sermon in the middle and go both ways. From now on nothing will keep me away except an emergency."

Carl grabbed my hand and my shoulder. "Rev'rend, you've done sumpthin' I didn't think possible. You bridged the gap between the solemnness of church and the fun of the cafe. You could be a stand-up comic."

"But he'd rather be a sit-down eater," Mrs. Grundy rolled up, gently bumping Carl aside.

I put my hands on my stomach. "Am I starting to show?"

Mrs. Grundy laughed. "No, but bend down so I can kiss you, Reverend." As her soft old lips touched my cheek, she whispered, "Innovative. Refreshing. You brought the saints out of the stained glass windows and down to earth."

The old leaper shuffled up the aisle and crushed my hand. "That's the best sermon I *never* heard. I never hear any of 'em, but I judge 'em by watchin' faces. You was funny with the communion, too."

I started to feel embarrassed again especially when his big old son came out and I glimpsed a purple stain on his bald head. "I'm sorry about spilling on you."

"Don't worry about it none, Rev'ren'. Most folks fergit about communion right away, but you sure made a lastin' impression on me." He punched me playfully in the shoulder and sent me crashing back into the wall. "At least it'll last till my bath next Saturday night."

Next came a very stern-looking old sourpuss. "Rev'rend, is it alright to laugh in church?"

"I think God will forgive us."

Her frozen face started to crack like thin ice, the sharp lines rearranging themselves into new patterns. Her pinched chest started to shake in a series of dry coughs.

"Are you all right, Ma'am?"

"Ya, ya, never felt better - haven't had a good laugh in years."

A short, roly-poly man came out, carrying the collection plates. "I'm Eldon Chance, the treasurer. Thanks for using my sermon tip." He gave me a big wink. "That's a purty sneaky way of loosenin' up the givers. The collection feels a lot heavier today."

"But —"

"That's alright, Rev'rend. That's our little secret."

Just then two purple-splattered men came out of the basement. I smiled gratefully at Ben and the Red Owl Manager. "Thanks, fellows. You saved my life - but you're lousy pourers. There was more juice on the trays than in the glasses."

"You shudda seen the kitchen!" Ben replied. "Rev'rend, I'll give you a tip. Never try fillin' those little shot glasses with a gallon pitcher - 'specially when you're ina hurry."

Ben lingered in the entryway while the Red Owl manager hurried home.

Two little old ladies came out with tears streaming down their wrinkled faces. The first stuck out a stick-like hand and sobbed, "That's the most touching' sermon I ever heard." Her carbon copy swallowed several times and finally choked out the words: "I was so moved - I was ready to be taken up to heaven right then."

As they went down the steps, Ben brought me down to earth. "Don't believe the McConnell sisters. They said that to the last sixteen preachers."

"I don't believe them, Ben. I preached on 'The Humor of Christ.'"

"You don't say? Well, it don't matter none - they cry over everything'."

George came out, grinning at me. "Uffda, Rev'rend, you caught me fair and square. That's the last time I'm gonna bring any books to church. From now on I'm gonna pay strict attention, so I don't miss nothin'."

My angel came sailing out and took George's arm. I felt a twinge. Were they married? Frantically I looked at her left hand. It was blessedly bare.

George looked at her proudly. "This here's my sister Arlene. She's the brains of the family - goes to the University."

For a moment I confronted the face that grew more beautiful every time I looked. "I want to see you every weekend -" I blurted out - "worshipping with us, of course."

Her dark brows raised a trifle, and I found out that I was wrong about her voice, for from her lovely red lips came a warm alto: "Of course."

If I had any lingering thoughts about her being an angel, they were dispelled by the way she descended the church steps. Definitely flesh and blood.

George was tapping my arm. "And this's my mother."

I looked upon a pink motherly face, the face of an older angel. "Rev'rend, welcome to Webber. I hope you like our little town."

"Yes, Mrs. Olson. I'd rather be here than any other place in the world."

"Well, get this, sheep-stealer, they're members of my church." Rolf Sorenson, Lutheran Pastor

7 Knowing the Competition

I drifted between sleeping and waking. Yesterday was my first Sunday, and I had survived - in spite of my pianist, my communion steward, and myself. I was lucky to have a congregation of such warm-hearted people and my own personal guardian angel.

I put my hands under my head and stared up at the cracked plaster ceiling. No, they don't make ceilings like that anymore. I rolled over and looked past the piles of dirty clothes to the clock - almost 9:30. This bachelor living was pretty nice. No mother to scold me about clothes all over the floor or about dirty dishes all over the kitchen. I was free to be my real self - a slob.

You've already heard my theology: "always leave them laughing," but now I'm going to tell you my philosophy, at least about housecleaning. I believe … that you shouldn't rush into dish washing. If your glasses and cups are dirty, drink out of a bowl. If your bowls are dirty, drink out of a saucer. Sylvester does, and that still doesn't exhaust all the possibilities: there are sugar bowls, gravy boats, kettles, and buckets. Why, I had even drunk milk out of a cake pan. It makes the milk taste metallic, but it saves you the bother of unnecessary washing. Now this morning, I planned to get by with empty salt and pepper shakers with two back-up thimbles.

Suddenly I heard a swarm of feminine voices, dominated by Birdie's firm tones, coming up through the register in the floor. "Effie and Thelma, you two start on the kitchen. Mildred and Carol, tackle the livin' room. Rose and Emily, you come upstairs with me."

"But, Birdie, what if the Rev'rend is there?"

"Oh, he's prob'ly bin gone for hours. It's almost ten o'clock."

There was a clatter of buckets, a whine of vacuum cleaners, and footsteps on the stairs. I was caught in the sack - with only my briefs on. I stood up in my sleeping bag, hopped toward the closet, grabbed the first shirt and trousers I saw, and started hopping toward the safety of the bathroom and the only lockable door in the house. Just as I was going out the door, someone was coming in. I fell, still in my giant bag, on top of a little lady. She screamed, and all the ladies came running.

She still thinks I was making advances when I was just trying to beat a hasty retreat.

Birdie and the other ladies laughed. "Rose, don't be foolish. You always think the men are after you. They didn't even chase you when you was young."

She got up and backed away from me. "Well, they's making up for it now."

"Rev'rend, sorry to disturb you," said Birdie. "We come to clean."

I got to my feet, still in my sleeping bag, and tried to hop - with dignity - into the bathroom.

While I was getting shaved and dressed, the women attacked the house. They cleaned everything at least twice. Sylvester lost half a pound of fur; the house lost three pounds.

When I went downstairs, I descended into a Sahara sandstorm of six vacuum cleaners and the clanking of the old wringer-type washing machine. I managed to skip over half a dozen cords and arrive safely in the kitchen. Birdie came out and tried to say something to me, but her voice was sucked up by all the vacuums. I decided it was time to head for the hills.

When I opened the door, Sylvester shot out, slipped through the hole in the screen door, and kited around the side of the house. It was too much for him, too. I stood on the side porch, wondering where I should go, now that I had been driven out of my own home. Well, I might as well face the music. I just couldn't put off going to the Red Owl any longer, even if it meant being collared by Brother Katzen, the smiling/condemning pastor of the Four-Square Gospel Tabernacle. After all, the Red Owl was the only chain grocery store in town, and I had to watch my expenses. I hadn't even been paid yet. Maybe I'd be lucky - maybe he wouldn't notice me.

I slipped back into the kitchen, got my list from the top of the refrigerator, and slipped out again. As I walked uptown, I glanced hopefully at Olson's house and enviously at the Lutheran parsonage. One was about as unobtainable as the other. I crossed the street and stopped by the sheriff's chair. Fred was fast asleep in front of Olson's Hardware. No robberies were in process, so I let him sleep. And then I noticed that across the street and midway down the block was Olson Jewelry. "I wonder if that's a relative of Arlene's," I muttered to myself.

"Ya, ya, Rev'rend."

I spun around and saw Fred, with his eyes now open.

"Hope I didn't scare you."

"Yes, you did. I thought you were sound asleep."

"That's what the bank robbers thought back in '44. They're still up in the state pen."

"I better be careful then."

"Ya, ya, watch your step, Rev'rend." He slapped his great thigh in accompaniment to his laughter. "But I guess it's no crime to give out information. The jeweler is Arlene's uncle, brother to her dad, God rest his soul."

"Oh, I didn't know her dad had died."

"Ya, ya, lemme see … 'twas the summer the drive-in movie screen blew down three times - must have been '48 or '49. Heart. Took 'im just like that. That's why I try to take it easy."

"Good idea, Sheriff. Well, I'll see you."

I walked across the street into the Red Owl. The minute I stepped in the door, the manager called out, "Rev'rend, good to see you!"

I held my finger to my lips. "Is *he* around?"

"You mean Brother Katzen? Ya, he's preachin' to the Indians back by the meat counter."

"I'm sorry, but I've forgotten your name."

"It's Frank."

"Frank, I want to thank you for helping with communion Sunday. By the way, how do you put up with Brother Katzen?"

"Tell you the truth, I can't afford to let 'im go. He draws all the Indians from the reservation in here - he can talk Sioux. They call him the Great White Father to his face and behind his back they call 'im Chief Sun-in-Storm."

"Very appropriate."

"And in between sermons, he's the best stockman I got. So I just put in these ear plugs and stand at the cash register and smile. Say, I think it's fairly safe to go shop now. He just started preachin'."

"Thanks Frank." I started down between the rows, keeping my head low and picking out what I needed. I had nearly completed my list when I heard the dreaded sound.

"Brother Rowe, is that you? C'mon over and tell me 'bout your Sunday service."

I reluctantly walked up to him. He was still on his soapbox, though the Indians were dispersing and disbursing.

"Well, how was it?" He looked at me with his fixed smile.

"It was, well, it was -"

Mrs. Grundy cruised majestically around the end of the canned goods aisle with a loaded shopping cart. "I can tell you, Brother Katzen. David had them rolling in the aisles."

"Praise the Lord, Brother Rowe." A waterfall of tears poured down over his perpetual smile. "You're turnin' those Methodists into a bunch of Holy Rollers." As he was clapping me on the back, Mrs. Grundy gave me a surprising wink and sailed back up another aisle.

No matter what I did during my ministry at Webber, I never could entirely live down Brother Katzen's good first impression.

As I was coming back from the Red Owl with my free groceries, my eyes were drawn irresistibly to the Lutheran complex. Did I tell you about the beautiful brick Lutheran Church just kitty-corner from my modest frame church? Well, it caused me many an envious twinge. And to top it off, the Lutheran parsonage was a new rancher with brick trim halfway up the front. What a lucky guy that pastor was!

Just then a man in a black suit came out of the Lutheran parsonage. He looked over at me. "Hey, Rowe, come over here."

The closer I got, the sterner he looked, which was surprising for a young man who had everything. "Rowe, I'm Sorenson," he said gruffly, standing at right angles to me and looking away.

"Nice to meet you." I juggled my grocery bags and extended my hand, but he reached up for his cigarette at that moment.

"I saw Dr. Hodgson's car and the mayor's car in front of your church yesterday." He swung around and stabbed at me with the burning cigarette. "Well, get this, sheep-stealer, they're members of *my* church."

I felt unjustly accused. My blood started to boil, and then decided instead to rise to my ears. "Listen, Reverend Sorenson, yesterday was my first Sunday. I don't even know all my own members - how could I know yours? What am I supposed to do - stand in the doorway and turn all non-Methodists away?"

"No." He flicked his cigarette away. "I guess you couldn't very well do that. I'm sorry I came on a little strong. Why don't you stop by this evening? I promise you a friendly chat." He stuck out his hand and gave me such a warm and contrite smile that my anger melted.

"Sorry I flared up, Brother Sorenson," I said, shaking his hand. "Yes, I'd be happy to come over tonight."

He started for his church but came back. "In fact, if you have time now, I'd like to show you around."

"Sure. By the way, my name is Dave."

"And mine is Rolf." We shook hands again as we walked toward his church. "We have quite an adequate physical plant. The brick structure is sound and requires little maintenance." We went up the steps and into the church. "I take special pride in my charts." He pointed to a series of charts and graphs done up on big poster boards in the entryway.

I had set my groceries down and was peering through the windows in the sanctuary doors trying to get a view of the interior.

"Brother Rowe, what goes on in there is recorded out here. On these graphs I track attendance and giving, which, after all, are the spiritual thermometers. Note that the general trend in my three and a half years has been up. I've increased attendance from a low of 44 to the current high of 138. That's why I felt a little put out about the mayor and the doctor being absent - I wanted to reach 140. Do you see?"

"Yes, Rolf, I think I see."

"And I've increased the giving. When I came, the church was taking in about $50.00 a Sunday, and now they're up to – " he got closer to his chart - "$161.37. Isn't that amazing!"

"Amazing!"

"And now I'll take you through the rest of the plant."

He had a lovely, high-ceilinged sanctuary with laminated rafters and warm wood throughout; he had bright and airy Sunday school rooms; he had a new parsonage; he had everything – except peace of mind.

We parted in front of the church. "Come on over about eight."

"O.K., Rolf."

When I got back to my house, I smelled fresh paint. The ladies had not only cleaned, they had also painted the living room. I couldn't believe my eyes. It was a green that had never been seen before - at least not on a wall. My appetite suddenly left me. I didn't want to look at food again.

After I hastily put the groceries away, I called Ben. "The ladies were over here painting. Do you know where they found that shade of green?"

"Ya, I do, David. You know, we ain't rich people. Everybody had a little leftover paint, so we just mixed it all together. Why? Is sumpthin' the matter?"

"Ben, you'll just have to see it, but don't come on a full stomach."

"I'll run over right now. Haven't had my lunch yet."

In a few minutes Ben walked in.

"Yuk. I see what you mean, David. Tell you what; let's go right down to Olson's and git some good paint. We'll slap it on tomorrow after this's dry, and the ladies'll never know the difference."

"Thanks, Ben."

A few minutes after 8:00 p.m. found me leaving my ramshackle old parsonage for Rolf's new brick one. Sylvester tagged along. From Rolf's front doorstep I was directly across the street from my angel's house. I turned back and rang the bell. In a few moments the door was opened by a young, colorless woman, evidently the housekeeper. Without looking up at me, she said, "Pastor Sorenson is in the study." Then she spotted Sylvester, and her anemic face lit up. "What a darling tiger! Is it yours?"

"Yes, that's Sylvester, king of Chicago's Northside and my only companion. He and I came across the country together."

Sylvester came up the steps and rubbed against the housekeeper's legs. She reached out her hand, passed the preliminary sniff test, and was allowed to pick Sylvester up. "Oh, I just adore cats, but Pastor Sorenson won't let me keep one."

"That's too bad. Well, you're welcome to come over and visit Sylvester any time. I see he gives you his Good Housekeeping purr of approval ... Just how long have you been working for Pastor Sorenson?"

"Ever since we were married." All the joy left her face. She put Sylvester down, and he went outside. "The pastor's study is right this way." As I followed her, I thought how strange it was for a handsome pastor like Rolf to be married to such a mouse. She looked so beaten and submissive. And why did he allow her to wear such shapeless old clothes? Now if I were married to Arlene Olson ...

"Pastor Sorenson is right in there." She pointed to a room filled with blue smoke. For a moment I couldn't see anyone or anything, and then Rolf came striding out of the cloud, clenching a small Bessemer furnace between his teeth. "David, I'm so glad you came. Deborah, put some coffee on for our guest."

"Rolf, I hate to say this, but one of the reasons I came to North Dakota was for clean air."

"Air? Oh, you mean the pipe. I don't mind, David. In fact, I'll leave it up here, and we'll go down to the recreation room." I followed him out into the kitchen where he stopped to tell Deborah that he wanted her to serve us in the basement. She was dreaming out of the kitchen window, and he had to speak to her several times.

The basement was furnished with wall-to-wall carpeting. At the far end were a davenport and some easy chairs grouped around a fireplace. On our way we passed a Ping-Pong table. Out of reflex I picked up a paddle and started bouncing a ball on it.

"Oh, do you play Ping-Pong?" I heard the suppressed excitement of the pro discovering a new victim.

"A little."

"Well, why don't we have a game while we're waiting for Deborah to bring the coffee?" He slipped off his black suit coat. "David, you have my special paddle. I got that for winning the tournament at seminary."

"Sorry, Rolf." I handed it to him and picked up a flimsier one. We took our positions, and he fired a serve across the net. I tried to return it, but it spun off the table. "Wow, you've got a lot of English."

"My major." He laughed. "We had a pretty fine group of Ping-Pong players at our seminary. While the pray-ers were up in the chapel, the players were having 'devotions' in the recreation room right below. I was one of the most devoted." He caught my next return and smashed it by me. "Ready to start?"

"Not for what you dish out."

"Don't feel bad, David. I'll spot you five points." We volleyed, and he won the serve. He sent his first serve straight down the middle of the table. I cut it with my backhand, and it landed on top of the net and rolled over. "Lucky return, David. One more for you."

His second serve came diagonally over to my forehand. Now I don't have much of a forehand, but sometimes I can sweep a forehand smash from my usual crouch. It worked. He stood there flat-footed as the ball ricocheted by him. He frowned. "That's two for you, plus the five I so foolishly gave you." His third service had everything on it but the proverbial plumbing. I make a despairing cut at it, not knowing where the spinner would land. The little spheroid seemed to become egg-shaped in the air, wobbling crazily under the impact of his spin and my cut. It floated down, just chipping off the edge of the table and dropping to the floor. When Rolf bent over to pick it up, it spun out of his hand.

"Eight-zero," he grunted. He must have been shook up - his next two serves overshot the table.

Thus it came to my serve at ten-zero. I gave Rolf a fast straight serve to his forehand. He returned it with the kind of high arc that I loved. I smashed it with my awkward punching backhand. After it shot by him, he laid his paddle down. "I have never seen a shot like that; I have never seen anyone so lucky; I have never been taken eleven to nothing." He turned his back to the table.

"Don't feel bad, Rolf. It happened only because you gave me five points. Why don't we play again? I'm sure you'll carry the day."

He turned back smiling. "Why, that's right. I did give you almost half your points." He picked up his weapon, ready to do battle. Thus began an unnumbered series composed of expertise versus blind luck. He fired every beautiful, professional shot in the books at me. I responded with awkward, fumbling, guesswork type shots, which would never be published. They had one common denominator - they were unreturnable.

He grew grimmer and grimmer as I won game after game. His speech was cut down to an angry scorekeeping followed by a repeated plea for "Just one more game." I hated to keep beating him, but he didn't want to stop. I tried throwing shots away; I tried my left hand. Nothing worked. I was "unconscious": I could do no wrong. And poor Rolf - he couldn't seem to do anything right. I watched him drop three years of seminary along with his clerical collar and sixteen years of other schooling along with his black shirt. He became a petulant pre-schooler. And that wasn't all. I saw him lose the veneer of 2000 years of Christianity and become a brutal savage.

Unfortunately Deborah came in carrying a tray with two coffee mugs and a plate of cookies. Rolf turned on her. "Get that slop out of here!" He gave her a shove, knocking the tray from her hands. With a sob, she turned and ran back upstairs.

I looked at the coffee soaking into the rug. "Shouldn't we clean that up?"

"Leave it!" he snapped. "You don't get out of playing that easily." So back we went to our series. About his longest speech after that was a complaint: "How can one person make so many net and edge shots?" Finally he collapsed on the davenport. I sat down in one of the easy chairs, grateful that he had called it quits before I dropped.

"Now, Rolf, I must confess to quite a run of luck tonight. Maybe we could play some other time."

"Never again, shark." He sat hunched over. I waited for him to say something else, but could see that he wanted to be left alone. "Good night, Rolf. Thanks for the good series. I think you're a lucky guy to have a new church and a parsonage like this." He was silent.

I went upstairs and called out, "Good night, Mrs. Sorenson," but the house was silent, too. When I closed their front door quietly, I glanced over at Olson's. All the lights were out. In fact, all of Webber seemed to have gone to bed. I walked to the corner and cut diagonally across the gravel street to Methodist territory. A dark shape detached itself from the old box elder and glided into my path. "Sylvester! Good old cat. Thanks for waiting for me." I bent down and scratched between his battle-scarred ears. "We must be the only spirits abroad tonight. Come on, Sylvester, let's turn in." With his tail straight up in the air, he followed me into the unlocked parsonage.

"Good night, Sylvester." I went up the worn steps, turned on the tub faucets, and stripped off my sweaty clothes. I was relaxing in the tub when I heard pounding on the front door. Maybe it would go away, but the pounding continued. Who could be out this late? I climbed out of the tub and wrapped a towel around myself. Dripping my way into the hall, I called down the steps: "Who is it?"

"It's Rolf. I've gotta talk to you, David."

I wondered what had happened to shake him out of his uncommunicative mood. "O.K., Rolf, I'll throw on some clothes and be right down." I dripped my way across the cold floor into my bedroom. Maybe if I put on pajamas, he wouldn't stay too long. As I went down the steps, I slipped into my robe.

Rolf was sitting on the floor with his face in his hands. He mumbled something.

"What's that?" I asked.

"She's gone." He rose up and handed me a note.

I unfolded it. "Dear Ex-husband, I'm tired of being your housekeeper. Go hire another. Good-bye. Miss (to you) Deborah Skarperud. P.S. I figure my housekeeping services come to roughly the value of the car - so consider us even."

"She's gone," he sobbed, "and she's taken the car - my beautiful red Olds - and she's ripped up all my charts. Oh, David, what can I do?"

"About Deborah, the car, or the charts?"

He looked up at me. "About Deborah, of course."

I was stumped. How could I, an unmarried pastor - without even prospects - advise Rolf? And then I remembered The Book. Bjorn had given it to me with the words, "Some day you may need this." I glanced at Rolf crying on the floor. It looked as if someone needed The Book right now!

"Excuse me, Rolf." I went to the study and began scanning the rows of books on my brick and board bookshelves. There it was: *Survival in a Parsonage* by Bjorn Nielsen. As I reverently lifted the volume from the shelf, I thought back to the wisest, most loving human being I had ever met. A real saint. That summer of clinical training in Illinois under Bjorn had been a growth in self-understanding and self-worth.

I walked back into the living room and handed the book to Rolf. "Here, this may help. It's based on Reverend Nielsen's work with disturbed ministers and their wives both in and out of mental hospitals."

He took it with reluctance and eyed it with distaste. "I've heard of this guy in seminary. They consider him a crackpot."

"Oh, they do, do they? Well, I bet some of those same guys are the first to turn to Bjorn when they need him. Just look at some of those chapter titles."

He opened the book and began reading: "'The Minister as Slave Driver or Shepherd ...Keeping Up Your Graven Image of Yourself ... When the Roll is Called Up Yonder, What Role Will You Play? ... Loving Yourself Properly ... The Minister's Wife: Partner or Housekeeper'- say, maybe this isn't so bad after all. I'll start reading it now. David, do you mind if I stay here tonight? I don't want to go back to an empty parsonage."

I knew all about empty parsonages. "You're welcome to stay, Rolf. I'll set up the guest air mattress." He was already absorbed in

Bjorn's book and didn't notice the motherly things I was doing for him. He didn't even respond to my "good night."

The next morning when I came down, Rolf was huddled in a ball on the air mattress, the book lying open near him. Evidently he had read about two-thirds of it. That meant that he wouldn't enjoy being called for an early breakfast. I went into the kitchen and put on the tea kettle. Let's see, what could I have for breakfast? There was half a pumpkin pie in the refrigerator, a quart of ice cream up in the freezer compartment, and some chocolate chip cookies in the cookie jar. Sounded good to me. That's what I called a nutritious breakfast. I dished up and was standing at the counter enjoying breakfast - my favorite meal - when I was startled by a voice: "Boy, Methodists sure eat differently from Lutherans."

I spun around. "Come on in, Rolf. There's enough for both of us."

"No thanks, I don't think I could handle it this morning, especially after I saw the sickly green of your front room."

"Oh, I forgot about that - I wonder if it looks any better this morning." After I walked into the living room, my stomach started doing flip-flops. "It's a vomit green."

"Don't be so refined, David. It's a diarrhea green."

When we went back into the kitchen, I put the rich desserts away. "Rolf, how does a little tea sound?"

"Good, just so it isn't *green* tea."

"No, it's orange pekoe." I poured two cups. "How are you feeling, Rolf?"

"Run over and deserted ... Thanks, Dave, for letting me stay here last night. Thanks, also, for Reverend Nielsen's book. He opened up a whole new world for me - makes my charts and graphs seem pretty superficial. What a man! I'd give anything to be able to meet him."

"Rolf, you can! I forgot to tell you last night - Bjorn has just transferred to Jamestown, North Dakota. He's the chaplain at the State Hospital. You can get there in a few hours!"

"I can?" Then his face fell. "But Deborah took the car."

"You can borrow my old clunker if you want."

"David, you're a prince. God sent you to Webber, that's for sure. I'll leave right away." He started for the door and stopped,

"David, would you mind calling Reverend Nielsen to see if he could see me today?"

"Glad to, Rolf. One thing I forgot to tell you: Bjorn is Lutheran, too."

"Perfect!" Rolf exclaimed. "Perfect!"

I went into the dining room and placed a long distance call to Jamestown for Chaplain Nielsen at the State Hospital. "Hello, Bjorn, this is David Rowe. Do you remember me?"

His rich Swedish voice came over the wire: "How could I forget my son?" His voice, as usual, warmed me to the depths of my being.

"Bjorn, I've followed you to North Dakota. I'm in a little town called Webber."

"That's good to hear, Dave. When can you come for a visit?"

"I hope to come soon, Bjorn, but I wonder if you'd help a friend of mine from Webber? He'd like to come up to talk to you. Are you free this afternoon?"

"All I have is a dreary staff meeting, which I will be delighted to miss. Send your friend here."

"Thanks, Bjorn. His name is Rolf Sorenson. Goodbye ... dad."

"Goodbye, son."

Warmed, I turned to Rolf. "It's all set. Bjorn will be expecting you this afternoon."

"That's great, David!"

"And here are the keys to the car. Just add a quart of oil every hundred miles."

"What?"

"It's quite an oil-burner, almost a diesel. You'll find a carton of oil cans in the trunk."

"Thanks, David. May I borrow The Book?"

"Keep it as long as you want."

"Goodbye, David." He picked up Bjorn's book and was out the door. I saw him drive the Buick over to his parsonage and go inside. In ten minutes, he came out dressed in different clothes and roared away in my car. Goodness, I was getting almost as bad as old Mrs. Larson, who was peering through her curtains at me peering through my curtains. I gave her a half-guilty wave and she withdrew hastily from her window.

That evening I got a call from Rolf, and he was bubbling and babbling. "Slow down, Rolf. Now start over again from the beginning."

"David, Bjorn is - is the closest thing to God on earth. He listened to me all afternoon. And he's just starting up a summer course in clinical training for pastors and their wives - get that, *wives*. So I called Deborah and asked her to run away from home with me for ten weeks in sunny North Dakota. She was thunderstruck. She even asked me to repeat my name. When she recovered from the shock, she said yes. David, do you realize this will be like a second honeymoon! Thanks, again, my friend. Now I've got to get going. Deborah is at her parents' home in Minneapolis. See you sometime, David. Bye."

Two mornings later I found the Buick back in front of my parsonage. In the trunk was a full case of oil. I patted the side of my old car. "You've gone many miles, and I think you've united two hearts. Well done, good and faithful clunker."

When I looked across the street, I saw a white piece of paper on the red doors of the Lutheran Church. By now I had completely become a small town citizen. Anything new excited my curiosity, so I casually crossed the street to read the note. It was written on the back of one of Rolf's old charts: "My wife and I will be gone for the summer to take a graduate course. In my absence attend the Methodist Church. If you need pastoral care, see my co-worker in the faith, David Rowe."

Pastors are strange people. A few days ago he had accused me of stealing a few sheep, and now he was turning over his entire flock to me.

"Eat whatever's set before you." David's mother

8 Occupational Hazards

I dreamt I was floating on a cloud … and then my air mattress went down. I woke up on a hard softwood floor with my back painfully flat. Then I thought of Arlene, a person who would never be able to lie flat or even stand straight. These daydreams were interrupted by Sylvester's Emergency Evacuation meow.

I rose like an old man, put my spine back in place, and, clad only in my briefs, ran barefoot down the worn steps. "Coming, Sylvester." I opened the door, and Sylvester shot out between a pair of blue legs. I followed the blue upward over a torso like a redwood tree and still upward to the broadest smile I had ever seen. Of course, it was the broadest face I had ever seen.

"Good morning," said the jolly blue giant. "I bring you furniture, ya?"

I retreated back inside, conscious of old Mrs. Larson peering at me from her house across the street. "Just a moment while I get dressed." I ran back up the stairs, but stopped to call down. "I'd offer you a place to sit, but I can't."

His deep bass reverberated up the stairwell. "I know - that's why I come."

A few minutes later I came down, clad in a T-shirt and khaki pants. "Now I'm more a man of the cloth. Did I meet you last Sunday?"

"Ya, it was me that got spilt on." He took off his cap and showed me the purple stain on his bald head.

I reddened. "I'm sorry, Mr., er …"

"Yonson, Yon Yonson."

"Nice to meet you, Mr. Johnson."

"But, don't worry, Rev'rend." He put his cap back on, and I could see that the issue was closed. "Would you like to see what I got?"

We walked out to his grain truck, which had the red wooden sides so typical of the breed. It was filled with what this good-hearted community could spare.

"I bin pickin' up stuff all mornin'."

I glanced at my watch - only 8:00 a.m. This was the second day in a row I had been caught in the sack. I was going to have to revise my schedule. "Did you load these all by yourself?"

"Ya sure you betcha."

"You must be very strong."

He grabbed a sofa and lifted it down effortlessly. "No, but my Fodder, there was a strong man." He settled comfortably down on the sofa as it rested on the gravel street. "When Fodder was 'bout sixty-five, he's out in the yard when the oil man come. Now this oil man's a stocky young fella and proud of his strength. He puts his arms around a fifty-gallon oil drum - it weigh plenty - and lowers it off of the truck onto the ground'. My Fodder, he says, 'I bet you t'ink you're the only one who can do that.' The oil man laughed. 'Old man, you couldn't even lift the bung outa the hole.' My Fodder gits real mad. He walks over to the oil drum, wraps his arms around it, and lifts it up onto the truck. The oil man was so su'prised he jumped inta his truck and roared away." He mopped his face with a red bandana as the couch shook under his laughter.

"Your Fodder, I mean, your Father, wasn't he the one that leaped up the steps Sunday?"

"Ya, ya, that's him. I bin tryin' to git 'im to slow down. Just the other day I caught him out in the field haulin' rocks. 'Fodder,' I sez to him, 'you bin farmin' this field for nigh onta seventy years. Why're you now startin' to pick rocks?' My Fodder, he stops for a minute with a boulder in his arms. 'Sonny,' he sez, 'I finally got tired of them rocks.'"[3]

Mr. Johnson struggled up out of the depths of the sofa. "Well, I suppose we better git these t'ings inside, ya?"

We unloaded the truck. Though I was twenty-four and, I thought, in shape, I had a hard time to keep up with Mr. Johnson. He may have exaggerated his father's strength a little, but I had the feeling that he was carrying me in with the furniture.

At last we were done, and I had to admit that the parsonage did look...well, fuller. I shouldn't have looked a gift horse in the mouth, but, in all honesty, the mohair sofa was more of a nohair sofa, the huge hall tree almost blocked my hall, and the chairs were lumpy, dumpy, and blob.

"One more t'ing - the yurnals for the ladies." Mr. Johnson disappeared toward the truck.

The urinals for the ladies? What in the world?

He came back with a stack of magazines. "Mrs. Yonson sent the yurnals for the Ladies' Aid."

As I took the stack of *Ladies' Home Journals* from him, light dawned. 'Thank you, Mr. Yonson.'

He turned his smile on high beam. "Now you got my name right."

Now that I had my home base pretty well set up I decided to go out and visit the rest of my parishioners. Sylvester and I drove over to see that wellhead of information, Ben Graves. I parked the Buick on the side of his garage and went into the gloom of the station. Ben was sitting at his old roll-top desk and making out the monthly bills.

"Ben, why don't you give me my bill now - then you won't have to mail it to me."

Ben looked up with a blank look on his lined face. "Who're you, you no-account stranger?"

"Come on, Ben. That Buick is a thirsty animal, and it uses more oil than gas."

"Don't worry, Rev'rend. I'll take it off of my pledge."

"Now I am worried." I couldn't resist teasing him a bit. "The treasurer says he has to use a magnifying glass to find it now. If you keep taking my gas and oil off your pledge, the church will wind up owing you money. Seriously, Ben, I'd feel better if you let me pay my account."

"And I'd feel better if you didn't."

"Stalemate?"

"'Fraid so. What can I do for you today, Dave?"

"Could you tell me how to get to the homes of our members?"

"Can do." He started looking through the pigeonholes of his ancient desk and blowing the dust off old papers. "Somewhere in my modern filin' system is just what you need - aha, here it is. Ever seen a plat book?"

"No." I moved behind his desk to get a better look.

Ben opened up an old book like an atlas. "This shows every parcel of land in the county and who owns it. You just take a membership list - here's one - and track down the members. As for the folks in Webber, I think I got a city map." He rummaged around some more. "There you go. This should be good for my business--you'll use plenty of gas and oil."

"Ben, you're a marvel."

"Uncut gem, remember?"

"A marvel and an uncut gem - but a lousy pourer."

"Never claimed to be perfect."

Armed with the plat book, the map, and the membership list, Sylvester and I set out to tour our parish. I found that the countryside was a great checkerboard. It was fun driving around the huge squares, each a mile on a side, each containing 640 acres of the fertile Dakota prairie.

As we rolled up to our first stop, John Schroeder's farmyard, dogs streamed out of the barn and around the corners of the buildings and ran barking toward the car. "What a nice friendly greeting! You better stay in though, Sylvester," I said as I slipped out of the Buick right into the jaws of a big black German shepherd. It was my first contact with farm dogs - and my most painful. I tried to get back into the car, but the dogs were blocking my way, and the shepherd was pulling me away from the car. Suddenly Sylvester shot out the window, landing near the shepherd and drawing his attention and teeth away from me. As the dogs converged upon Sylvester, I hobbled into the car and tied my handkerchief around the wound.

I looked out the window and saw a striped tornado at the center of the pack. Sylvester was paying me back for years of free room, board, and kitty litter. He seemed to have a way with dogs - knew just how to stroke them. He laid into them with lightning lefts and rights that a mongoose wouldn't have seen coming. A number of his canine opponents suddenly seemed to lose interest in the battle and fled the scene. Still, he was badly outnumbered by his dogged opponents and taking some punishment himself. In a sudden change of strategy, Sylvester sprang into the air and landed with a skid on the top of the car. I could hear his claws scrape furrows in the paint.

The dogs yelped victoriously as they ran around the car and dared Sylvester in the clearest possible terms to return to the fray. He accommodated them by streaking through the air and making an eighteen-claw landing right on the back of the German shepherd. The shepherd raced in high gear into the barn, from which emerged a series of snarls, hisses, and yelps. Then the shepherd appeared without his rider and disappeared over the hill. But what had happened to my brave cat?

Sylvester came to the door of the barn, paused to lick his wounds, and sauntered toward the car. The remaining dogs orbited around him - but not too closely.

When I opened the door to let him in the car, he tried to lick my calf with his file-like tongue. "No thanks, Champ." I lifted him carefully away and held him in my arms. "Sylvester, you're a wonderful cat; you're a great cat; you're a Magnificat."

Farmer Schroeder, wearing slippers and carrying a gun, came out of the farmhouse. "Don't know what you're sellin', stranger, but clear out."

"Just trying to sell a little faith." I handed him one of the cards my folks had had printed up for me.

He studied it closely, forming the words with his lips as he read, "You must be the new preacher."

"Almost the late preacher. Well, I hate to bleed and run, but I had better get to the doctor."

"Rev'ren', if I had knowed it was you, I wouldn't have took my time."

As I drove away, I wasn't worried about my leg - I knew that it would heal - but I was afraid the finish on my car roof was ruined.

When we got back to town, Sylvester and I made two medical calls. Old Doctor Hodgson shook his head. "Preachers rush in where angels fear to tread. In the future, Reverend, you'd better stay in your car until the farmer comes out and talks to you. When the dogs see that you are treated as a friend, then they will accept you."

"Thanks, Doctor; I could have used your advice earlier. How much do I owe you?"

"Nothing, Reverend. Just trying to lay up some treasures in heaven."

Then we went to the vet. He was the opposite of tiny Dr. Hodgson; he was a big black giant. The vet was the first black man that had ever lived in Webber. Farmers said that he picked up cows and put them where he wanted them. Someone may have been slinging the bull, but, as I looked at all 6'7" and 370 pounds of him, I became a believer.

He was very gentle with Sylvester, though, and stitched his right ear and bandaged his left hind leg. He could handle all creatures great and small.

"Thanks very much, Dr. Samuels. How much do I owe you?"

"There's no charge, Reverend."

"But –"

"I can imagine just how difficult it must be for a minister to make ends meet."

Since I didn't want to go to the mat with him, I left. But if this kept up, how was I going to spend all of my salary?

As we came out of the vet's office, we bumped into Arlene.

"Oh, the poor baby." She scooped up the battered old fighter and held him to her bosom. "He's so soft and cuddly."

"He, ah, probably thinks the same about you," I mumbled.

"What did you say, Reverend Rowe?"

"Never mind…and please call me Dave."

"I wouldn't feel right about that, Reverend."

Somehow I felt I wasn't making much progress with Arlene.

In my farm calling I came to the Rowlands. Their road was the exception to the rule that all roads are on the section line and therefore straight, for their farm lay back against one of the lakes scraped out by a glacier some thousands of years ago. My old Buick took a terrible beating as it lurched over the crooked road, which was covered with rocky outcroppings like the droppings of some ice age mammoth. After scraping bottom many times and almost rattling apart, my car pulled up to a leaning barn which evidently existed in a gravity-free zone.

Mrs. Rowland, obviously pregnant, came out of a chicken coop to the right of the car. I assumed that the house lay somewhere back in the trees behind the barn. "Hop in, Mrs. Rowland, and you can direct me up to the house."

"It's right here, Rev'ren'." She pointed to the chicken coop.

"Oh, I'm terribly sorry - I guess it was blocked by my car." How could I make it up to the poor woman?

"Come on in, Rev'ren'. Lowell and the children would love to see you."

As I followed her into the house, I saw that my first impression was not too far off. There were chickens everywhere plus dogs and cats and both kinds of kids.

"Lowell, we got company."

There slept the man of the house, his head leaned back against the sofa. A cat was curled up in his lap; several chickens perched on the back of the sofa; a mother pig laid next to him with her numerous piglets guzzling sloppily. Another was grunting and delivering more piglets in the corner. The floor of the room was covered with a living carpet of dogs, children, pigs, goats, and strutting chickens. The monarch of this fruitful kingdom slept on, a man in harmony with nature.

"Lowell! Company!"

I have never seen a person wake up so fast. His heart must have gone from zero to sixty in two seconds. (I would have had a heart attack for sure.) As he sprang up, the sea of animals parted under his feet. Miraculously he landed on bare floor and stood face to face with me, his plump red face beaming, a right jolly old elf.

"Lowell, it's the new minister," said his wife.

"Rev'ren', it's good to see you. Welcome to my castle." He shooed some chickens off a lumpy chair. "Here, have a seat. Well, this's an honor to have the minister to call. Not many visitors git up our road - the truant officer mostly." He laughed. He was one of those self-taught men who are great talkers - always smiling and winking and jabbing the air or your ribs.

"My grandfather was banished from his village in Wales 'cause he couldn't spell the name. That was right embarrassin' 'cause he was the schoolmaster."

"That's strange. What was the name of the village?"

"Llanfairpwllgwyngyllgogerychwyrndrobwllllandysiliogogogoch." His eyes twinkled.

"I can see why."

"She has a lovely sound and a lovely meanin', she does. She's the 'Church of Saint Mary in a hollow of white hazel, near a rapid whirlpool, and Saint Tysilio's Church of the red cave'. Grampa left the old country, which we call Cymru, and he come over here to Dakota Territory and found this paradise." He leaned forward and whispered confidentially. "Other settlers had passed it by 'cause they didn't find *The Treasure*. C'mon, I'll show you."

I followed him through the sea of animals, much as the Israelites had followed Joshua through the Red Sea. He led me into the kitchen where his missus was nursing two babies at once. "We hope you can stay for dinner, Rev'ren'," she said.

I looked at the flies and the dirt and the rest of the zoo. "Well, I really should be getting back."

Tears came to her eyes and trickled down her plump cheeks. "That's what all the ministers say - none of 'em have ever stayed to dinner."

My heart was softening - what would a few ounces of dirt and germs matter? After all, these people were bustling with health. In fact, everything seemed pregnant, exuberant, bursting with vitality. It couldn't be too risky to eat here. "Thank you, Mrs. Rowland. I'd be happy to accept your invitation."

"Oh, Rev'ren', it's such a honor. Lowell, be sure and bring up sumpthin' special for the Rev'ren'."

"Don't worry, Mother." He bent down to a ring in the floor and lifted up the cellar door. "Now wait just minute while I light the kerosene lamp. O.K., now watch your step, Rev'ren'." He disappeared into the depths. I peered down but couldn't see anything other than the glare of the lamp. "Ain't you comin' down, Rev'ren'?"

"Yes, but I can't see how to get down."

"Sorry, Rev'ren'. Guess I know my way so well. Here, I'll come back up for you." He emerged from the depths, looking as ruddy as if he spent his nights shoveling coal into the furnaces of Hell. "You can have the lamp."

I took the sooty lamp and held it down into the blackness, which backed away a few feet and revealed a frail looking ladder.

"Go ahead, Rev'ren'. If it'll hold me, it'll hold you."

Carefully, I lowered one foot onto the top step. It creaked alarmingly but seemed strong enough to hold my full weight, so I took the leap of faith and went down. When I got to the dirt floor at the bottom, Mr. Rowland was standing right behind me.

"If you lemme have the lamp, I'll show you where The Treasure is." I followed him through the cobwebby darkness. "You know, people think this's a poor farm 'cause it don't raise much in the way of field crops," his voice echoed through the cellar, "but I'll show you how productive it is." He opened up the double doors of a huge cupboard. "Here it is - my Small Game Preserve." In the flickering light I could see small bodies floating in glass jars. "What'd you like for supper? Squirrel, possum, gopher, skunk, porkypine? Now here's a real treat." He took a jar down from the shelf. "Muskrat."

As I saw the specimen with its long rat tail turning around in the jar, my stomach started turning. This was too much like biology lab. I grabbed a post for support and uttered a silent plea heavenward: Get me out of here! I had been raised to eat only animals that moo or oink. Well, sometimes I've been known to eat things that cackle or gobble, but even the thought of lamb or venison is enough to send me running out of the room, and this stuff ...

"Act - actually, I like all of them about the same." I thought that was both a wise and diplomatic thing to say, but it backfired.

"Good! Most folks don't like my Small Game Preserves. Just for you, we'll take up one jar of each. Here." He started handing me jars. The muskrat turned and stared sightlessly into my eyes. I closed my eyes and somehow made it back upstairs with an armload of jars.

"Mother, the Rev'ren' here loves all small game."

"Oh, that's just wonderful! My prayers is answered!"

And that was a little unfair of the Lord. Why was he ignoring my prayer and answering hers?

"You menfolks just go in and relax, and I'll whip up supper in no time. Patience, set the table." One of the runny-nosed, dirt-caked children reached up into the doorless cupboard and pulled down a stack of tin plates. She walked over to the table, which evidently was a favorite nesting spot. I waited for her to chase away the chickens and wipe off the abundant animal matter, but she just plunked the plates down around the chickens.

Lowell and I went back to our old places in the living room. ('Living' was right - everything in there was living.) The animals flowed around and absorbed us.

Lowell leaned back and lit a sickening pipe. "Make it myself - an ol' family recipe." (I could just imagine what was in it.) "Rev'ren', I've watched animals all my life and I figger they're purty smart." (Not smart enough to stay out of glass jars, however.) "You know how people say you can tell how cold the winter's gonna be by how thick a beaver builds his house?"

"Yes, I've heard that."

"Well, I've found out how the beavers know." He leaned forward and pointed at me with his pipe. "They watch us humans to see how much coal we put in our basements."

"Oh, is that a fact?"

"Yep, and do you know my wife ain't had a single child?" I blinked. "No," he slapped his knee in glee. "They've all come in twos and threes and one set of four."

I looked around at the walls. The plaster had fallen off the lathes, and I could see into all rooms. Sex must be no mystery in this house.

"How many children do you have, Mr. Rowland?"

"'How many children do we got, Mother?" He yelled through the remains of the kitchen wall.

"Sixteen fully baked and at least two in the oven."

"My wife's sorta modest when it comes to – to … being in the 'family way'."

"You can come to the table now, gents."

"After you, Rev'ren'."

I went without eagerness into the kitchen. The table was covered with steaming glass jars surrounding the living centerpiece of the nesting chickens. It was a battleground of wild smells, both living and dead.

Mrs. Rowland was smiling, so happy to have snared her biggest game of all, an elusive preacher. "Here, Rev'ren', you git the chair."

Mr. Rowland boomed out, no longer the jolly old elf but now the stern patriarch. "Remember, nobody eats till the preacher says grace."

"O Lord -" My voice cracked and I tried again. "O Lord, may we remember Peter's vision of the great sheet containing all creatures great and small and how You commanded him to (gulp) eat. And how Peter didn't want to eat because he thought they were (gulp) unclean. Help us remember, Oh help us remember, that what You have cleansed we should not call unclean. Amen." (Acts 10:9-16) My mind believed - I was just trying to convince my stomach.

Mr. Rowland beamed at me. "That was a beautiful prayer, Rev'ren'. After supper would you read that Scripture to me a couple of times? I wanna memorize it. And then I'll recite the *Gododdin* and sing 'Rhyfelgyrch Gwyr Harlech' to you. Here, have some—"

"Please, Mr. Rowland, don't tell me what they are. I think I'll enjoy the meal much more if everything is a surprise."

"Suit yourself, Rev'ren'. Say, you'll hafta come out for more of these feasts. Alright, everybody, dig in." Dozens of hands shot out, and a few snouts and muzzles poked their way onto the table. I was the slowest draw, and that's probably why I'm still alive. I really prayed that day: O Lord, help me to eat this, this - You know what it is - and not get sick till I get over the hill. I ate slowly of the wild, gamy, greasy, tough, stringy, slippery, repulsive stuff, and I did make it over the first hill as the Buick pitched and weaved sickeningly. Then I had a long period of communion with nature while I knelt over a ditch. After wiping my mouth, I drove straight to Doc Hodgson. He pulled me through.

To this day, I can't eat anything in a glass jar. I can hardly stand to drive by a Game Preserve.

I resolved never to take Sylvester out to the Rowlands' farm. I didn't want him to wind up treading water in his own juice.

"I wondered if angels ever needed reviving." David Rowe

9 Revive Us Again

One day when I was mowing the lawn, a VW bus whined up in front of the parsonage. I looked up to see Ron! "What are you doing out here?"

He came toward me, grinning broadly. "I finally persuaded Dottie and the kids to move."

As we were shaking hands and pounding one another on the back, I could see Mrs. Larson almost fall out of her upstairs window.

"Come on in, Ron, and tell me all about it."

Ron walked in and looked around the parsonage. "This makes me feel right at home. My parsonage is furnished in the same period, Early American Junk." With derring-do he dropped his chunky body onto the davenport.

"Where's your church, Ron?"

"Over at Rock Creek. Know where that is?"

"No, where is it?"

"It's about twenty-five miles east of here."

"That's not far at all."

"No, in fact I couldn't have gotten any closer and still stayed Methodist. Say, Dave, I hope you can come over tonight. We're starting revival services, and I'm trying to drum up attendance. Bring all you can. The new District Superintendent - have you met Victor Hanson yet? No, well, he gives gold stars to the church with the biggest attendance. You might even get a star in your crown for helping me out."

"Thanks for the invitation, Ron. I'll see whom I can line up." I wondered if angels ever needed reviving. Well, it wouldn't hurt to ask. "Can you stay for some coffee and baked goods? I'm pretty well stocked."

He patted his ample stomach. "Love to, but I've got to rush to Devils Lake to meet the evangelist and the song leader. Have you ever heard of Brother Bob and Joe Armstrong, 'The Man with Muscles in His Vocal Cords'?"

"No, I haven't."

"They're supposed to be pretty good. My predecessor lined them up, so I guess I'm stuck with them." He got up and started toward the door. "Hope to see you tonight, Dave."

"I'll sure try. What time is the service?"

"Eight o'clock." He hoisted his bulk up into the bus which sped away in a cloud of dust.

After an early supper, I drove the Buick over to Arlene's house and walked up to the door. I felt as nervous as a kid on his first date. Come to think of it, I was a kid on his first date. Arlene opened the door, and I grabbed the railing for support. She had on a red suit with a short jacket over a white blouse. Generally suits are severe, but the only severe thing about that little suit was its effect on my heart.

"Ask the Rev'rend to come in," Mrs. Olson called out.

"No, mother, I think Reverend Rowe is in a hurry. Good-bye, mother." She hurried down the steps to my car, and I had to move fast to open the car door for her. "Thank you, Reverend. Most of the boys I date let me do that for myself."

Strange things were happening to me as we drove toward Rock Creek.

"So you go to the university, Ar - I mean, Miss Olson."

She laughed. "Please call me Arlene. Miss Olson makes me feel so old. Yes, I go to the University of North Dakota in Grand Forks. Of course, I'm off this summer."

"Ah, what's your major?" I glanced over at her delicate profile.

"Business education. I'm going to be a secretary."

Outside the fields of wheat and barley and flax flew by, but they weren't half as lovely as her shoulder-length brown hair blowing in the wind.

"Uh, what year are you? When do you graduate?"

"I just finished my junior year; I'll graduate next spring."

That would make her about twenty or twenty-one compared to my twenty-four. "And then what?" I probed. "Marriage? A job?"

She laughed. "I'll probably be an old maid secretary all my life."

"I can't believe that!" I looked over at her incredulously.

"Excuse me, Reverend, but you just passed your turn."

"Oh, sorry, guess I wasn't paying any attention to the signs." I stopped the Buick at the first crossroads and turned around.

"Don't worry, Reverend; I'll direct you."

When she called me Reverend, it made the three or four years between us seem like thirty or forty. I felt like the Ancient of Days.

Thus we came to Rock Creek, a town even smaller than Webber, with only 1147 people. Arlene showed me where the church was, but it was dark. I glanced at my watch. "Only two minutes after seven. Why don't we stop in at the parsonage?"

"Do you think we should bother Reverend Wright and his family? They're probably pretty busy."

Just then Ron came out of the parsonage on his way to the church.

"Hey, Ron, I made it."

Ron came smiling toward the car. "Good! I hope you have a car full."

"No, but I have Arlene Olson."

Ron came around the car, reached his big hand in the window, and surrounded Arlene's hand. "This is better than a car full. Where did you find this beautiful babe?" Arlene went as red as her suit. "Sorry to embarrass you, Arlene," Ron said.

"It's just that I'm not used to hearing a preacher flirt."

Ron laughed. "I consider myself more of a realist than a flirt. Why don't you kids come into the parsonage for awhile. I'll be back as soon as I open up the church."

Arlene and I got out of the car and walked up to the parsonage. I knocked. In a few minutes the door was opened by an attractive, slender blonde who was carrying a baby. "Mrs. Wright, I'm David Rowe, pastor at Webber, and this is - "

"Oh, come in, Rev. and Mrs. Rowe." Arlene flamed up again just as Ron came up the steps.

. "Well, you see we aren't married yet - I mean this is just our first date." I babbled, becoming almost as red as Arlene.

"Oh, I'm sorry - you two looked so right for each other."

Ron boomed out, "Just because you've found Mr. Wright doesn't mean that Arlene has. Appearances are sometimes deceiving. Now take David here - he manages to hide the ravages of his secret drinking, whereas Arlene, through the arts of make-up and plastic surgery, shows no ill effects from her years of dope addiction."

"Ron, Ron." Mrs. Wright shook her head in mock despair. "Sometimes I think you don't have a serious thought in your head."

He yelped in delight. "That's my Dottie." He picked up his wife and child and spun them around. "That's my gorgeous little Dottie."

Arlene whispered to me, "I've never seen a preacher act like that before."

Ron must have overheard, because, on his next revolution, he came back grinning. "David, I think you have a problem. A beautiful problem, but a problem nonetheless."

Arlene looked at me. "What did he mean by that?"

"I, ah, er, think he was referring to my existential identity crisis."

We were suddenly invaded by a series of shrieks and giggles dressed in pajamas. Three or four little kids surrounded Ron and Dottie, and started chanting, "We love mommy, but we love daddy more, 'cause there's more of daddy to love."

Ron set Dottie down and gathered up the gigglers in his big arms. "Children, meet another preacher by the name of David Rowe and another lovely lady by the name of Arlene Olson." That silenced them for awhile until one of them pointed at Arlene. "Is that his mommy?" Arlene, by this time, was developing a permanent pink glow.

"No, you rascals. Now back to bed, or I'll make you go to the revival service." He set them down, and they scampered away.

"Dottie, you should see David's huge parsonage. Boy, that could really hold our growing brood. How many bedrooms do you have, David?"

"Five, though I use one as a study."

A wistful expression came over Dottie's face. "Five bedrooms...and we have only two for the seven of us."

Ron pretended to be stern. "You don't doubt the wisdom of the bishop and the superintendents, do you?"

"No, but it would be so nice to have room."

"Well, maybe someday ... but we get by. Come on, I'll show you around the parsonage."

We followed Ron through the small dining room into a large kitchen which had seven doors. He pointed to one of the doors.

"That one leads to the privy in the back yard. This is the only parsonage on the district with five rooms and a *path*."

"And how do you like our stove?" Dottie pointed to an old wood-burner. "My scotch husband disconnected the gas stove and put it out on the back porch."

"But, Hon, you know we couldn't afford the gas bills. Besides, it's healthier for us." Ron patted his stomach. "That's not all flab. I'm a lumberjack on the side."

"He means that he trims trees for people."

"Don't destroy the glamor." Ron laughed. "It brings in a little money and a lot of free wood."

Ron opened another one of the seven doors and motioned Arlene and me to go through. We found ourselves on a narrow stairway, which we followed to the two bedrooms on the second floor. Ron and Dottie - with the baby - came up behind us.

"How do you like the double-deck bunks I made?" Ron asked.

"Very nice." I replied, noting that installing bunks was the only way to get four kids into the small room.

"Hey, what's this?" Ron pointed to one of the top bunks. The covers were raised up in a tent, and light was glowing through the sides. Ron tiptoed to the bunk and pulled the covers back. There was his eldest, a little pixie of five or six, holding a flashlight and looking at a picture book. "So that's how my flashlights get worn out."

I came up to the pixie. "Is this the Ron Wright Reading Readiness Method?"

Ron smiled. "Princess, you know you can read all day long."

"But it's more fun at night, Daddy."

Ron pulled the covers tenderly over her tousled blond head.

"All right. Good night, Princess."

We passed into the second small bedroom, which was almost filled with wall-to-wall beds.

"Here's the beginning of the production line," said Ron, "from double bed to crib to double-deck bunks."

"Ron!" Dottie exclaimed.

He put his arm around her. "I'm not entirely sure how it's done - I think it happens when I put my shoes under Dottie's side of the bed."

She gave him a playful slap, and he hugged her.

"Oh, yes." Ron released Dottie. "There's a reason why I lured you kids up here." He went over to the wall, undid a hook, and swung open a little door. "Be right back." He got down on his hands and knees and crawled out of sight. We heard the sound of something heavy being pushed across the floor, and then we saw an old mimeograph machine slide out of the opening, followed by Ron.

"There it is - the original, the one that mimeographed the Ten Commandments, and it still works."

Ron got up and brushed off his knees. "Do you have a mimeograph at Webber?"

"No," I replied.

"Well, then, what am I bid, David?"

"Hmm, I don't know."

"Just think, David, you could put out a beautiful Sunday bulletin and a monthly newsletter and even a Christmas letter. Every pastor has to put out a mimeographed Christmas letter."

Arlene was swept up. "And I could type the stencils for you!"

"O.K., then I bid $20."

"Sold for $37.50 - remember my starving family."

"O.K., Robin Hood."

"Your church will probably pay for it anyway. I'll even put it in your trunk for you."

When we went downstairs and were settled in the living room, Ron said, "Did I tell you about the letter I got today from my dad's old friend, Harry Peterson. Harry is a customs man up in Dunseith." Ron reached inside his brown suit coat and pulled out the letter. "Harry made quite a catch last fall, just south of the border. A bus pulled up to the customs office - it's located in an old motel - and a couple of hunters from Kansas came in -"

"Excuse me, Ron dear." Dottie looked from Ron to Arlene and me. "Would you like some coffee? I think Ron is set for one of his long stories."

We shook our heads. "Well, maybe you'll want some after the service. Sorry to interrupt, hubby."

"That's O.K., Dot. See how she knows me, but still tolerates me. Well, these two hunters came in, and Harry asked them if they were bringing anything back from Canada. They said eight ducks each - that's within the legal limit. Harry went out to look at their bus, which was fixed up as a deluxe camper. Now Harry has quite a nose for contraband. He sensed something was wrong, so he whipped out a screwdriver and began unscrewing panels all over the inside of that bus. He found over 400 ducks in little refrigerated compartments."

"Wow; that's quite a haul!" I said.

"And the clincher was that the hunters were big in the conservation movement in Kansas. One of them was the secretary of the

Audubon Society, and the other was the head of a task force to preserve our wildlife."

"Evidently that didn't extend to Canada," I said.

I glanced over at Arlene. She seemed entranced by the Wrights. "I hope you don't mind my asking," she said to them, "but how did you two meet?"

Dottie shifted the baby to her other shoulder. "One day, I was walking along past Ron's church on my way to the library when I heard this loud wolf whistle."

"Now, Dottie, I don't want these impressionable children to get the wrong idea. Actually I had just come out of choir practice and was whistling the anthem. Can I help it if the first two notes just happened to be the same as a wolf whistle?"

"So my old wolf is trying to pretend that he's an innocent lamb," Dottie teased.

"Misunderstood by all - that's me." Ron hung his head and sniffed. When he raised his head, his eyes were twinkling. "She's always been whistle bait."

"So you admit you whistled?"

"Of course, beautiful." Ron glanced up at the cuckoo clock. "Well, I'm afraid we have to break up the party and go face the music."

We stood up, though Arlene seemed perplexed by such goings on in a parsonage.

While Dottie put the baby to bed, the three of us went next door to the church. Ron's church was made of field stone, gray and cold. Inside, the people were strangely subdued, not at all like the friendly folks in Webber. No one greeted Arlene and me. Maybe they did need reviving.

The two of us made our way down to the first pew. Even the pews seemed cold. I glanced up at the ceiling, a patterned metal surface, much like an old general store. Up on the platform Ron was talking with Brother Bob and Joe Armstrong, "The Man with Muscles in His Vocal Cords." Then Ron came and sat next to us. He leaned over and whispered, "I'm leaving everything up to them. I'm just going to sit back and enjoy the service."

Brother Bob walked up to the pulpit. "Welcome to my ninety-seventh revival that I've conducted all over this great land of ours, mostly with Brother Joe. 'Fore I start, I want you to pray for my wife.

She's ill - praise the Lord. In the hospital - bless His name. Right at death's door - O Lord, pull her through."

As Brother Bob launched into a long prayer, I glanced at Ron, who rolled his eyes heavenward. I, too, wondered if Brother Bob knew what he was saying.

"Tonight we're gonna have a lotta singin' and prayin' and preachin' and cryin'." There was a scattering of half-hearted "Amens." "Come on, now - I can't hear you. What did you say?" The "Amens" became louder. "That's better, but I thought you were supposed to be Shouting Methodists. Come on, shout it out so the Lutherans can hear you in the next block!"

From behind us came a tremendous wave of sound, carrying on its crest some "Amens," a bunch of "Preach the Words," and a cacophony of "Hallelujahs."

I looked uncomfortably over at Ron. The muscles in his jaw were tense, for we were right there on the firing line.

Brother Bob frowned at us. "Well, now, I think we're gonna have a problem gittin' our revival off the ground when your own pastor ain't 100 percent behind it. Brother Wright, I bin talking to some of your members, and they tell me you ain't never had an altar call. Brother Joe, come over here and see if we can't pray some religion inta this preacher."

Joe Armstrong and Brother Bob descended on Ron. They were big husky men, and each grabbed an arm and hoisted Ron right out of the pew. They began marching Ron up and down the center aisle and double-teaming the embarrassed Ron with prayers. Brother Bob would cry out: "Ignite this preacher's cold heart." Brother Joe, in a voice that shook the chandeliers, would follow with his thunderous plea: "Fill him with the Holy Spirit and with fire."

This went on for half a dozen trips up and down the main aisle until Dottie came up the side aisle and slipped in next to Arlene. Then Brother Bob shifted targets. "And Lord, we pray for this preacher's depraved wife, that Scarlet Woman setting there in The Lord's House with her lipstick on like Jezebel. Convict her heart of sin. Make her repent of her frivolous spirit and painted face."

Brother Armstrong had just taken a deep breath in order to join the attack when Ron called out: "I have a message from the Lord."

Brother Bob cried out, "Hallelujah, our prayers is answered. Come, Brother Joe, let's set and listen to what the Lord has given to

Brother Ron." They went back to the platform and sat while the grim-faced Ron went to the pulpit.

"Yes, I have a message from the Lord, but I think it's a different message and a different Lord from theirs." He glanced back at the evangelist and the song leader. "My Lord is a gentleman. He stands at the door and knocks. (Revelation 3:20) He doesn't muscle his way in and drag us off. He says, 'Come unto me all you who are weary and heavy-laden, and I will give you rest.' (Matthew 11:28) He gives invitations not commands. He is the Lord of love and laughter and joy, not a God of gloom and doom and punishment."

Out of the corner of his eye Ron caught some movement behind him as the evangelist started to get up out of his chair. Ron spun around and held up his hand. "No fair - I demand equal time. You've had your say long enough." There was something in his eye that made Brother Bob sit down again. "I didn't mind your criticism of me, but when you started on my wife, that was too much. Dorothy dear, would you please stand up." All eyes swung toward Ron's lovely wife. "There, have you ever seen anyone that looked better than that? 'Dorothy' means 'gift of God,' and Dorothy is God's gift to me and to you. You can share in her beauty and goodness. As far as I'm concerned, I think her beauty is heightened by her lipstick, which I call her 'Red Badge of Courage'."

Ron walked to the side of the pulpit. "How many of you wash your cars after they get muddy? I've seen a lot of people wash their cars and wax them lovingly until they bring out the shine. If we take such good care of our cars, how much more should we care for our bodies which are temples of the Holy Spirit. Just as we decorate the altar with flowers, we should also decorate our faces with a little color."

Ron's face lit up in his usual grin. "Now I'm not recommending that men start wearing make-up, but it wouldn't hurt any of us to decorate our faces with a smile. In the words of that old gospel hymn, 'Brighten the Corner Where You Are.' If you want dull, drab sermons, ignore my advice, but if you want joyful, inspiring sermons, you can brighten your faces and your hearts. That will inspire me and make you feel better, too. You may sit down now, darling."

Ron turned back to his platform guests. "Brother Armstrong, how about using that magnificent voice of yours in singing 'Brighten the Corner Where You Are'?"

The song leader looked uncertainly over at the evangelist, but found him fast asleep. Brother Bob never could listen to anyone else speak for over two minutes.

On the way home, traveling over the dark roads with my non-sealed beam headlights, I asked Arlene what she thought of Ron and Dottie.

She snuggled her legs up under her. "Mrs. Wright is wonderful, and Reverend Wright is … the most serious pastor in North Dakota."

"It was an electromagnetic storm as the 'presence' met the 'aura'."
David Rowe

10 Charles Meets His Match
(Princeton 21 - Radcliffe 21)

"Ben, I just saw the strangest sight."
Ben looked up from his roll-top desk. "What's that, Rev'rend?"
"I saw a man, dressed in a suit coat and tie, riding on a tractor."
"Oh, that's Charles Barrett - he's a Princeton man."
"Well, what's he doing out here in North Dakota?"
"When his folks died, he came home to run the family farm."
"Amazing, does he always dress up like that?"
"Ya, ya, he always wears a tie for dear old Princeton."

■■

The post office was the center of community life in Webber. All the townspeople had to come in to pick up their mail. The farmers had mail delivery, but came in to mail packages, buy stamps, sell livestock, or wait out bad weather. Because of this, the post office had not only atmosphere but also soil. Seeds germinated in the cracks between the floor boards, were watered by inaccurate spitters, and were fertilized by rich boot scrapings. The lobby was never swept, but it was mowed once a week. All this in turn added to the atmosphere, making a rich mix of hay, manure, sweat, and tobacco. No one seemed to mind - that was the way it was in Webber, North Dakota.

One day I was in the post office and dialing the combination of my mail box when the suit-coated Charles Barrett strode in. He was a tall, heavy-set, gray-haired man of about forty.

I walked over to him. "Mr. Barrett, I'm David Rowe, the new Methodist preacher."

He directed an imposing gaze toward me from his Olympian height. "Delighted to make your acquaintance. I hear that you are making quite an impact upon the natives with your unique communion services and obstreperous cat. Why don't you come out to my domicile some time so that we can discuss the Dead Sea Scrolls? I would like to get your view on the disputed 'Teacher of Righteousness' of that ancient monastic community."

"Well, er, perhaps." He had really snowed me under about the scrolls.

"Splendid, Mr. Rowe. I'm really looking forward to our little colloquium. The only bad part of my self-imposed exile to the hinterlands is the lack of intellectual stimulation."

I wandered over to see Ben - it was only two blocks - and told him about my meeting with Charles Barrett. Ben laughed. "Charlie enjoys snowin' the experts. You should hear what he done to Old Doc Hodgson - dazzled 'im with quotes from the *A.M.A. Journal.* Same way with the county agent - made him sign up for some refresher courses."

I toyed with Ben's display, which contrasted a good and a bad shock absorber. "Well, that makes me feel a little better."

"Now, Dave, you're lucky.' He's tipped his hand to you on the Dead Sea Scrolls business. You can do a little archeological diggin' 'fore you go out to see 'im."

"Good idea, Ben."

"You'll find that behind his dignified exterior, he's just an ordinary guy."

"Yes, an ordinary guy ... who always wears a tie."

But thoughts of visiting Charles Barrett were put off by another visitor.

It was one of my bachelor evenings in the big white parsonage. I had fried up a mess of hamburgers. Since I was out of bread, I tried them between crackers - the crumbiest meal I had ever eaten. Fortunately Sylvester cleaned up under me. Then we retired for a quiet evening in the front room. Sylvester curled up in the Great Depression in the nohair sofa. I sat in the uneasy chair and tried to find a place without projecting springs.

Ring, ring. I padded across the old rug from J. C. Penney's fitting room into the dining room and picked up the phone. "Hello." I tried to speak with ministerial dignity. "Methodist parsonage, Pastor Rowe speaking."

"Davy-boy, it's Aunt Ellie."

"Aunt Ellie," I said with real pleasure, "it's good to hear your voice. How are you?"

"Frankly, at my wit's end. I was just wandering around the house, wondering what to do with myself - since Herbie died there's nothing happening - when I thought of my poor little nephew way out in the wilds of North Dakota ministering to all those Indians and Eskimos."

"Now, Aunt Eleanor -"

"I knew you wouldn't pull up grubstakes and come here, so I decided to go out there on a safari."

"But aren't you afraid of getting scalped?"

"I'll bring some wigs."

"When are you coming?"

"I'll be there on the Monday afternoon stagecoach."

"What?"

"The Great Northern pulls into Minot at 3:15 Monday afternoon."

****

I was late, so I left my old Buick in a NO PARKING zone outside the depot. I had the CLERGY sign displayed prominently inside the windshield. "See you soon, Sylvester."

I walked through the waiting room onto the train platform. As the train pulled in, I thought of Aunt Ellie. Her interests had run the gauntlet from yoga, ballet, belly dancing, isometrics, Weight Watchers, motorcycling, and scuba diving to more sedentary things such as bridge and skydiving. And now she wanted to see Webber. Would the town ever recover from the shock of her brilliance, bounce, and beauty?

Suddenly, she appeared at the top of the steps in an expensive black dress and a huge feathered hat. She was a master of the grand entrance - and she didn't look forty-two. Every man in the place turned to look at her. There was something about her that made men fall all over one another trying to help her. As the conductor tipped his hat, the porter brushed off the steps, and an old redcap dropped a priest's suitcase and tottered over to her.

"Davy, darling." She glided down the steps and gave me her perfumed and powdered cheek to kiss. All the men on the platform glared jealously at me.

"Hi, Auntie Mame, I mean Aunt Ellie."

"Davy, you're looking absolutely splendid - though slightly hayseedy - and you've filled out, too."

She turned and fluttered her eyelashes at her following. "You aren't going to let this poor old redcap struggle with all this luggage, are you?" Six men in business suits surged forward. Like a queen, she directed them in proper baggage handling. As we moved toward the waiting room in single file, I realized that she must go everywhere in a safari.

When we got outside, there was a policeman writing me a ticket. I looked for the CLERGY sign, but Sylvester must have knocked it down. The men in the safari positively turned up their noses when they saw my old blue Buick with the claw marks on the roof. Aunt Ellie sidled up to the policeman. He looked up and instantly was caught up in her fragrance and aura. He tore up the ticket. "Better move your car, ma'am."

"Certainly, captain," she said, awarding him a battlefield promotion. The policeman opened the door for her, while I was left with the job of loading over a dozen suitcases into my car. When I got back inside, I asked, "What are all those bags for, Aunt Ellie?"

"Oh, most of those are filled with old newspapers and cardboard. I've found that men like to carry things."

As we drove away, Sylvester was giving out with a rare purr. She affected all males.

We drove into Webber's main street with Aunt Ellie enthusing, "How delightfully frontier-ish. I feel like a pioneer." Then she slipped into one of her roles. "How long 'fore we reach the homestead, paw?"

"'Fore sundown, Matildee." I replied.

"How many folks in this here settlement?"

"About 2400 souls." I turned before the dairy and drove a block. "Here's the church."

"How rustic!"

"And here's the parsonage."

"How delightfully dilapidated!"

As we got out of the car, I caught a flicker of curtains from across the street. At her post of duty - as usual - was Mrs. Larson, The Eye That Never Sleeps. I went up the walk and swung open the parsonage door. "Welcome to the home place."

Aunt Ellie went from room to room. "I adore it - just like the movie set for 'The Egg and I.' Oh, Gramma used to have a sofa like that - and it sagged in almost the same place. Oh, the curtains are right out of *Better Homes and Garbage*."

When we got to the kitchen, I thought I'd better warn her. "Don't move the kitchen table, Aunt Ellie. It has only three legs and has to lean up against the wall. And be careful sitting in that chair." I pointed to the weakest of the tube chairs. "Don't lean back. I flipped over in that one once.

"Now if you'll come into the dining room, I'll show you how the table doubles as a Ping-Pong table." I lifted up the tablecloth to show a piece of plywood resting on two sawhorses.

Aunt Ellie looked at the rug and gave a squeal of delight. "This rug must be at least 100 years old."

"No, I think it's pretty recent. It came out of the fitting room at J. C. Penney's."

"All this junk must have taken years to accumulate."

"Actually, it arrived one morning on the back of a big Swede. Come on upstairs and I'll show you your room."

She went lightly up the steps like the ballerina she once was and peeked in all the rooms. "Why, there's only one bed."

"You can have that, Aunt Ellie. I'll sleep on the air mattress."

"Oh, no, Davy. Don't you remember about my bad back? I sleep on a board at home, so the floor will be just right for me."

Next morning the smell of frying bacon and fresh bread drifted up to me, making me think that mom must be fixing me a big breakfast. But when I opened my eyes, the bare room seemed unfamiliar. Where was I? Chicago? Seminary? No. Realization dawned with the dawn - I was in Webber, my first pastorate.

I slipped on my robe, padded downstairs, and stopped in the kitchen doorway. It was "Again Pioneers". Aunt Ellie had exchanged her black sheath for a calico dress and a flour sack apron. She was rolling out dough on the kitchen table, and the counters were covered with pans and flour and loaves of fresh bread. Bacon was sizzling and coffee was bubbling. "Smells great. When do we eat?"

She spun around. "Soon, Revander - Matildee just 'bout ready." Role-playing was more real to her than reality.

"Great, I haven't had a hot breakfast since I left Chicago."

She cleared off a corner of the kitchen table and started bombarding me with food. "Here's some hot bread." She slapped butter on it. It went on like liquid gold. "And here's some of my famous raspberry jam." She dropped two tablespoonfuls on each slice. Then followed bacon, pancakes, coffee, and a little coffeecake to wash down the coffee.

An hour later I shoved the chair back. "Enough, enough! You're worse than my congregation of Methodist 'Jewish mothers'!" She started to look downcast. "No, it was absolutely delicious. It's just that there's no more room in the <u>in</u>. Well, what would you like to do today, walk around the town or visit some of the farms?"

"Maybe later, Davy. I haven't got time today. I noticed the bedroom windows seem pretty dirty and the basement needs straightening."

And she was off. For four days I caught only glimpses of her as she flew by me with mop, hoe, or ladder. She was spading the old garden, beating the rugs, painting the weathered wooden shingles, dusting the chimney. And in between those operations there flowed out of the kitchen the most savory pies, cakes, and breads. This temporarily reversed the trend of baked goods flowing into the parsonage. For the first time we became exporters. Those who came to give were met at the door, stripped of their gifts, and sent away with double what they had brought. In fact, for four days the sales at the bakery hit a slump - and then she slumped.

When I came downstairs on Friday morning, she was sitting cross-legged on the living room floor, practicing her yoga. I tried to tiptoe by. "Da-a-a-vy, I'm bored. There's nothing to do."

I quickly shifted into a parental role. "Well, daughter, we could go calling."

"And get manure on my $100 shoes?" She sat hunched over. "Isn't there a night club or a movie or even a high school play?"

"I'm afraid there isn't much to do in Webber." We both slumped. And then, while I was listening to a car crunch its way down the gravel street, a revelation hit me. I'm sure Moses was no more excited when he saw the burning bush, or Nebuchadnezzar more awestruck when he saw the handwriting on the wall. I spun around. "How would you like to meet a Princeton man?"

She looked up in disbelief. "Here, in the boonies? Is he alive? Does he live here, or is he just visiting? You wouldn't kid an old woman?"

"No, Charles Barrett is a real live Princeton man - who always keeps his tie on for dear old Princeton."

"Is he married? Is he good-looking? Is he –"

"Come and see for yourself."

"Now?"

"Now!"

I had heard of levitation, but had never before witnessed it. She rose from the floor all the way up the stairs. I heard the clicks of her four real suitcases opening up simultaneously and pouring their rich wares onto the bare floor. I braced myself for the inevitable.

"But I don't have a thing to wear."

"Improvise!"

As the old Buick lumbered its way over washboard roads, I glanced over at Aunt Ellie in her mauve dress. She was radiant and singing some aria in her mezzo-soprano. I hoped that my idea would not fall flat. I would hate to see her slide back into depression. We drove east of Webber for about ten miles and turned south until we came to matching statues of a strange two-faced god - I suppose to watch people coming and going. The Barrett farm was the only one with a Latin motto.

"Aunt Ellie, do you know what Barrett's motto means?"

"Fortunately I minored in Latin at Radcliffe. It means roughly 'hoping against hope'. Very puzzling."

I thought so, too, but soon forgot it in the pleasure of riding along Barrett's blacktop road between its edging of white stones. The fields we passed seemed unusually symmetrical and geometrical. The farm buildings were freshly painted, including the biggest barn and longest ranch house I had ever seen.

Around the corner of the big barn bounded a Great Dane, followed by a tractor with an enclosed cab. The door to the cab slid open and down climbed Charles Barrett, looking as if he had just come out of the Princeton library. He had on a navy sport coat and light blue slacks. He strode over to the car and tipped his blue fedora. "Excellent timing, my dear medicine man." He saw the Great Dane eye Sylvester through the rear window. "Begone, Cerberus." The great creature bounded away.

I reached my hand out the window, but Barrett hesitated before he shook my hand. Afterward, he looked carefully at his right hand, touching each finger.

"What are you doing, Mr. Barrett?"

"After I shake hands with a minister, I always count my fingers."

We were off to a good start.

"Um, Mr. Barrett, I brought some company. This is my Aunt Eleanor." He went around the car, opened the door with a sweeping gesture, and handed Aunt Eleanor down, much as a nobleman would have helped a lady from her carriage. He bent over her hand and kissed it. As he straightened up, he saw her face for the first time and was thunderstruck.

There ensued the longest period of silence since Charles Barrett had learned to talk. I could hear his brain spinning behind his eyeballs as the great wordsmith was searching his file cabinets. When he finally regained speech he said: "How toothsome, winsome, lissome, and buxom! Surely this young creature can't be your Aunt!"

"Brother, has this guy got a line of patter, but I hope he keeps it up."

Charles tried to recover some of his composure. "May I show you around my tenant farm?"

"I'd like to see your place. Wouldn't you, Aunt Ellie?"

She looked down at her open-toed shoes. "Just so we don't step in any manure."

"Ah, you mean 'growth medium'," corrected Charles. "We may as well commence with the Nerve Center." He grabbed Ellie's arm and conducted her into the immaculate barn, a sharp contrast to the Webber Post Office. There behind glass was a milking parlor done in white tile. Several men were applying milking machines.

"It's fascinating to see them put the machines on the cow's te -" Aunt Ellie was cut off by Charles saying, "Tut, tut, here we call them 'milk dispensers.'"

Aunt Ellie drawled, "It's nice to meet a real gentleman farmer."

The barn was the cleanest I'd ever been in. The farm equipment was the best in the area. Most of the tractors were even equipped with air-conditioned cabs. It was a model farm that had been written up and photographed in the *Fargo Forum* and the *Minneapolis Tribune.*

"Mr. Barrett, I noticed how straight the rows are in your fields."

"There's a text for that: 'No man who puts his hand to the plow and looks back is fit for the Kingdom of God.' (Luke 9:62) You should know that, Rev. Rowe."

He always made me feel so uneducated. I tried to cover my embarrassment by saying, "It does have a familiar ring."

"Why don't we go up to the shanty for some refreshments?" The "shanty" was a new eighty-foot rancher.

"You don't mind perching here in the kitchen, do you?"

"Not at all," Aunt Eleanor answered for both of us. We sat on soft leather bar stools and looked around the dream kitchen with its gleaming counters and shining fixtures. "Boy, I wish I had a kitchen like this," said Ellie.

"It's even better than the parsonage," I observed.

"While we're waiting for the coffee to percolate, would you like to take the guided tour?"

"Ya sure you betcha," Ellie said.

Both Charles and I gave her a surprised look.

"I'm trying to blend in with the locals," Ellie replied.

"Impossible, my dear," said Charles. "You can no more blend in than a diamond among dirt, than a cardinal among sparrows, than a —"

"What a line of patter! The 'growth medium' is piling up pretty deep in here." (But I knew she was secretly pleased.)

Imperturbably, Charles switched to a travelogue: "Now here is the living room, with a few sticks of kindling from the East." The living room ran thirty or forty feet up to a big stone fireplace. It was a forest of many shades of green.

"Lovely," said Aunt Ellie, "but my decorator says that there should be just one shade of green."

"Come over here, my dear." Charles was pointing out the picture window. "Just take a look at how The Great Decorator does it. How many shades of green do you see?" They stood before the picture window, looking over the panorama of the Barrett farm, from the gardens with their varied plants to the varieties of trees in the shelter belt.

"One, two, three … why, there must be at least seven or eight," said Ellie.

"Ten."

"Think you're pretty smart, don't you?"

"*Summa cum laude* from Princeton," he answered smugly.

"Which has become *summa cum lard*." She dropped her eyes to his paunch. "On behalf of the superior graduates of Radcliffe, I challenge you."

There followed a free-wheeling, free association intelligence test. I was amazed because I am usually so tongue-tied around the opposite sex. It was an electromagnetic storm as the "presence" met the "aura".

ELLIE: "What do you think of Neanderthal Man?"

CHARLES: "Low brow."

ELLIE: "Dante?"

CHARLES: "Infernal."

ELLIE: "Pasteur?"

CHARLES: "I prefer homogenized."

ELLIE: "Uneasy lies the head…"

CHARLES: "That wears a frown."

As they were lunging and parrying, they were moving closer and closer together.

"Now switch," cried Charles. "Haste - "

ELLIE: "Makes weight."

CHARLES: "Too many cooks - "

ELLIE: "Get stewed."

By this time they were slugging it out chin to chin.

CHARLES: "A riddle:" said Charles, puffing, "what would you call a housewife from the Midwest?"

ELLIE: "A - a midwife."

CHARLES: "Good - you liked that kitchen? Well, you can have it -"

ELLIE: "With apron strings attached, I suppose."

CHARLES: "Yes."

ELLIE: "Well, this is a bit sudden, and Herbie is hardly cold in his grave, but I did see your motto, and I -"

CHARLES: "Quit prattling woman. What's your answer?"

ELLIE: "After due consideration, I think I'll say -"

CHARLES: "Yes, yes?"

ELLIE: "Yes."

"You took long enough." Charles glanced at his watch. "It is now 4:33. I believe that we will just make it to the courthouse before closing. David, why don't you go light the candles on the altar, and we will meet you there at approximately 5:27."

I looked incredulously from one to the other. "Are you both serious?"

They nodded. "And over twenty-one," said Charles.

"Several years over twenty-one," added Ellie. They laughed.

Charles put his arms around Ellie. "I don't believe I heard your last name."

"It doesn't matter," she replied. "I won't have it more than fifty-four minutes."

I left on their laughter.

You never know how a pastoral call is going to turn out. And this one - the only known football game between Princeton and Radcliffe - had ended in a tie and a tied knot.

I rushed home, put out the cat, put on my navy suit, and hurried to the church. Good - they weren't there yet. And now for a quick look at the order of service. I pulled a hymnal out of a pew rack and began leafing through the pages. Where did they hide the marriage service anyway? Let's see ... The Lord's Supper ... Baptism ... Reception of Members. Ah, there it was: Matrimony. Good - it ran only three pages, from 546 through 548. Strange - it was right before the Burial of the Dead. I wondered if there was any significance to that.

While I was reading, they came in chattering like teenagers. Charles strode ponderously down the aisle to me. I was one step above him on the platform, but even so we were eye to eye. Ellie soon joined him.

Charles handed me the license. "I assume you'll take care of this."

"Er, I suppose so, but first I better tell you that I've never married anyone before."

"My dear young cleric," Charles responded, "I do not want smoothness - I want speed. This poor woman hasn't long to live, and she should have the privilege of spending her declining years with me."

"Declining years! Why, I'm younger than you are. I'm only ... thirty-nine."

"Don't perjure yourself, my dear. Never fear - I will take care of you. I will employ around-the-clock nurses."

"Humph, if you think I'm on the brink of senility, why do you want to marry me?"

"For intellectual stimulation - what else? I haven't been challenged like this since I had to match wits with my childhood sweetheart, Irene Lucas, back in elementary school. But, alas, she has shuffled off this mortal coil, leaving you, my dear, as the only living woman anywhere near the Barrett I.Q."

"Davy, why don't you marry this ego to his I.Q.? Then they can live happily ever after in that big empty house." Ellie scooted to the far end of a pew and turned her back to Charles.

They were having their first marriage spat, and they weren't even married.

Charles frowned and went over to sit next to Ellie. "Don't fly away, my dove. We can roam the world together: a honeymoon in Paris ... several leisurely months on the Riviera ... a tour of the Eternal City led by my good friend Cardinal Leone ... a cruise to the Enchanted Isles ..."

While Charles was singing his love song, I glanced at the marriage license. There was something wrong. I looked again - then called out to the two lovebirds. "I'm afraid I can't marry you two anyhow. This license is from the wrong county."

"Wrong county!" I pulled them back from their world cruise to Webber, North Dakota.

"Yes." I savored this little moment of one-upmanship over Charles. "You need a license from Prairie County, where our church is located."

"Oh!" Charles sank back onto the pew. "I assumed I needed a license from Rose County, where my farm is located."

"That's the way with you bachelors," said Ellie. "So inexperienced."

Charles muttered, "And now the Prairie County Courthouse will be closed until Monday." With his dignity and high spirits gone, he looked like a little boy in stage make-up.

The three of us sat slumped in the pews.

Suddenly Ellie bounced back. "Davy, can't you perform the ceremony in Charles's house? That would be in the right county."

"Aunt Ellie, you're smarter than both of us. Right, Charles?"

"Well, I'm prepared to give ground on that one point."

"O.K., everybody," said Ellie, "let's get going."

We left the church and climbed into my Buick. I looked down at the furry bundle on the front seat. "I guess Sylvester wants to be part of the wedding party, too."

"Sure," said Ellie. "He can be a witness."

We drove east from Webber until I slowed to make the turn south. Suddenly Charles yelled, "Stop!"

I slammed on the brakes. "What for?"

"Getting cold feet, lover?"

"On the contrary, we have just passed the county line; we can have the ceremony right here."

"But," said Ellie, "we're already halfway to your farm."

"Yes, but neither of us has much time left, and I want to spend it married to you."

"Why, that's the nicest thing you've said yet, my impetuous lover. O.K., Davy, let's have the service here, though I would have preferred an intimate little ceremony in St. Paul's Cathedral."

I pulled the Buick into a field. All of us got out and stood next to the car, except Sylvester who leaped to the roof and sat there eyeing us. I opened the hymnal and began reading: "'Dearly Beloved, we are gathered together here' (namely in this field) 'in the sight of God and in the presence of these witnesses' (actually just one witness, namely this cat) -"

"Don't add words, David," Charles complained. "Cut, cut!"

"Yes, sorry ... 'to join this man and this woman in holy matrimony –'"

"We know why we're here, David. Get to the meat of it." Charles was spinning his hands.

"O.K., skipping, skipping. Here's something that looks important. Now, Charles, take Ellie's hand and repeat after me: 'I, Charles, take thee, Eleanor, to be my wedded wife, to have and to hold, from this day forward, for better, for worse, for richer, for poorer –'"

"You can leave out 'for worse' and 'for poorer.' It's going to be 'for better' and 'for richer.'"

"Here's 'hoping against hope,'" said Ellie.

"You've stolen my motto - along with my farm."

I shook my head and glanced back at the book. "'... in sickness and in health, to love and to cherish, till death us do part, and thereto I plight thee my troth.'"

"'Plight thee my troth?'" Ellie looked at me questioningly. "What does that mean in English?"

Charles opened his mouth, probably to give a long discourse on the etymology of the term, but instead muttered something about "tempus fugit" and looked at me.

"It means 'pledge you my faith.'"

"Then I say 'ditto'."

They were rushing me.

I looked back at the hymnal. "Now we come to the giving of the ring."

Charles struck his forehead. "Ye gads, I forgot the ring."

"Charles, you can use one of mine - I've got eight."

"No, thanks. May I borrow your class ring, David?" I slipped it off and gave it to him. "Eleanor, my dear, I'll let you pick out your engagement and wedding rings when we get to Paris."

"Now slip it on her ring finger and repeat after me: 'In token and pledge of the vow between us made, with this ring I thee wed: in the Name of the Father, and of the Son, and of the Holy Spirit. Amen.' Let's see now. I guess we can skip down to -"

"Wait!" said Ellie. "I want to give Charles a ring, too. Which one do you want, dear? The ruby one, the one with twined serpents, or what?"

Charles shuddered. "I shall have to teach this woman everything about taste. They're all equally bad." He forced a smile. "But I shall cherish whatever you give me."

"How about a good swift kick?"

"Tut, tut, my dear. You're holding up the ceremony."

"All right, kids, you can go back to your corners to wait for round two."

"Really, David, can't you recognize a little innocent fun?"

"O.K., if you two really want to get married, then join hands."

They looked at each other for a moment, appeared to weigh all the factors, and decided to get married anyway. After they joined hands, I put my hand on top of theirs. "'Forasmuch as Charles and Eleanor have consented together in holy wedlock, and have witnessed the same before God' and this cat, (skipping, skipping) 'I pronounce that they are husband and wife together.... Those whom God hath joined together, let not man put asunder. Amen.' All right, Charles, you may kiss your bride."

"David, would you be a good lad and turn your back?"

Just as I turned away, a truck pulled up, and an old, capped head peeked out. It was my old trucker friend who had stopped for me during my first trip to Webber. He called out, "Havin' car trouble this time?"

"No," I replied. "That's just Charles's motor racing."

"Every time the organ swelled, a heavy-set, older man would stand up." David Rowe

11 Strangers in Our Midst

One Sunday Miss Osgood, fortunately without the sequined turban, was playing the pump organ. She could really draw music out of the old relic - a case of one antique playing another. No one else could play the old organ - not even my angel. Miss Osgood alone knew how many rubber bands to put on each stop, though sometimes they flew over at me. Communication was difficult, for she could neither hear me nor see me. She was as apt to strike up a hymn during the middle of my sermon as to sit there motionless when she should be playing the offertory music..

That Sunday I noticed that we had several strangers. One, I found out later, was quite a golfer. She wasn't paying much attention to the service … just meditating about the fairways when our tenor soloist startled her with the a *cappella* beginning of his solo. "For," he sang out, and the lady golfer instinctively slid down in the pew and covered her head. When she realized that she was in church, she became very red-faced. (In later years I saw drinkers forget themselves like that at communion. Sometimes they would toss their drink back and hold out their glasses for seconds.) The lady reformed - she never came back.

Miss Osgood usually upstaged the soloist. Because of her bad eyesight and vanity about not wearing glasses, she had to squint right up to the music stand to find the notes, which she found sometimes, but never on Sunday. Between the wrong notes and her head bobbing and weaving, who looked at the soloist?

But that Sunday both the soloist and Miss Osgood were upstaged by another stranger. Every time the organ swelled, a heavy-set, older man would stand up. He was an imposing looking old man, almost episcopal in his appearance, with a snowy, shaggy mane and bushy white eyebrows. He never got to stand very long, however, for a lovely white-haired lady would yank him down by the sleeve. But then when the organ would swell again, he would rise again. For once no one was looking at Miss Osgood.

By the end of the service (four hops later), I was curious to meet the old gentleman. "You're new in this area, aren't you?"

He gave me a surprisingly firm handshake. "Ya, ya, Brother Rowe, we just retired at last Conference and thought we'd settle down here. We served this church years ago - when was it, Martha?"

"It was 1929 to 1931, Lars," the lovely white-haired lady said.

No wonder - I should have known. A retired preacher was like an old war horse who bridled for action at the sound of martial music. "Well, Brother and Sister ..."

"Olson."

"Olson, I'm delighted to welcome you back to your old church and hope that you will help with the services."

"Thanks, Brother Rowe, but it feels good just to set back and relax."

"Except when he jumps up," said Martha.

"Sorry, guess it's just a habit after forty-four years of Sunday services."

Martha squeezed my hand. "We'd like to have you out to our home - it's just a mile past the airport, the old Barstead place. Could you come tomorrow night about six?"

During the meal Lars had said little. He seemed determined to get the food down as fast as he could. About the only thing he did say was, "Pass Brother Rowe the pepper and the Psalter."

I wondered about his quaint expressions until I found out that he had never been to seminary. He had taken a correspondence course, a fairly common practice in his day.

Now we had finished dinner, and Martha was pouring us our third cup of coffee.

"Martha, why don't you sit down and relax after all your work?" I pointed toward her chair.

"Why, I do think that I better sit down before I fall down. Are you sure you don't need anything more?"

"Maybe less." I rubbed my full stomach.

Lars laughed. "Know what you mean, young fella, 'cause I bin eatin' her cooking for forty-three years."

Martha dropped wearily into her chair. "You forget, Lars. We haven't always had good eating. Remember back in the Depression when your salary was $600 a year - and we weren't getting all of that."

"Now, Mother, let's not look back -"

"The Depression when little Chris was born." She stared off into space and seemed to drift back ... "Chris and I are the only ones on the second floor of the hospital. Where's the nurse? She must be down on the first floor with the other patients. There's a crash from the nursery. Chris is crying. I ring the buzzer; I call out. There's no answer! I must go to him." She stood up, reached out and stumbled into the bedroom. "Oh, my baby, my baby. It's all right now - Mommy's here." On the mantle the clock ticked the years away, but for Martha no time had passed.

I looked uncomfortably over at Lars, and wondered what to say.

Lars pulled out a handkerchief and wiped his eyes. "She's never gotten over it." He looked up at the clock. "Guess I've never gotten over it neither. It happened right here in the Webber Hospital. Martha tried to git outa the hospital bed - in those days they kept mothers flat on their backs for ten days. When Martha swung her feet over the edge of the bed, she fell onta the floor. That woman actually crawled down the long hallway to the nursery. She found our Chris lyin' on the cold floor. An ice storm had smashed the window and blown over his basket." He turned his face away for a moment. "Little Chris was blue and shiverin' and cryin'. Martha put him in the basket and crawled back to her room, pullin' the basket all the way. By the time I came up to visit, she had little Chris in bed with her, tryin' to warm 'im up. After she sobbed out the story to me, I carried both of 'em outa the hospital and took 'em home."

Martha came out of the bedroom with a doll. She sat and rocked it, crooning softly.

Lars watched her sadly. "Martha held little Chris over the floor register in the parsonage tryin' to keep 'im warm. All night she held him on her shoulder so he could breathe. Chris was coughin' almost all the time by then. She held 'im over the floor register until ..." Tears flowed down their wrinkled cheeks onto their black clothes. They had never come out of the Great Depression.

Martha laid the doll aside and looked at me blankly for a moment while the years spun up to the present. "Lars, tell David something funny. Let's not be gloomy. Tell David about the mistake we made in Winnipeg."

"Oh, ya. Well, David, we always served churches in Nort' Dakota when it was against the law to serve alcohol in eatin' places. When we went upta Canada, we figgered they'd be the same way. We didn't have much money, and the only thing on the menu we could afford was 'high ball, 35 cents.' We ordered two of them, and they was delicious. When we got home, we told some of our members about the great bargain we found. They really poked fun at us. Guess we were pretty naive then."

I didn't say it, of course, but I thought they still were.

"Martha, I really enjoyed that pork roast - it's my favorite."

"Thank you, David."

"By the way, how did you folks like the service?"

Martha looked over at Lars, and he cleared his throat. "Well, we realize that you're young, and prob'ly they told you to do things that way at seminary, but for me, I like the Saint James Version of the Bible better than all those modern ones because it's more sacrilegious."

I kept a straight face because I couldn't laugh at these devoted old people. They had labored in the Lord's vineyard before I was a seed.

"And another thing, David, there's something missin' in the lethargy."

I wasn't sure that I had heard him right. "Did you say 'lethargy'?"

"Ya, ya, don'tcha know, the ritual. There's sumpthin' missin' in the lethargy, but I can't quite put my finger on it."

"Well, let me know if you think of it."

During the evening I had been dropped into depression, and now I was being raised to laughter. I had to get outside to relieve myself. "Well, I hope you folks will excuse me. I'd better be getting back. Good night, Martha; good night, Lars."

"Good night, David."

"You're always welcome here."

The next time we had communion the mystery about the "lethargy" was solved. Lars helped me with the communion, which he did with a practiced air. He didn't mix up the words as I had done, but he did have one trouble that I hadn't noticed before. When he gave the dismissals, he whistled through his bridgework on the S sounds: "Arise (whistle) and go in peace (whistle) and may the God of peace (whistle) go with you." That wasn't too bad, but at one point his false teeth went shooting out of his mouth. He grabbed them in midair and shoved them back in, right in front of the astonished congregation.

After the service he came up to me, and he was looking very pleased with himself. "I found what was missin' from the lethargy. It was the tedium."

"The tedium?" I blinked.

He pointed to the hymnal, and I read: "Te Deum Laudamus (We praise thee, O God)."

"See," he said triumphantly, "you can't have real lethargy without the tedium."

He had the gift of tongues.

In spite of the language barrier, Lars and I got along very well. We had only one difference of opinion that developed into a major issue. I believed that a pastor's place at a funeral was with the family: therefore I did not lead the casket or ride in the hearse. Instead I walked with the family and rode with the family. On the other hand, Lars felt that his place was with the deceased. He led the casket, rode in the hearse, and even stood at the graveside till everyone left the cemetery.

In late July Old Mrs. Morgan, the communion steward, passed away. (I hope it was nothing Lars or I did at the communion services.) At her funeral, Lars went his way, and I went mine. He stood next to the grave while I rode away with Mr. Morgan and his two daughters.

Irene Morgan looked back as we were pulling out of the cemetery. "Oh, look at Rev'rend Olson, that faithful old shepherd - he's still standing there at mother's grave."

Everyone glanced back with love and admiration.

Maybe I was wrong. Maybe Lars did have the right idea. I looked back again, but Lars had disappeared.

"You had better turn around," I said. "I'm afraid the faithful old shepherd has fallen into the hole."

We made a U-turn, drove back to the grave site, and helped Lars out of the grave. The only injury he had was to his dignity.

"The pursuit of higher education, huh?" Ben Graves

12 The Library Opens

In early August the townspeople were gathered in front of the fire hall for the dedication of the library. Tillie had done a good job of publicity on the phone, and Alf had driven the fire truck around the city with siren and loudspeaker blaring. Now the crowd, cordoned off by old fire hoses, was waiting for the ceremony to begin. Beyond the barrier blinked the sheriff's car, though the sheriff himself was sitting in his usual chair, now transplanted to the fire hall. At Alf's feet lay Old Flame, his tail drumming an excited beat. Mrs. Grundy, Mrs. Larson, and the other library volunteers were standing in front of the fire engine along with the rest of the Coffee Gang, also known as the Webber Town Council, also known as the Volunteer Fire Department. Today their role was clear - they had on their yellow slickers.

The Honorable Carl Lysne (it was his turn to be mayor that year) raised his megaphone. "Quiet, quiet, please. Thanks, folks. We're gathered here today for the official openin' of the Webber Public Liberry, an idea thunk up by Rev'rend David Rowe and carried out by a corps of volunteers headed by Mrs. Grundy and Mrs. Larson."

There was a small wave of applause. Mrs. Larson jerked her head at the unfamiliar sound, and Mrs. Grundy turned and smiled at me.

Carl continued: "I wanna thank alla those who gave books and helped with the liberry, 'specially George Olson who turned over his collection of three hunerd westerns and supplied the lumber for the shelves." George didn't even raise his head from his latest western, *Gunslinger.* "Our thanks go also to the firemen who cleaned out the loft and painted the entire fire hall." Gone were the cobwebs from the rafters; the whole place gleamed like the fire engine.

"The Liberry Committee would like to award a special citation to the person who contributed the most time and effort to the liberry." He paused while everyone wondered who that could be. "Will Hannah Larson please come forward?"

For a moment she was frozen, and then as the applause washed up in warm and unexpected waves on the dry and frozen shore of her soul, she began to melt - from the eyes downward. Ben and I took her by the arms and led her over to Carl, who was holding out a scroll. Carl lowered the megaphone and said, "Hannah, this's just a small token of the appreciation and affection we feel for you." Into her surprised hand he placed the scroll.

"Read it," someone called from the crowd. Others began to chant: "Read it, read it."

Hannah unrolled the scroll and tried to focus on it, but at that moment the best eyes in Webber were blinded by tears.

Carl took the scroll and glanced at it. "Tarnation, never could read that Old English script. Mrs. Grundy, you wrote it - you ought to be able to read it."

As Mrs. Grundy took the scroll, the entire crowd quieted down, for they knew that they were in the presence of The Teacher. "Hannah Larson, we honor you for your sharp eyes that functioned undimmed by dust and small print; for your willing arms that lifted tons of books; for your tireless legs that climbed the steps countless times. For all these simple deeds we honor you, because they add up in our minds to greatness." Mrs. Grundy rolled up the scroll and handed it to her old enemy. "Hannah, please accept this with our love."

Hannah stood there, her mouth working, her eyes brimming, unable to cope with her first honor in nearly a century. As Mrs. Grundy clasped the stick-like Hannah to her ample bosom, the free citizens of Webber raised such a cheer that Old Flame actually rose to his feet for a minute. It looked as if he, too, were showing honor.

After Mrs. Grundy released Hannah, I handed her some Kleenex, which she immediately began to use with loud honking and sniffling.

Carl whispered to her, "Soon's you're ready, we'll have the ribbon cutting'." She finished mopping up and nodded. Carl raised his megaphone. "And now our award-winner will cut the ribbons which are blocking both the bottom and the top of the stairs."

Mrs. Grundy pulled a pair of scissors out of her bag and handed it to Hannah, who started walking toward the base of the stairs. Her hand darted out and snipped the ribbon in two. More applause.

"'And now," said the mayor, "Mrs. Larson's beginnin' her - near as we can figger - 145th trip up that long flight of steps." We watched her ascend with surprising agility - without even once showing her ankle. At the top she cut the other ribbon, which parted fluttering.

"Mrs. Grundy will now join Mrs. Larson at the top of the stairs."

Dozens of eyes shuttled between Mrs. Grundy's hips and the narrow stairs; people shook their heads. Undeterred, Mrs. Grundy turned and rolled around the side of the fire engine and stepped into a tractor tire attached to three steel cables, which in turn were hooked to a longer cable. This ran clear up to a pulley affixed to the ceiling and down to a motor-driven winch on the fire hall floor. Alf started the motor, and there was a whirr as the tractor tire rose up in the air. As it rose, we saw a canvass sling unfold under the tire, completely surrounding Mrs. Grundy. The crowd gasped as she went up like an overweight Mary Poppins to join Mrs. Larson on the upper level.

"And now the liberry's open for business, and Alf's elevator's open for rides. The liberry's free, but the elevator costs $1.00 each way, proceeds to go toward buyin' books. Good readin' and good ridin'. That'll give us good 'rithmetic. Oh, ya all prob'ly can't git up to the liberry at the same time, so the Firemen and the Ladies' Auxiliary has set up some booths in the back of the fire hall. Be generous in your spendin' - all profit goes into the liberry fund. You'll find homemade cakes and pies, coffee and punch, and a su'prise treat, B.K.P.S. Ya, Curt Winter's donated two pigs to the liberry, and Busia Kowalski's made 'em into her prize-winnin' sausage."

The crowd could stand on ceremony no longer. They streamed around the fire truck, past Alf's sign that read: LIBERRY HOURS 1:00 to 4:00 DAILY EXCEPT SUNDAYS AND FIRES. Some went up the stairs to the library, some to Alf's elevator, and most to the booths at the back, especially to the booth where Curt and Busia were dishing out sausage.

Ben tapped me on the shoulder. "Quite a day for Webber. You really done sumpthin' for the town, Dave - 'specially for Old Hannah Larson."

"I guess I'm not so bad, after all."

"Nope, not by a long shot. C'mon and I'll treat you to coffee and B.K.P.S."

And then I saw a pair of very trim, un-Victorian ankles ascending the steps. "Excuse me, Ben, but I think I'll go up to the library first."

"The pursuit of higher education, huh?" He nodded wisely as I started up the steps after Arlene.

The narrow library was crammed with bodies. "Excuse me, Miss Osgood. Pardon me, Miss McConnell. Sorry, George." Finally, I worked my way through the crowd to the far end where Arlene was talking to Mrs. Larson and Mrs. Grundy at their check-out desks.

Mrs. Grundy looked up at me. "Oh, Reverend Rowe, I have a special library card for you." She reached into the center drawer of her desk and handed it to me. Two things caught my eye: the number at the top, #1, and a typed note across the bottom: "No book limit - no fines -no expiration date."

"Thank you, Mrs. Grundy. That's really very nice."

"It's only right, Reverend. You're the father of the library, and Hannah is the mother."

"Guess I'm not too old to have kids then." Hannah clutched her scroll and smiled.

I turned to Arlene and stammered, "Would - would you like anything to eat?"

"Thank you, Reverend Rowe, but I'm a pound overweight now."

I couldn't help looking and wondering where. "You look fine to me. How about a cup of coffee or some punch?"

"O.K., then we can come up later to get some books after the crowd thins out."

I liked that *we*. "Yes, that sounds good. Do you want to walk down or ride down?"

"It might be fun to ride."

I looked down and caught Alf's eye. He nodded. The next time his elevator came up, Arlene and I stepped in. When the tire rose into the air, we were thrown together inside the canvass sling. There was only one thing to do - I put my arms around Arlene. Alf, I thought, you're a mechanical genius, and this is the best dollar investment I ever made. On the way down, she apologized. "I'm sorry for bumping into you like this, Reverend, but I can't help it."

"That's all right, Arlene. I forgive you."

When we reached the bottom, I handed Alf my last dollar bill without regrets. We then went over to the beverage booth. Mad Ole, who had changed all the way from a white coat to a white apron, grinned up at us. "What'll it be, hot or cold?"

I looked at Arlene and she said, "Black coffee for me." Turning back to Ole, I told him, "Two coffees, one black, and one white."

"Yes, sir, Rev'rend." He went back to an urn and poured them. "That'll be ten cents."

I gave him a quarter and told him to keep the change. I was feeling high.

Arlene held the steaming coffee, closed her eyes, and breathed deeply. "I love the smell of fresh coffee."

"I'm hooked on it, too."

"It's wonderful of you to do this."

"It cost only a nickel."

"No, I mean the whole library idea."

"If you like it, then it's all worth it."

She looked at me strangely. "Not just me, but Mrs. Larson, Mrs. Grundy, Mr. Lysne, and all the others. And there's the sheriff enjoying Busia's sausage."

I glanced over at Fred chomping his way through a plateful. "My business is making people happy."

"And you're very good at it." It was my turn to look at her strangely. "Yes, you are. From the moment you steamed into Webber with your overheated radiator; and later walked down Main Street dressed in furs on a hot June day; and 'shed your body' at communion; and bowled over Miss McConnell in your sleeping bag; and got Charles Barrett, the confirmed bachelor, married to your aunt; and -"

"Hey, wait a minute. Don't I have any secrets?"

"Not very many, I'm afraid. Rowe–watching has become a community pastime. There's only one mystery - what did you do to the Lutheran pastor?"

"I can't tell even you yet - because I'm not sure how it's going to turn out. Can you wait till the end of summer?"

"Of course ... it's just nice to have coffee with a man who is a legend in his own time."

Where the time went I don't know. I was content just to be with her, and she appeared to be content to be with the 'legend', or me, or both.

"Please lift your feet, Rev'rend."

"What?" I turned away from Arlene's angelic face to see Alf pushing a big broom toward me. "Oh, sorry." Glancing around, I noticed that the crepe paper was down and the fire hall was empty, except for one or two people in each booth clearing up and counting up.

Arlene and I stood up, carried our chairs over to the side, and stacked them with the others. As she straightened, she brushed her shoulder-length hair back from her lovely face. "We better get upstairs to get some books before they close up."

"Do you want to ride?"

She blushed. "We better walk."

I enjoyed walking up behind her - I could have kept walking forever. When we got to the top, the shelves were empty, and Mrs.

Grundy and Hannah looked worn to a frazzle. Their desks were covered with charge cards from all the books.

"You're too late, my dears," said Mrs. Grundy.

Hannah nodded. "Ya, we're cleaned out. Everything's gone - even the old auto repair manuals."

I walked toward their desks. "That's amazing."

"No," said Mrs. Grundy, "that's sausage." She pointed to the sign: FREE LINK OF B.K.P.S. FOR EVERY 5 BOOKS.

I smiled at Arlene. "Perhaps the way to people's minds is through their stomachs."

"Well, I hope they'll digest these books," Hannah snapped. Mrs. Grundy looked despairingly at the two mountains of charge cards. "Hannah, let's save these till tomorrow."

"Suits me, Mabel." (I had never before heard Mrs. Grundy's first name, but the knowledge would do me little good. I would never be able to call The Teacher "Mabel.") Hannah got stiffly to her feet.

"May we give you a hand, Mrs. Grundy?" Arlene asked. As Mrs. Grundy tried unavailingly to lever herself up, Arlene and I grabbed her arms and lifted. She rose slowly like an arthritic elephant.

"Why, thank you, children. You can see that I'm very tired."

We walked with her to the elevator. Alf dropped his broom and hustled over to the winch. With a powerful whine it lifted off the tractor tire and raised it up to the balcony. We helped Mrs. Grundy into the tire.

"Do you want to ride down with me, children?"

Arlene and I quickly shook our heads. Two was company, but three would be suffocation.

"Well, I'll meet you downstairs then."

As I watched her sail away, I marveled that she did not let her prodigious body imprison her free soul.

At the end of her trip, we helped her out of the tire. Though she was nearly exhausted, she turned to Alf. "Thank you, Alfred, for giving me wings."

Alf hung his head, and I could see the color creep up the back of his neck into his ears. "Shucks, Teacher, I – I -"

"And you gave wings to David's dream, too." Then when he still hung his head, she said, "Forget the past, Alfred."

Alf straightened up. "Ya, ya, Teacher."

Ben came walking up, holding an adding machine tape. "Anybody here curious 'bout how much we made today?" The rest of the Coffee

Gang, Birdie, Hannah, Mrs. Grundy, and a few ladies I still didn't know gathered around the tractor tire.

"Don't keep us in suspense, Ben," Carl said, tiredness making his voice sharp.

"This's just a preliminary count, of course." Ben stretched out the tape.

"Are you gonna tell us or not?" Mad Ole made a snatch for the tape.

"Alright, I figger we made "$3,787.12.""

Curt asked, "Did you say three *t'ousand*?"

"Ya, ya, $3,787.12."

"That's more than we got in the city treasury," Carl said.

Mrs. Grundy looked heavenward. "Thank goodness. That makes us one of the best endowed small libraries in North Dakota."

Tiredness left everyone; good spirits returned.

"Ole, you got any more of that good coffee?" Frank asked.

"Near half an urn."

"Well, start pourin' then. Drinks are on me." Frank pulled the chained wallet out of his back pocket and fished out a $5.00 bill. "Here, hope this won't mix up our moneyman."

We trooped back to the coffee booth. As fast as Ole was setting them up, the Coffee Gang and the others were grabbing them. They sure could hold their coffee.

I felt a gentle tugging on my sleeve. "Pardon me, Father." It was Busia Kowalski. "How you like sausage I gave you?"

"Well, ah, I don't really know - the gypsies got it." Suddenly the hall grew very quiet.

"Then is good I save last three pounds." She handed me a grease-stained package. "Be careful of gypsies, Father."

I looked around at the Coffee Gang. Fred was holding his stomach and looking a bit green. "I think it'll be safe now, Busia. Somehow I feel that the gypsies won't bother me today. Besides, the sheriff himself will walk me home."

The laughter of the rest of the Coffee Gang almost drowned out Fred's groan.

"There's a man crawlin' up your sidewalk." Hannah Larson

13 The Superintendent Drops In (A Crashing Bore)

One morning I made my usual walk to pick up the mail at the post office. On the way I passed Arlene's house and gave it a quick glance, with the hope of catching sight of her or at least a member of her family. That would increase my chances of seeing her. However, no Olsons were to be seen.

Then I heard the familiar bellow of Yon Yonson. "GOOD MORNIN', REV'REN'. COME ON OVER AND TALK TO MY FODDER."

I looked across the street and saw Yon standing in the box of his truck, parked behind the dairy. He tossed a twenty-gallon cream can down to an older, smaller version of himself. When I had seen his father leap up the church steps, I had no idea that he was over ninety. As I crossed the street, I tried to observe signs of his father's great antiquity. Of course, the noxious vapors from the old man's pipe partially hid him, but even when I got close I saw little indication that the elder Yonson was ninety-one.

"FODDER, DO YOU 'MEMBER THE REV'REN'?"

The old man peered closely at me. "YA, YA, I REMEMBER."

"Nice to meet you again," I said, but the old man cupped his ear.

"YOU'LL HAFTA SPEAK UP, REV'REN'. MY FODDER'S A BIT HARD OF HEARING."

I was driven back by the sound of his voice. As my ears started to ring, I wondered whether Yon's yelling was the result of his father's hearing loss or the cause of it.

I said, "NICE TO MEET YOU AGAIN."

The elder Yonson's face split in a familiar grin. He puffed a tobacco cloud at me and extended a crushing handshake.

Now I was sure that Yon hadn't exaggerated his father's strent, I mean strength.

"You'd better give up smoking," I joked, "or it will shorten your life."

"WHADDA YOU SAY?" The father again cupped his ear.

Yon spoke up for me, his voice increasing in volume. "THE REV'REN' SEZ SMOKING WILL SHORTEN YOUR LIFE."

All traffic stopped on Main Street. I felt the ears of the entire community pointing my way. The old man pounded me appreciatively on the back. "THAT'S A GOOD ONE, REV'REN'."

I escaped as quickly as I could from the well-meaning Yonsons, with my eyes watering, my back aching, and my ears ringing.

Sometimes it's good to maintain a certain distance from one's parishioners. In the Yonsons' case, the right distance was about two blocks - upwind.

The Red Owl Manager was out sweeping his sidewalk and chuckling, "I hope you don't declare Welch's Grape Juice harmful to health."

When I darted into the post office, the postmaster beckoned me over to the window. "Heard you were comin', so I got everything outa your box." He handed me a stack of letters - then held up a postcard to the light. "Your aunt - you know, the one that married up with Charles Barrett - she sent you a card from, lemme see, Cork, Ireland. She writes - no, it's Charlie's handwriting: 'Thanks, David, for marrying me to the most fascinating creature on earth!' Now, here's her message – 'Charles is over here recharging the Blarney Stone. Be back later this century.'" He finally relinquished the card to me. "Oh, ya, they sent you a package, too." He ambled over to a big table and came back with a package. "Be sure and bring your aunt in. I'd like to meet the woman. Things git purty dull around here - some days we don't even get a post card."

I assured him I would and went around the block, carefully avoiding the dairy and hoping I would undergo no more invasions of privacy.

However, as I was passing the newspaper office, I noticed that my shoelace was untied. While I was tying it, I happened to overhear the editor speaking to his only employee, "Ernie, what's our biggest type?"

"Seventy-two point Roman, Sam."

"Then set this headline in seventy-two point Roman: METHODIST MINISTER BEGINS CRUSADE AGAINST TOBACCO."

Was there no privacy? Was everything known? With cheeks burning - not entirely in embarrassment - I hurried home, slamming the door behind me. Now I was going to have a little time to myself, away from the prying eyes of Mrs. Larson and the rest of the community. I even pulled down the living room shades.

I settled down with the mail and worked my way through it: there were ads for pulpit robes, book sales, advent dime folders, and a new Methodist Publishing House catalog. Just one semi-personal letter - it was from the new District Superintendent, Victor Hanson - and it concluded with a handwritten note: "I'll be flying up that way next week and will drop in to see you."

Now for the package. It was from Germany. I took it into the kitchen and set it carefully on the three-legged table. Grabbing the scissors out of the drawer, I began the long process of cutting open the well-wrapped package and unwrapping layer after layer of paper. It must be glass. It - there revealed before me was a beer stein. Just what I didn't need; just what I could never show. Why, if anyone saw this stein, they would immediately assume I was an alcoholic. I could just see the next issue of the *Webber Wolfcall*: CRUSADE TURNS INTO BINGE - PASTOR GOES FROM IN HIS STEPS TO IN HIS CUPS.

But it would be a shame never to use this beautiful stein. Just one quick toast to the bride and groom, and I would hide it away forever. I went over to the refrigerator and looked inside. All I had in the way of beverages were milk and root beer. Milk would never do for a toast - it had to be something stronger. I opened the root beer and let it gurgle its way into the depths of the stein. The whole bottle barely covered the bottom. I believe the term is "one finger." I raised the stein - it took both hands - and said: "To Charles and Ellie, wherever they are, may they have short storms and long rainbows."

The phone rang, and I went into the dining room with the stein.

"Rev'ren', this's Hannah. You can't see this 'cause your shades is down - but there's a man crawlin' up your sidewalk. 'Scuse me, I gotta git back to the winder -"

I let the phone fall back into the cradle. "Oh, no, what next?" I supposed I should go take a look, though, so I walked into the front hall and peeked through the window in the front door. *There* was a man crawling up the sidewalk, a man in a black suit. Suddenly I remembered the letter from the new D.S. Opening the door, I called out to him, "Are you Victor Hanson?"

The man raised his head, nodded, saw the stein, gasped, and collapsed.

I set the stein down and rolled him over - his clothes were torn and burned, and he had some cuts and burns. He was unconscious. What could I do? Aha, I had it. I grabbed the stein and poured root beer on his face.

He came to, spluttering and coughing, and looked at the stein. "I hope you can explain that."

"I think so, but first let me help you into the house." After I helped him to his feet, he put his arm around my shoulders, and we both staggered into the house. "Do you want to lie on the davenport or what?"

"No, just let me sit down for a moment." He sat down in the uneasy chair and shot up again. "Don't you have anything more comfortable?" He eyed the lumps in the chairs and the Great Depression in the davenport.

"Sorry, I'll get you one from the kitchen." In my haste and confusion I got the chair with the weak back and hurried back to my boss. "Here, try this."

He sat back and kept on going, his feet going right over his head, a perfect somersault, but maybe he didn't feel up to it after his plane crash.

He lay there, unmoving. I again knelt beside him and rolled him over. "Are you all right?"

He looked up. "You aren't going to pour any more beer on me, are you?"

"Oh, no - besides that was only root beer. I was just - er - drinking a toast to ... well, it's hard to explain."

"Never mind, I'm taking an inventory of my bones. Well, everything seems to function pretty well ... despite the plane crash and your chairs. I'll just lie here on the floor while you call the ambulance."

Just then we heard a loud siren with a counterpoint of clanging. Webber's fire truck pulled up in front of the parsonage, and seven figures dressed in yellow tumbled off. They ran in with hatchets and a big hose.

"Where's the fire?" Fred yelled.

For a moment I was stunned. "Fire? There's no fire."

Carl pointed at the D.S. "But this guy looks burnt."

The D.S. raised himself up on one elbow and pointed with his other arm. "My plane crashed - at the end of the street."

"You guys go check the plane," Ben said. "I'll stay here. But hurry back to take him to the hospital."

The rest of the firemen ran out, jumped on the fire engine, and clanged away.

Hannah came hurrying in and looked at the D.S. lying on the floor. "How's the poor drunkard? Elmer was afflicted the same way - God rest his soul."

"I am not drunk, Madam. My only drinking was involuntary when this - this person dumped his beer stein on me."

"It was just root beer," I said.

"I thought I saw a stein when we pulled up." Ben went outside and came back in carrying the huge stein. He sniffed at it. "It's root beer a 'right."

"How would I know?" the D.S. said primly. "I never touch stimulants."

"I just got the stein from Charles and Ellie -" I looked from Ben and Hannah to the D.S. "You see, my aunt is in Europe on her honeymoon, so I thought I'd drink a toast to her and her new husband."

Ben grinned. "I knew you could explain it O.K."

"Of course," said Hannah, "you oughta know the Rev'ren' wouldn't of done no wrong."

"Pardon me for interrupting this testimony meeting," rose a sarcastic voice from the body on the floor, "but I feel I need some medical attention."

"Sure enough," said Ben. "Soon's the fire truck gits back we'll take you to the hospital." Ben turned to me. "Who is he, Dave? Do you know him?"

"It's Victor Hanson, the new D.S."

"Oh, sorry, I didn't recognize you, Brother Hanson. You look sorta diff'rent, all stretched out there like that with your clothes torn and burnt -"

"Now before the Keystone Cops come back," the D.S. cut in, looking at me grimly, "I would like to give you a message: Brother Omdahl has just had a heart attack, so I am naming you as dean of the junior high camp next week. He hasn't lined anything up, so you'll have to do everything. If I survive, I will be the inspirational speaker." He gritted his teeth and shuddered. "And another thing, Mister Rowe, I would like to have absolute *quiet* in the hospital - that is, *without* company."

His wish for quiet was not to be granted so soon, for the fire engine pulled up with its bell ringing and siren shrieking.

In rushed the Coffee Gang, with Mad Ole and Curt bearing a stretcher. They lifted the D.S. onto the stretcher, and The Coffee Gang hurried out again.

I watched them perch the stretcher on a narrow catwalk on the side of the fire engine and then roar away in a hail of gravel. What a way to make an impression on a D.S., the man who had the power of appointment or disappointment. It looked as if I would face a lifetime of "challenging" (problem) churches - at least during Victor Hanson's term of office. And on top of that, I was supposed to be dean of a camp that I had never seen. I didn't know where to start. How could I possibly get ready by next week?

I blinked. There walking toward me again - this time in shorts - was my angel. How did she know just when I most needed her?

She extended a bare round arm toward me. "Reverend Rowe, I finished typing the stencil for the bulletin."

I then had another inspiration. "How would you like to be a counselor at camp next week? Scratch that - how would you like to be co-dean?"

"I'd love to," she answered in her soft warm voice.

I glanced down at her beautiful legs and thought to myself: And I would love to see you running around in shorts for a week. I was a religious genius! I did have aptitude for this job.

"Put on therefore ... bowels of mercies ..." Colossians 3:12 (KJV)

14 Camp

Camp taught me the difference between boys and girls.

Right after the Sunday service I grabbed a quick bite, threw my stuff into the car, and drove over to Nordahls' to pick up their daughter Valerie. Her whole family came out of the little house. One carried a big suitcase, another a shopping bag, another a sleeping bag, and still another a crinoline petticoat on a hanger. Then I drove over to the Adamses' place. Karen had almost the same luggage - a beach bag substituting for the shopping bag. Lastly, I stopped at Olsons' to pick up Arlene and her younger brother Teddy. Arlene had the standard female luggage, including some blouses and skirts on hangers along with the inevitable crinoline. I was able to get everything into the trunk except the beach bag. Of course, the crinoline petticoats and Arlene's clothes went inside on the clothing hooks, though it would have been more accurate to say that they filled up the entire back seat from port to starboard.

"I guess we can squeeze two in the back seat," I said, "but it's going to be scratchy."

Arlene turned to her brother. "Where's your luggage?"

Teddy reached in his pocket and drew out a clean pair of socks. Ah, I thought, there he stands in the shoes of Brother Berdahl, the walking circuit rider. And now I knew the difference between boys and girls.

"Oh, Teddy, you'll need more than that." Arlene went back into the house. "Mother, guess what Teddy's done!"

About five minutes later Arlene and Mrs. Olson came out with a hastily-packed suitcase and a hastily-rolled sleeping bag. "I'm sorry, Reverend Rowe. Will you be able to get these in, too?" Arlene looked beseechingly at me from under her dark eyebrows.

"I think so." I pulled everything out of the trunk and looked at it. As I began to repack, the miracle happened - everything went into the trunk. Even Teddy's stuff; even the beach bag. But not the crinolines.

Mrs. Olson asked, "Teddy, do you have your jacket?"

"No, Ma."

"Just a minute, Rev'rend." She went inside again.

While she was gone, the girls were trying to get Teddy to sit in the back seat between the petticoats. "No," he yelled, "I'd rather die!" This sent them into screams of laughter.

The seating arrangement worked out well: Karen and Valerie in the back seat, and Arlene and Teddy in the front. Teddy claimed the seat by the window; otherwise he thought he would get car-sick.

That put Arlene right next to me. Teddy was a valuable man to have around.

Mrs. Olson came hurrying out. "Here's your jacket." She leaned in and gave Teddy a kiss.

"Ma!"

Everyone chorused good-bye and waved until we turned the corner.

Thus we came to camp.

Right away Arlene and I became involved in registering several hundred kids from all over the state. Cars arrived all afternoon, disgorging excited campers and soon-to-be-suffering counselors, 'prisoners' and 'guards' in the language of that year.

"Hey, Warden!" boomed Ron's big voice.

"Ron!" I stood up and stretched my back back to normal. "It's good to see you. I haven't seen you since ... the revival."

"We've got to get together more often, Dave. Oh, hi, Arlene. You're co-warden, aren't you?"

"Co-dean." She looked up smiling.

"That sounds too much like a drug, which could become habit forming."

"Say, Ron," I asked, "would you give us a hand with the registration?"

"Sure, as long as you don't put me down in The Swamp."

"And why should you get better treatment than the rest of us?"

"O.K., I'll help anyway."

In this way, Arlene and I recruited helpers in the process of trying to get 200 yelling kids straightened out.

In the late afternoon, Ron came over to my table. "How about going outside for a breather, Dave? I think the others can handle it for awhile."

"Good idea, Ron." I leaned over to talk to Arlene, but she was deeply involved with the group from the Williston church, all of whom wanted to stay in the same cabin.

Ron and I walked outside and up the hill behind the registration building. On the hilltop a wind cooled us delightfully. Around us spread the panorama of the camp: the hills ringing the lake, the cabins on the lower level ringing the chapel and the dining hall. The whole lower level was dotted with lovely old trees.

"Umm, it's great up here," I said.

"Sure beats being indoors."

"Just look at the kids running over the hills and all around the camp."

"They're curious and energetic. Just thought of something, Dave. What's the proper term for a group of junior high kids?"

"I give up. What?"

"A 'rash of adolescents' or a 'brace of teenagers'."

I laughed. "Ron, it's good to have you around. I really appreciate your pitching in at the last moment."

"Glad to, Dave. It was unfair of His Holiness to hit you like that."

"Well, I suppose he blamed me for the plane crash."

"It's his own fault - that's the third crack-up I've heard about. It's a miracle that he walks away from each one."

"Or crawls," I amended.

"Victor clings to the past - that's why he's known as 'The Reverend Victorian'. Did you know that he was called 'The Flying Chaplain of World War II'?"

"No, I didn't."

"Well, The Flying Chaplain has now come to earth." Ron pointed to a long black vehicle negotiating the tight turn into the camp.

"A hearse?"

"Victor never could pass up a bargain. He couldn't turn down a Cadillac for 200 bucks."

From the hills and out of the registration hut streamed a crowd of curious campers. Ron swept his arm toward the arriving hearse. "What say, old chap; shall we go view the remains of our late superintendent?"

"After you, Ron." We trooped down the hill to the parking lot. Ron walked up to the driver. "How are things, Mrs. Hanson?"

"Not so good."

"Miriam, have you met David?" She shook her head. "David Rowe is the new pastor at Webber."

"Oh, yes, where Victor had his last crash."

"I'm sorry, ma'am."

"It's not your fault. I've been after him to get rid of that flimsy old plane and get some suitable transportation - but he got this instead. I'm so embarrassed, having to drive him all over in this hearse. He's taking a nap - all stretched out in the back like a corpse. Oh, I wish I could do something to disguise what this is."

"Don't worry, Miriam. Some night Dave and I will paint it red and hang ladders on the sides."

We went back and joined the curious who were peering in at the sleeping superintendent.

"Looks peaceful," I noted.

"Remarkably lifelike."

Just then Victor opened his eyes and sat up. Several campers screamed; a bunch went over the hill.

"He moves," I said.

"He rises," Ron added.

"The day of resurrection is at hand."

Ron moved around to the rear of the hearse and swung open the rear door. "Lazarus, come forth!"

Victor smiled. He may or may not have heard us - he seldom listened to anyone. Still he enjoyed being the center of attention. "Did you notice how I've fixed this up?" He pointed to a refrigerator and stove, all done in tasteful black. "I even have a hat rack."

"Wow," I said, "a live-in hearse."

"What a way to go!"

Victor looked at us with his approximation of a smile. "I'm glad I caught you boys. I need both of you to help me get the service set up for tonight."

Ron gave me a pained look.

"Hop in. Miriam will drive us down to the barn."

I felt odd climbing into the hearse, but at least I was going in under my own power. Victor picked up a speaking tube. "Navigator to pilot, navigator to pilot, take us down to the barn. Over and out."

As the big Cadillac started up, I felt very conspicuous before the eyes of all the campers - I wasn't the exhibitionist that Victor was.

The hearse rolled smoothly down the hill to the lower level of the camp and then veered off into the trees to stop at a badly-weathered barn, the only original building left from the old Folson farm.

Victor eased out of the hearse, fished out a key ring, and went up to the barn doors. "I hope everything is still intact. I haven't seen the stuff for years." He unlocked a chain around the bar. "Here, give me a hand with these doors."

The doors opened with an unwilling screech, and we entered the cool gloom. Victor started rummaging through a bunch of old stage sets and separating them into piles.

"Now, here's the flight plan: I'm going to do my old series on the history of Methodism entitled 'An Endless Line of Splendor'. This first pile is for tonight. Set it up in the chapel." He glanced at his watch. "I'm going to supper, and I'll see you in the chapel at 1900 hours."

He walked out with an attempt at a military bearing, which is hard for a rubber ball to do. When we heard the hearse pull away, Ron kicked Pile One with his toe. "I don't see how we'll ever get this junk to stand up."

"Yes, it's as spineless as a cobweb."

"Well, Dave, let's give it the old seminary try."

The next two hours passed slowly as Ron and I made trip after trip between the barn, work shop, and chapel. First we tried making wooden supports, but the old sets were too frail. Then Ron suggested 'skyhooks,' so we rigged up some wires and finally got Pile One transformed into Set One.

"Not bad," I said.

"Not bad? You mean a *miracle!*"

About 6:30 Arlene came walking in with two chicken dinners. "Reverend Rowe and Reverend Wright, how would you like some supper?"

"You're an angel." I looked from one delectable sight to the other. She blushed.

"And I'll eat to that." Ron started digging in.

"Arlene, I'm sorry I went off without saying a word. That's been bothering me for the last two hours."

"That's all right, Reverend. I understand. Reverend Hanson told me you two were helping with the evening service. Well, I had better get back to our children - I mean the campers." She hurried out the door.

Ron waved a half-eaten chicken leg at me. "That co-dean of yours is kinda cute."

"Cute! Are you blind? She's the most gorgeous woman I've ever laid eyes on!"

"Aha, do I detect some feeling in that remark - some love interest, perhaps?"

I sighed. "Yes, but it's all one way."

"Oh, yeah? Well, contrary to what a certain pastor thinks, I'm not blind. I see the way she looks at you - like you're one of the twelve apostles or even J.C. himself."

"Really?"

"Yeah, I think you two kids have got a bad case of 'pedestalitis'."

"What?"

"You've got each other up on pedestals. Yes, the Reverend and his angel, the awed couple. Someone's going to fall off, and I hope it won't be too hard on either one of you."

"Well, what should I do about it?"

"You should - I say this as an old married man who has just had his ninth anniversary - you should fall off the pedestal as soon as you can. That's why they call it falling in love."

Before I had time to finish my supper, Victor came striding in. "It's almost time for the service, and we haven't gotten the lights and sound effects worked out."

We groaned, but we went to work. After all, he was the boss.

At 7:00 the campers started coming in. We were working frantically back stage. At 7:30 the campers were becoming fidgety. Finally we finished and gave Victor the cue. Dressed in a black robe, he strode out on stage and began to speak in his most ministerial tones: "Tonight we begin a great trip through our past. I present to you 'An Endless Line of Splendor'."

Backstage Ron blew at one of the flimsy sets and whispered, "He means 'An Endless Line of Squalor'." I clapped my hand over my mouth and bit my cheek to keep from laughing.

Thus began (was it only?) two hours of boredom: Victor was Wesley; Victor was Asbury; Victor was the horse.

Ron and I were handling the lights and sound effects, so we had to stay awake, but the audience had no reason to postpone sleep. Victor had violated the first rule of night production – never turn out all the lights. The kids slept peacefully, tired out from their first day of running around the 160-acre camp. When the lights finally came on, we had to wake them up to get them to bed.

Every afternoon found Ron and me rebuilding the past for The Reverend Victorian, and every evening found the two of us backstage. We were Victor's *deus ex machina* (God from a machine). Just as, the old Greeks had saved their heroes by the intervention of the gods, we were called on to speak in thunder and lightning or to produce the Holy Spirit like a dove on the end of a fishing pole. It was exacting but not exciting. I was embarrassed that the kids were getting enough sleep at my camp.

Friday noon Ron grabbed me and led me behind the barn. "Dave, we've got to do something - I can't go through two more nights of this."

"I agree, but what can we do?"

"A little clever sabotage. Now listen ..."

Later that afternoon, Ron went up to Victor. "How would you like to use some animals to heighten the realism?"

"Excellent!" said Victor. "Now you're getting into the spirit of the thing."

That evening we were ready. Victor was portraying the westward spread of Methodism, when the side door opened. In came a cow led by Ron, determined to do a little spreading of his own. The cow let fly with a large liquid pie. In a pasture on soft grass, it wouldn't have been such a smash, but on a concrete floor! Like a soft-nosed bullet, it spread on impact and kept spreading. The cow evacuated the chapel of 220 people in seconds. Ron was the last one out, and he slammed the door shut. "Can you imagine what that would do if it got outside?"

That ended indoor services at camp.

About midnight I heard a tap at my window. I arose sleepily and glanced over my dozen small charges. Ron was standing outside the open window. "How did you like the special effects?"

"Spectacular! But did you have to get so messy?"

"Maybe I did give her too much prune juice."

"Prune juice!"

"Yes, just in case there was an obstruction in her 'bowels of mercies'."

"And the Word became flesh and dwelt among us ... " John 1:14
"The best way to get across an idea is to wrap it up in a person."
Anon.

15 The D.S. Strikes Again

In startling contrast to The Reverend Victorian was Kim, a college student from Korea sent to us by the Board of Missions. He was as small as the junior high boys and as energetic, whereas the D. S. was as active as a giant sloth and as up-to-date.

The next morning we were sitting outside the chapel, for still obvious reasons. Miriam Hanson, as Conference Missionary Secretary, got up to introduce Kim. Miriam was a sweetheart: lovely, gracious, and filled with southern charm. Somehow Victor had snared her during his years at Asbury Seminary in Kentucky.

"We are privileged to have Kim, who has come all the way from Korea, to speak to us. Let's give him a warm welcome as an ambassador from across the seas."

The kids clapped and cheered as Kim came forward.

"Thank you, thank you." He bowed from side to side. "You and I are of different races. In our world there are also other races. How can we get along? How can we live in peace? Let me tell you an ancient story that I call 'The Five Fighting Fingers'.[4]

"Once upon a time the five fingers had a fight. Each one thought that he should be the leader of the others. They argued and fought until they were tangled up.

"'Listen,' gasped the thumb, 'let's go see the Wise Man and ask him to pick the leader.'

"The fingers untangled themselves and set off for the Wise Man's hut, which was on the top of a high hill. Somehow they climbed to the top.

"'Well, fingers,' said the Wise Man 'what brings you here?'

"'All of us disagree,' answered the thumb. 'We have come to ask you to pick the leader. Why don't you pick me? I am different from all the others, those more or less identical brothers.'

"'I should be the leader,' said the index finger. He waved himself right in front of the Wise Man's face. 'Without me the teacher could not teach. Without me the preacher could not preach.'

"'No, no,' said the next finger. 'I have a better idea. Let's line up to see who is tallest. There, since I am the tallest, I should be the leader.'

"The fourth finger looked angry. 'Just let me ask one question. When people get married, where do they put the wedding ring? On me, of course. I should be the leader.'

"'Wait,' cried the little finger, 'pick me, pick me.'

"The other fingers laughed.

"'No, listen! When a person goes to church, he folds his hands and bows toward the altar. Since I am the closest one to the altar, I must be the closest one to God. Make me the leader.'

"The fingers turned to the Wise Man. They found him staring out of the open door of his hut toward the eternal mountains.

"'Tell us, tell us, which one should be the leader?'

"He turned and smiled at them. 'There is not just one leader. There are four leaders.'

"'Oh,' said the thumb, 'then tell us which one is the servant of the other four.'

"'Each one,' said the Wise Man."

Kim gave us an especially radiant smile. "I am here as your servant."

He won our hearts.

As the kids crowded around Kim, Ron came up to me. "I was watching them - they were hanging onto every word."

The Reverend Victorian went by, mumbling to himself. "Why did that go over? That little foreigner had no props, no sets, no lights. He didn't even use a pulpit."

I spoke to his retreating back. "It went over because *he* was the message - and there was nothing to get in the way."

Reverend V. was still muttering. "I just can't understand it. He's just a kid, and I've been a preacher for forty-one years. I just can't -" He stopped dead. "I'm really going to have to come up with something now." He bustled away.

"Victor," I called.

"Save your breath, Dave." Ron grabbed my arm. "Victor doesn't listen to anyone. He is partly deaf and completely dumb."

But Victor made a U-turn and came back to me. "Brother Rowe, I was distressed by the folk dancing last night, the immoral contact of bodies."

"I see, but how about that game where you sat on the girls' laps? That had even more body contact than dancing."

"Not the same thing at all," he spluttered. "There was no music."

I was already late for the next event on the schedule, so I hurried back to my cabin. The boys from my side and the girls from Arlene's side were already gathered in the center classroom for our "The Sky's the Limit" discussion group.

"Why don't we all go outside under the trees?" I suggested. That met with immediate approval.

"What would you like to talk about today?" Arlene asked the kids as they lay or sat or sprawled around in a rough circle under a big elm. "War and peace ... race relations ... dating?"

No one reacted.

"Any other ideas?"

No response.

I came to Arlene's rescue. "Come on, kids. You don't want to sit and stare at my big nose for an hour, do you?"

"I wish I had a big nose ..." Teddy sighed. "And a big body to go with it."

Karen lamented. "You can have my big, ugly, flat body if you want. I look like a boy, anyway."

Around that circle of young, attractive, healthy youngsters came confessions of terrible deformities: of eyes too close together or too far apart, of flat feet or pigeon toes, of off-color hair or pimpled complexions, of knock knees or bow legs. One girl surprised us by saying that she was too short from the knees down. We looked, and her legs seemed long enough to reach the ground. Arlene thought that her own calves were too skinny, although I silently disagreed. Amazingly, everyone had some physical defect, even though no one else could see it.

The hour flew by - I had unwittingly started our best discussion by my chance remark.

Arlene brought it to a close. "God will correct many of our so-called deformities by the natural process of growth. I was late to ... develop, but the miracle happened. For the rest, learn to accept yourself as you accept others and as others accept you."

I liked her theology. I wished Reverend Victorian shared it.

After lunch I had my first free afternoon - without being a stagehand. I wandered over to the cabin, but all my "family" was gone. When I came out, I saw Arlene sunbathing on a blanket and reading. I stood there admiring her as she lay on her stomach, her slender legs extending out behind her.

I dropped down next to her.

"I don't think your calves are skinny."

She jumped. "Oh, you frightened me, Reverend Rowe."

I wasn't making much progress - I was still at the Reverend level. I lay back, put my hands under my head, and looked up at the clear blue sky. "Sorry, Arlene, I didn't mean to startle you." I heard her close her book. Silence, not entirely uncomfortable, grew between us.

"Arlene, tell me about yourself." I pulled a blade of grass and stuck the tender stem between my teeth.

"There's not much to tell. I was born in Webber and lived there all my life until I went away to college."

"Please go into more detail than that, Arlene. Tell me everything - from the beginning."

"O.K., if you really want to know ... . My mother sent for Doctor Hodgson one October 16. She had been washing clothes and had been going up and down the basement steps all morning. I guess I was premature - I weighed only three pounds."

I rolled onto my side and looked at her. "You've filled out well."

"Please, Reverend." She blushed.

I tried to relieve her of embarrassment. "Three pounds - that's less than my nose!"

"Reverend Rowe, I wish you wouldn't make so many remarks about your nose. You're always saying things like 'Eagle Beak' and 'Deacon Beacon.' I - I think you look very distinguished - and ruggedly handsome." She sat up, and her ivory face was suffused with color, which was starting to spread over the cream of her bare arms and legs.

I was touched. "Thank you, Arlene. No one has ever said that to me before. Boy, five minutes around you and even Cyranno would stop thinking about a nose job." I jumped up. "Sleeping Beauty, how would you like to go for a walk?"

"O.K., if you stop running yourself down."

"O.K., if you stop calling me Reverend."

She laughed. "All right."

"Will you shake on it?" I extended my hand. After a moment her small hand slipped warmly into mine. "Now say my name."

We stood there near the big elms as I watched her try to form the words. "All right, Rev ... Re ... I mean, David." A warm glow spread through me. My name sounded very good on her lips.

"All right, you two, now march!" We spun around at the sound of Reverend Victorian's voice, but he wasn't talking to us. Instead he was pushing a boy and a girl in our direction. The kids were stumbling across the uneven field with Reverend V.'s heavy hands on their shoulders. It was Arlene's brother and Karen.

"Well, co-deans, I caught these two sparking in my hearse."

"Sparking? What do you mean?" The Reverend V. always sounded so antiquated.

"I mean they had sneaked into my hearse and were - were osculating."

"Osculating?"

Reverend V. drew me aside, careful to put his back to Arlene. "They were k – k - kissing." Then he resumed his normal tone, which was amplified to reach the back pew of the largest church. "Co-deans, I want you to chastise them severely for trespassing and – er - lowering camp morals. Now I'll leave the culprits with you while I get ready for my special service." He started away and turned back, sweat glistening on his porcine face. "Brother Rowe, I want you to gather all the campers at Vesper Point right away!" He waddled off.

I looked helplessly at Arlene and then at the kids. Reverend V. seemed dedicated to ruining everyone's love life.

Teddy hung his head and kicked at the grass. "Sorry, Sis, I was just goin' inta the dinin' hall and heard Karen cryin' on the phone. She was so homesick. All I did was put my arm around her. Then we went outside to get away from the other kids, and the hearse was right there, so we just slipped inside for some privacy. 'Fore I knew it, we were huggin' and kissin'."

Karen nodded her head fearfully. "It's my fault, Rev'rend Rowe. Teddy was so nice that I -"

"Don't worry about it, kids. What you did is the most natural thing in the world, what the scripture says is 'the way of a man with a maiden.'" (Proverbs 30:19) I looked over Teddy's tousled head at Arlene. She was wiping a tear from her eye.

The two kids looked up at me, and their fear was gone. "You mean you ain't gonna punish us?"

"Punish you? No, Teddy, I'm proud of you for trying to comfort Karen."

"Thanks, Rev." (And the word was a short, snappy one syllable.) Teddy squared his shoulders and held his head high. Though he was only five feet tall, he looked like a big man at that moment.

I glanced at Karen. She had a pretty face atop her long lean body. "Are you still homesick?"

"Gosh, no!" She gazed adoringly down at Teddy, who reached out and took her hand.

"Can we go now, Rev?" Teddy asked.

"Sure - just one word of advice. You can 'spark' anywhere - just stay away from the hearse - you don't want to cause any more combustion."

They skipped away hand in hand.

"David, thanks. That was a beautiful thing you did."

"You're welcome, Arlene. Before this summer I might have been tougher on him, but I'm getting to understand 'the way of a man with a maiden.'" And if I played my cards right (to use an un-Methodist expression), that young man was going to be my brother-in-law.

"Well, duty calls. I hate to leave, but I have to get everyone to Vesper Point."

Arlene already had her back to me and was folding up the blanket along with the precious moment.

I turned and ran toward the dining hall, fuming to myself. Darn that D.S. He has the sensitivity of - of a frozen mastadon. And then I ceased feeling so guilty about what we had done to his indoor pageants.

In the dining hall, I flipped on the power unit for the P.A. system and grabbed the microphone. "Attention, all campers; attention, all campers. Please go immediately to Vesper Point."

When I got to the point overlooking the lake, about half of the campers were already there. Ron came up to me. "What's up?"

"Your friendly neighborhood Superintendent. I don't know what he has in mind. He just said to gather here right away."

"That could mean anything." Ron made an elaborate show of searching the lake, the shoreline, and the sky. "He could even parachute in."

I laughed. "I guess we have to be prepared for anything." I turned back to the assembled campers. "Everyone please sit down on the grass and wait for the superintendent." I looked around for Arlene, but didn't spot her, so I sat next to Ron.

Away to my right some cattle were coming down to the lake to drink and graze on the grassy hillside. I thought I recognized the cow that had delivered the *coup de grace* to Reverend V. "Ron, is that the one?"

"It could be - she still has double the output of the others."

I leaned back on the grassy bank. "Isn't it peaceful out here, watching the cows graze?"

For once Ron was serious. "As the Psalmist says, 'For the cattle on a thousand hills are God's.'" (Psalm 50:10)

Suddenly the silence was shattered by the blast from an out-of-tune trumpet. We turned to see The Reverend Victorian approaching in a small boat. While the lifeguard strained at the oars, a brown-robed Reverend V. was tooting his own horn, which he hadn't played in twenty years.

"What in the world!" I exclaimed.

"I hope it's not The Last Trumpet," Ron declared. "No, I do believe that Reverend V. is going to have a Galilean service."

"What's that?"

"He'll preach to us from the boat."

"Oh, no - not that unstable character!"

The approaching horn got louder but not better. It was free-association noise, good only for cleaning the wax out of our ears. The birds flew, the frogs hopped, and the cattle stampeded away in panic. Unfortunately this mass exodus of mobile life did not include the poor humans on the shore.

Ron leaned toward me. "The D.S. strikes again."

And there we were - pinned down on an empty hillside without even a bush for cover. The menace was unsteadily approaching, and we were trapped. I didn't even dare laugh in front of my 200 teenagers and the more serious members of my staff.

As he got closer, I could see that Reverend V. was having trouble - his fake beard was getting in the way of his playing. The kids were quiet, enthralled or apalled, I don't know which. Finally the Showboat hit the shore. The lifeguard, a Nordic god, jumped out, tied a rope around a big rock, and ran up the bank.

The Reverend Victorian rose majestically in the boat and began to quote from the Sermon on the Mount: "'And why are you anxious about clothing?'" He was gesturing far too widely. "'Consider the lilies of the field, how they grow; they neither toil nor spin-n-n-n ... .'" We watched in fascination as his hands flailed the air and the boat slowly turned over. His 300 pounds of brown-robed and bewhiskered dignity hit the water, raising a spout like a blue whale. The boat kept turning, and in a moment The Reverend Victorian came up covered with mud and green algae, the whiskers now transplanted to his bald dome.

Ron thoughtfully completed the verse for him: "'Yet I tell you, even Solomon in all his glory was not arrayed like one of these.'" (Luke 12:27)

Laughter swept the hillside. As The Reverend V. sank again, the lifeguard, true to his name, made his first and last save of the week by helping the exhausted Superintendent up onto the shore. He saved Victor's life, but he couldn't save his face.

After the initial laughter, Ron and I felt bad. We followed Arlene down to where Victor lay and knelt beside him. I asked, "Are you feeling O.K., Victor?"

"A little shaky, Dave." For the first time he was looking directly at me.

Ron spoke up, "I'm sorry I laughed, Vic."

"That's all right, Ron." He smiled for the first time that I had ever seen. "It must have been pretty funny."

He was not only looking directly at each one of us but also carrying on a real conversation. I sensed that something had happened under the water, something like a baptism. Maybe he was like Peter. As long as Peter could walk on the water, he didn't cry out for help - only when he went under. Perhaps The Reverend Victorian was drowned, and the real Victor was raised.

"Fellows, this whole week has been a disaster. Where did I go wrong?"

Ron looked at me, so I tried to break it to the D.S. gently. "Well, Vic, I think you upstaged yourself with things."

Ron cleared his throat. "Kim came across so forcibly because he was his message – 'the Word made flesh'" (John 1:14)

"You mean ... that if I got up in front of the campers without my sets and props, that they would accept me, I mean, just me alone?"

There was no need for talk. I squeezed his shoulder, Ron clasped his hand, and Arlene dried his face with a towel.

"Thank you, brothers and.sister. Let me lie here for a few minutes, and then I think I can make it back to the cabin."

That evening I walked into the mess hall, and it was no longer a mess. The permanent staff had shoveled out the mud and mopped the floor clean. The kids had decorated the hall with crepe paper and put candles on the tables. But the biggest improvement of all was the campers themselves. It was Dress-up Night, and they had.

I raised my hand for attention. "Before we return thanks, I want to tell you something I'm thankful for. I got tired of seeing all of you running around in grubby jeans all week. In fact, I thought I was down here with 200 boys, but now I see that half of you are girls."

They responded with boos and hisses.

"When I drove down here, my car was wall-to-wall petticoats. I can see now that they were justified." Laughter and whistles marked the end of my speech.

After the prayer, I walked over to our family's table. One look at Arlene nearly bowled me over. Arlene, who looked good in anything, was wearing a red peasant blouse - and did she have nice shoulders! I couldn't keep my eyes off her. I don't remember what was on the menu.

"Rev'rend Rowe, Rev'rend Rowe, would you please come forward?" Startled, I looked around. Teddy had taken over the P.A. system and was beckoning to me. I extricated myself from the bench and went up to stand by Teddy. He smiled confidently at me and held the mike to his lips.

"This's my first camp, and I thought it would be borin' down here with my pastor and my sister watchin' every move I made, but I found out diff'rent." He glanced over at Karen, who smiled shyly back at him. "In fact, this has been the best week of my life! I hate to see it end. I've been talkin' to a lotta kids who feel the same way. We all wanna thank you, Rev'rend Rowe, for makin' this camp possible." A cheer went up, with a counterpoint of feet-stamping and table-banging.

Teddy turned to me again. "We wanna give you and Rev'rend Wright a little gift." Ron struggled out of his bench and joined us. "We know that you went outa your way to help us kids, so we wanna give you this bucket of prune juice." Ron and I looked a little sheepish (or, more properly, cowed) as Karen handed Teddy the bucket and he passed it to me. I quickly gave it to Ron, and then looked around for Victor, but he wasn't there. Miriam gave me a surprising wink.

Laughter spread through the assembled campers, just as the story must have spread.

"May I have the mike now, Teddy? Thanks. I want to thank all of you This was my first camp in North Dakota, and I will never forget you. Tonight is our closing campfire. I suggest that each of you come prepared to throw something on the fire, something which symbolizes a bad habit or sin or whatever you want to get rid of. And if the fire gets out of hand, Ron can pour on his bucket of prune juice. See you tonight at 9:00 at Vesper Point."

After all had changed into their old clothes, Ron lit the fire near the large cross. Youth and adults started streaming from all over the camp toward Vesper Point and the campfire. Most clutched a small object of paper or wood or cloth in their hands. We trudged our way up the hill, burdened by more than gravity. One by one all the campers threw the objects into the fire and walked away feeling lighter.

Victor approached me, and I looked at him closely to see if he had recovered from his harrowing afternoon. He spoke softly, "Dave, may I say a few words to the campers?" I nodded.

Victor went and stood before the fire. "Young people, I've been in the ministry for forty-one years, and I've accumulated a lot of things. You've taught me something this week - that things can get in the way, can block communication. Now I need you to help me clean house. Dave, Arlene, Ron, and Kim, would you lend me a hand? And Teddy and Karen - would you help an ashamed old man? And the rest of you - I'm sorry that I haven't taken time to learn your names - I need your help, too." He was looking directly into our eyes, more alive than he had ever been.

Ron and I stepped forward. I thought I caught sight of tears in Ron's eyes, but it was hard to tell because mine were brimming. Kim also came forward, radiating his special joy. A soft hand slipped warmly into mine, and I turned to see Arlene. Her smile put even Kim and the fire in the shade.

We followed Vic down the hill to his hearse - it was filled with old stage sets. "Take everything out of the back. And, Ron, would you please take a group of campers and get the sets that are still in the barn?" Each one grabbed a panel and followed Vic back up the hill. He threw a crumbling panel onto the fire, and we followed his example.

It made a merry blaze.

"One more thing," Victor said, "I'm donating my hearse to the camp - I think it'll make a first class pickup."

"Thank God!" said Miriam.

Arlene stepped forward. "Let's all sing, 'You Are the Light of the World'." As we sang, the D.S. put his arms around Ron and me. "Camping keeps us young. Right, brothers?"

"Right, Vic."

Even District Superintendents can be saved.

"It was the tail end of summer, and the fields had ripened to a golden brown ..." David Rowe

16 Picnic

Right after I got back from camp, Mrs. Larson called. "Rev'ren' Sorenson's back, and I hate to tell you this gossip ..." (I knew how she hated to tell me.) "... but Mrs. Sorenson ain't with him. Instead he's got some - some *sexpot*."

"Come now, Hannah, where did you ever get such a word?"

"Well, sometimes we gits books that ain't fit to be put on the liberry shelfs. Our committee's gotta read 'em to see if they's fittin'. It was one of them that's got the word."

"I see. Well, I wouldn't be too worried about that 'sexpot,' as you call her. If you'll take a closer look, I think you'll find that it's really Mrs. Sorenson."

As soon as I hung up, the phone rang again. "Rev'rend, this's Tillie. Don't believe 'em. That Liberry Committee's passin' around shady stories amongst theirselves - and they won't lemme in on it."

"Now, I do see."

The phone rang for the third time. This time it was Ben.

"Welcome back from camp, Dave. How're things goin'?"

"Not so good, Ben. I just found out that our Library Committee is running an underground circulation of risqué books. Ben, I've created a monster."

"Don't feel bad, Rev'rend. It ain't your fault, and anyway, it keeps 'em off the streets by cuttin' down on senile delinquency."

When I went up for the mail, I decided to stop in at the Sorensons'. Rolf opened the door, grasped my hand wordlessly, and pulled me inside. "Brother Dave." He grabbed me in a bear hug. "Debbie," he called, "guess who's here!"

Fortunately Mrs. Larson's call had prepared me, for down the hall came a completely different Mrs. Sorenson. Gone was the colorless drudge. Here was a vibrant, attractive young woman. She, too, threw her arms around me. "David, I can't thank you enough!"

"My thanks are in seeing you two together. You both look terrific!"

All three of us began chattering at once about the summer and the parish and the three of us.

"David, you've got to stay for coffee - that's the Lutheran communion, you know. Deb, why don't you take David into the living room while I pour the coffee?"

It was a pleasure to follow the new Mrs. Sorenson. "That's a pretty dress. Is it new?"

"Yes, Rolf loves to buy me new clothes. You should see some of the nightgowns he's bought me. Rolf calls them my 'negligible negligees'." A pleasant pink brightened her formerly anemic complexion.

Rolf came in carrying a tray with three coffee mugs. "Debbie," he teased, "you needn't tell David everything."

"But David is just like one of the family."

"You're right there, Sweetheart."

Around the corner came a striped cat, a miniature version of Sylvester. As the cat jumped up into Debbie's lap, Rolf looked proudly at his lovely new wife. "You see how I'm putty in her hands." He spread his hands - then leaned forward. "This summer was even better than I had hoped: it was a second honeymoon and a new birth! I tell you, David, the real heart of religion is relationship: man's relationship to God and man's relationship to man."

"Don't forget man's relationship to woman." Debbie gazed meaningfully at Rolf over her coffee cup.

He looked at her with adoring eyes. "The most important relationship of all! And, do you know, David, none of these can be charted."

"It sounds as if you learned quite a bit from Bjorn."

"Volumes! Did I tell you that Papa Nielsen sends his love?"

"No, but thanks for the message. I think I'll go up to see Bjorn next Monday."

"He's gone - just left for Norway on a three month trip. Bjorn hasn't been back to his homeland for over thirty years, but you probably already knew that. The class chipped in and bought him a pair of skis."

"Wonderful! I remember Bjorn telling us how thrilling it was to shoot down a snow-covered mountain."

They were looking deeply at each other again. "Well, you two lovebirds, thanks for the coffee, or should I say 'communion'?"

"You're welcome," they responded.

I stood up. "You know, the house even smells better."

"That's probably the romantic perfume Rolf gave me."

"Or maybe the lack of tobacco smoke," Rolf added. "I don't need smoking any more, now that I've discovered the joys of marriage."

"And we have an announcement to make." Debbie looked down at her stomach.

"Really?"

"Yes, in about six months," Debbie said proudly.

"And if it's a boy," Rolf said, putting his arm around Debbie, "we're going to call him David Bjorn."

"I don't know what to say. I -"

They held out their free arms, and I walked into their wordless embrace. I hugged both of them and kissed Debbie on the cheek. "Take good care of my Godson."

They were so full of love that I almost flew across the street to see Arlene. I rapped eagerly on her door. Someone was coming … the door was opening … but it was only Mrs. Olson's maternal face peeking out. "Rev'rend, come on in. Here, let me pick up these magazines so you can set down."

I sat on the edge of the davenport, and Mrs. Olson collapsed into a big brown chair. "Arlene and Teddy bin tellin' me about the wonderful time they had at camp."

"That's good. Uh, is Arlene home?"

"Ya, she's out back hangin' up the clothes."

"Would you mind if I go out to see her?"

"No, go right ahead, Rev'rend. Excuse me for not movin'."

I walked over the worn linoleum through the dining room and kitchen, pushed open the screen door, and went around to the back of the house. Just the top of Arlene's head was visible, moving between the lines of wash. I entered her row and followed her down.

"Aha, I caught you with three sheets to the wind."

"Oh, Reverend, you scared me!"

"I'm sorry - I always seem to be doing that."

"That's all right, Reverend."

"David, remember?"

"All right, David, but you caught me looking like such a mess."

I looked carefully at her plaid shirt, one tail hanging out over her jeans, and at her rich brown hair being swirled by the wind around her beautiful face.

"Do you realize that ninety-nine percent of all women would like to be in just that kind of a mess?"

"Why, thank you, David."

"Once you said that you were curious about the Sorensons." She nodded. "Well, I'll tell you the rest of the story - if you come with me now on a picnic."

"A church-wide affair?"

"No, a two-person aff - I mean event. And I can provide the food. The 'Jewish Mothers' have been bombarding me again."

"O.K., but I have one more load to hang up."

"Good, that'll give me a chance to pack a picnic basket." I started back down the row, but stopped and called back, "This is a come-as-you-are picnic, so don't change a thing."

"But -"

"You look great just the way you are."

Her frown turned into a smile. "See you soon ... David."

Things were progressing nicely. We were moving closer and closer together - we had even held hands at camp. And now I was going to be alone with her on a picnic!

Sylvester followed me out to the car. "Oh, no, you don't, Sylvester. I don't go on your dates, do I?"

He turned tail and stalked off.

I put the picnic basket and thermos jug on the floor between the seats and drove over to Arlene's. She came running down the steps and into the car. I noted with pleasure that she hadn't changed. Mrs. Olson waved from the door.

"Where do people picnic around here, Arlene?"

"Wildcat Lair."

"Sounds ominous."

"No, it isn't. It's just a thicket of bushes and trees south of town. I can show you how to get there if you want."

"If you're with me, I won't be scared."

"No wildcat has been seen there since the Coffee Gang were children."

"That's good."

As we came to a stop at Main Street, Arlene told me to turn right. Fred looked up from his chair and waved - the short, fat arm of the law had a vigilant eye. I turned right and went past the dairy and the barber shop. Busia Kowalski, up on a ladder painting her sign, waved so hard that I thought she'd fall; Alf was hosing down the fire engine and nodded at us; Ben looked up from pumping gas and grinned. I really didn't mind being seen with Arlene. I waved at all of them, for I knew they had nothing but good will for us.

We bumped across the railroad tracks and rolled along the highway out to the airport road. Lars and Martha Olson were just turning and heading toward town. We waved at them, too.

"Turn south on the airport road."

I did until Arlene said, "Slow for a right hand turn."

"Right here?"

"Yes, it's just a few miles – there, that thicket up ahead."

It was the tail end of summer, and the fields had ripened to a golden brown, the promise of a rich harvest. Soon we came to the edge of Wildcat Lair and got out of the car. I pulled out the thermos and picnic-basket and turned to gaze at the tangle of bushes and trees.

"Where to now?"

"I'll show you. Do you mind if I take your blanket? There aren't any tables."

"Help yourself."

She reached in and took the blanket off the back of the rear seat, where it covered Sylvester's rips. "I see your cat's been busy."

"Yes, he loves something he can get his claws into, but that thicket looks like something even Sylvester couldn't penetrate."

Arlene laughed. "Follow me."

I followed her gladly through the maze of trails. I was glad that women had discovered slacks. From any angle my angel looked good. The path opened out into a little clearing next to a river. Across the river the thicket continued, making a private oasis in the middle of the dry plains.

"This is lovely," I said, "but the only thing that mars it is the trash. If this keeps up, the earth will soon be covered with bottle caps and broken glass."

We set down our burdens and cleaned up the area, restoring it to its pristine purity. We loaded the trash into a trash bag. Then Arlene knelt on the bank and washed her hands in the river.

"Good idea." I knelt beside her and followed her example. "Uh, been here often?" Every man likes to think that he is the first, that the girl was newly-created for him alone.

"With a lot of groups."

After Arlene spread the blanket on the grass, we sat on it and bowed our heads in prayer over the picnic basket. Surrounding us was the sleepy bum of the humblebees. "Thank you, Lord, for this food and for my being here in the beauty of your creation with this beautiful girl. Amen."

"Thank you, David."

"You're most welcome." I opened up the basket. "And thanks to the good cooks of Webber, we have fried chicken, slices of roast beef, homemade rolls, potato salad, blueberry pie, and apple pie. And thanks to me, we have hot cocoa. Help yourself, Arlene."

"Umm, it all sounds so good - and it smells so good, too. I think I'll have a little of each, if I may."

"Take all you want. You're a long ways from obesity." She got to her knees and started dishing up. I poured her a cup of cocoa. "Darn!"

"Reverend!"

"Sorry. I forgot to bring marshmallows."

"That's all right."

After I dished up for myself, Arlene said, "How about the story?"

"What story?"

"About the Sorensons."

"Oh, yes. I'll tell you, but please don't tell anyone else."

"I promise."

"Have you seen the Sorensons since they got back?"

"I saw him, but I'm not sure about her. I mean, I saw a very attractive woman, but ..."

"That was Mrs. Sorenson."

"It was!"

"And that's how it turned out."

"But what did you do?"

"Played Ping-Pong."

"David, you aren't explaining anything."

"I better go back to last June. After my first Sunday, Rolf Sorenson jumped me for being a sheep-stealer."

"Whatever for?"

"He had seen the doctor's and the mayor's cars in front of our church."

"That was terrible of him."

"Well, he relented and invited me over that evening. When I got there, I made a terrible mistake. I took his wife to be the housekeeper."

"Oh, David!" She covered her mouth with her graceful hand.

"Well, you know how she used to look - so drab and subservient. Then Rolf and I played Ping-Pong, but I was very lucky and beat him every game. He got terribly angry and took it out on Debbie. She left him."

"But I thought they went to take a graduate course."

"They did, later, but first she ran away."

"Really?"

"Yes, she even tore up Rolf's charts and took his new car."

"He must have felt awful."

"Yes, he did. He came over to the parsonage that night."

"What did you say to him?" She rose up on her knees.

"I really didn't know what to say, but then I remembered a very special book."

"The Bible?"

"No, it was called *Survival in a Parsonage.*"

"You mean - I would think that it would be heaven to live in a parsonage."

"Not when a person is alone."

"But they were two, man and wife."

"Correction - man and housekeeper."

"Oh." Arlene sank down.

"Rolf loved the book, so I introduced him to the author."

"You what?"

"The book was by a good friend of mine, my former teacher and counselor, Bjorn Nielsen."

"You've had counseling?" Her eyes grew wide.

"Yes."

"But you seem so mature."

"Many of us lead almost normal lives - as long as we get plenty of TLC. Fortunately there's an abundant supply in Webber, but I don't think there's much in Ron's church."

"No, it seemed so cold and unfriendly."

"Rolf went to see Bjorn and found real love and understanding. Bjorn was about to start a course for pastors and their wives, and Rolf got so excited about it that he was able to talk Debbie into taking it with him. That's what worked some changes."

"I should say so - from the looks of Mrs. Sorenson."

"I think you'll find them very loving people now."

"I'll make a point of visiting them. David, you have such a way with people. Look what you did for the Superintendent and what you've done for Mrs. Larson and Charles Barrett and the Rowlands - I heard that you actually ate dinner at their house."

"Please, Arlene, not while I'm eating." I set my plate down.

"I'm sorry. Oh, David, you take such a warm pastoral interest in all your flock." She impulsively grabbed my hand. "No wonder I think of you as a brother."

It was one for Guinness. I had gone from "Reverend" to "brother" in only three months.

"Some are born mediocre; some achieve mediocrity; some have mediocrity thrust upon them." Anon.

17 Memorials

I was working on my sermon when I heard the front door open and Ben's voice call out. "Rev'rend, are you home?"

A lot of people didn't bother knocking on the parsonage door - it was, in a sense, community property. Quite a contrast to my parents' Chicago apartment with its buzzer system, double locks, and peephole.

"In here, Ben," I called back from the study.

Ben shuffled in and perched on a folding metal chair.

"What's up, Ben?" I laid my pencil down in the center of volume eight of *The Interpreter's Bible* and rubbed my eyes.

"There's sumpthin' I bin meanin' to tell you, but it always slipped my excuse for a mind."

He handed me an envelope, a very impressive-looking envelope - aside from some greasy thumb prints - from the bishop's office in Aberdeen. I pulled out the letter and opened it up. It was so crisp that it crackled in my hands. Underneath Bishop Shears' crest (a lamb straddling a large pair of shears), was the date. Noting that it was almost a year old, I began struggling through the greasy redundancies: "I have before me your gracious invitation … be most honored to participate in the festivities … am looking forward with real anticipation to the seventy-fifth anniversary of your church."

"Ben, you mean the Bishop is coming?"

"Ya, ya, next month."

"And our church is going to have a seventy-fifth anniversary?"

"Ya, ya, but no need to git in a lather. Our ladies bin bakin' and freezin' and cannin'. We already got 'bout half the locker plant filled up."

"Whew!" I sat back in my chair till another question hit me. "But where are we going to put the bishop? There's no furniture in the other parsonage bedrooms."

"With the Bird Sisters."

"Oh, that's good … but the letter, says something about a special memorial for Brother Berdahl. What's that?"

"This." Ben handed me a plastic bag. "I wouldn't open that up if I was you. It's his socks."

An odor of locker rooms rose up from the plastic bag. The once white socks had turned gray with age and chemical reaction, yet they weren't completely gray, for they had been darned many times in many colors. I pushed them to the front of the desk.

"I'm takin' 'em upta Olson's Jewelry to have 'em bronzed – that should kill the smell. Birdie's already washed 'em twice. Then I'm gonna build a glass case for 'em and give 'em a proper burial."

"Good idea, Ben."

"Like I say, I bin meanin' to tell you, but never could catch you when I 'membered. You was always off doin' sumpthin' like your liberry project or youth camp. Fact is, you're the going-est preacher we ever had. 'Fraid you got too much horsepower for our one-horse town - 'fraid the bishop'll move you to a bigger place."

"I hope not, Ben. I want to stay in Webber for a long time." The tears came to my eyes, and I pulled out a Kleenex.

"Sorry, Rev'rend. Didn't mean to upset you."

"It's not that - " I said with dripping eyes and flooding sinuses. "It's the socks."

"Oh, sorry." Ben grabbed them, jumped up, and headed for the door.

"If there's anything I can do for the seventy-fifth …"

Ben stopped and turned around. "Nope - well, ya, there is. You could pick up the invitations this afternoon from the newspaper office."

"Glad to, Ben."

And he was gone … but Brother Berdahl lingered.

After lunch I walked up to the bustling office of the *Webber Wolfcall*. A hundred per cent of the work force was on duty - both Sam and Ernie. I went up to the counter, and Sam, the editor, came over to me.

"I've come for the invitations."

"Wedding invitations?" Sam teased.

"No." I smiled. "The invitations for our church anniversary."

"O.K., Rev." Sam reached under the counter and pulled out a box. "Here, you wanna see one?" He pulled out an invitation and laid it on the counter. "How'd you like that?

On the cover of the card was a line drawing of the church. "Mrs. Grundy did that. We're gonna use it on the cover of the history she wrote, too." The members had been busy. Inside, in Old English script, was the actual invitation: "You are cordially invited to the Seventy-fifth Anniversary of the Webber United Methodist Church on October 18.

Dedication of the memorial to Brother Berdahl by Bishop Pontius J.
Shears at eleven o'clock. Luncheon following. R.S.V.P."
"For your fine work, you two get the first two invitations."
"Thanks, Rev," said Sam. Ernie called out thanks, too.
I picked up the box. "You can send the bill to - "
"I know - Eldon Chance."
"I guess you know nearly everything that goes on in Webber."
"Purty near, Rev, purty near."
"Good-bye, Editor."
"So long, Newsmaker."
As I left the office, I thought of the perfect person to help me send
out the invitations, so I slipped down the alley to her house. When Arlene
came to the door, she was wearing blue jeans and a sleeveless blue blouse.
"Arlene, I just got the invitations for the seventy-fifth anniversary,
and I thought - what are all these boxes for?"
"I'm getting ready to go back to college."
I sank into the only empty chair.
"To college - so soon?"
"Yes, classes start next week." Arlene took some books off the
piano bench and bent over to put them in a box.
To think that I wouldn't see her moving through my life for nine
months. Oh, how I would miss her!
"Arlene, I ..." My mouth grew dry; my bones turned to wax.
"Arlene, I've got to tell you - " I jumped up and tapped her on the
shoulder. Startled, she spun right into my arms. Wide-eyed, she looked up
at me, her lovely lips just inches from mine. "First, I'm not your 'brother'.
Second - " I kissed her.
There was a moment of paralyzing warmth, and then she twisted
away from me, cried "Reverend Rowe!", ran into her room, and slammed
the door.
I stood there, still clutching a packet of invitations in one sweaty
hand. How I wished I had been blessed with blarney like my new uncle,
Charles Barrett. He would have known what to say *before*, so that he
wouldn't have had to say anything *after*. I kicked a couple of boxes on the
way out. "Oh, d - " but I couldn't say that. I was a real case - a preacher
who was tongue-tied - and it looked as if I had ruined my chances with
Arlene. I had fallen off the pedestal, all right, and about a mile into the
ground.

When I came out of Arlene's house, I bumped into the editor, who looked up at me curiously.

"I was just delivering these invitations - that's all." He glanced at the box in my hands.

"Oh, I still have them, don't I? Uh, Arlene couldn't help with them because she's getting ready to go back to college. She was packing until I … came."

The editor nodded knowingly, whipped out a notebook, and jotted down a few notes. Then he made a beeline for the newspaper office. His next issue had a line in the "Editor's Eyeful" column: "Your editor was out walking within one block of this office when he distinctly heard the sound of wedding bells." I plunged into the anniversary preparations to try to forget, hoping that no one figured out "for whom the bell tolled."

My next duty for the anniversary was more pleasant. I called Ron. "How've you been since camp?"

"Fine, Dave. How about yourself?"

"I seem to have stumbled into a big anniversary celebration."

"I could have told you," said Tillie.

"You must be very busy, Dave."

"Not really. I've got a board chairman who has things pretty well lined up. I hope you and Dottie can come."

"When is it?"

"Sunday, October 18."

"In the morning?"

"Yes."

"Well, I can come, but Dottie can't. She fills the pulpit when I'm gone."

"Too bad, Ron, but I bet the congregation welcomes it."

"Some do, though others think a woman should be silent in church, but I don't see why she should make an exception of that one area."

"You're making Dottie out to be an old nag."

"Hey, Old Nag, come over here." There was a long silence broken by some sounds of kissing. Then Ron came back on the line. "What were we talking about, Old Buddy?"

"Our seventy-fifth."

"Oh, yes. Well, I'll be there. Service is at eleven, I suppose."

"Yes, and we'll have a lunch following."

"See you then, if not before."

"Greet Dottie and the kids for me - especially your nighttime reader."

"O.K. Greet Arlene and the kids for me."

I couldn't tell him about Arlene - the wound was still too fresh. I hung up sadly, hoping Tillie hadn't heard Ron's last remark.

No use moping - I decided to call Vic and Miriam. "Tillie, would you get me Reverend Victor Hanson over at - "

"O.K., Rev'ren'."

The electricity that raced over to Minot returned with Miriam's soft southern drawl. "Hello."

"Miriam, this is Dave Rowe."

"David, how nice to hear your voice."

"It's nice to hear a southern belle, too. I was wondering if you and Victor could come to our seventy-fifth anniversary."

"We'd like to. When is it, David?"

"October 18."

"Oh, that's too bad. Victor and I will be in New Orleans then. We're flying down for our fortieth anniversary."

"That's a shame."

"What's a shame?" Victor's strong voice joined us.

"It's too bad you'll miss Webber's seventy-fifth anniversary on October 18."

"I think we can arrange our schedule to do both. How about it, dear?"

"Certainly, darling."

"Dave, we'll plan to land in Webber about 8:00 a.m. on the eighteenth."

"I'll meet you at the airport."

"Thanks. Did you know that I have a new plane, a Cessna?

"No - that's great!"

"Actually I don't own all of it. It's a three-way partnership with a doctor and an implement dealer."

"Good idea. It'll be wonderful to see both of you again."

At last the great day came, or actually the day before the great day. The bishop was due sometime on Saturday, the seventeenth. He was going to spend the night in Webber and then leave immediately after our service to "consecrate" a new church in Fargo. (Nothing could be "dedicated" until it was paid for.)

From breakfast onward, I kept looking for the bishop. Every time a car came crunching down the gravel street I looked up. I even asked Mrs. Larson to keep her eyes peeled - perhaps the most needless request I've ever made.

Noon came. Still no bishop. By late afternoon, I was worried, so I asked Tillie to call the area office. She found out that the bishop and the public relations director had left Aberdeen around 10:00 a.m. They should have arrived by now. Well, if they hadn't arrived by 6:00, I would call the sheriff.

On Main Street, the sheriff dozed in his captain's chair in front of Olson's Hardware. From the east, a high-powered black car came whizzing into Webber, zoomed the length of Main Street at well above the legal limit, made a bootleg turn, and came roaring back to stop with the front bumper against Fred's knees.

The lawbreaker had at last come to the sheriff. The problem was that Fred had been hoping to get through the year without issuing a ticket.

"Hey, Fatso," the driver called out, "wake up and give us some directions."

Fred tilted his hat back. "I'll give you some directions alright. First - move that tank back two inches. Second, gimme your driver's license."

There ensued a war between church and state with the result that Fred threw the driver and his passenger into jail for speeding, reckless driving, creating a nuisance, resisting arrest, and use of foul language - no doubt a misunderstanding of some ecclesiastical terms.

I received a phone call about 5:30. "Rev'rend, this's Fred. There's a couple of guys down here in the jail who wanna see you."

Oh, no! I hung up with a feeling of apocalyptic gloom, afraid that it was the end of my world.

I hurried over to the courthouse and went down the steps into the basement. Fred was sitting in an oversize chair with his feet up on his desk. Behind him and behind bars were the two culprits.

"Bishop Shears, welcome to Webber - I mean, I'm sorry about this mix-up."

Fred put his feet down. "There ain't no mix-up - these are the two guys that came inta my town like Al Capone and his hatchet man."

The bishop spoke through clenched teeth. "Rowe, if you have any influence with this minion of the law - "

"More of his fancy cussin'," Fred grumbled.

The bishop glowered at the sheriff. "I say, if you have any influence, I'd appreciate an expeditious exit from this dungeon. Don't even consider that your future depends on it."

My knees felt weak. "Fred, please let them out."

"Are you postin' bail?"

"No, I don't have any money with me." Then I thought of something better than money. "You can have the last two pounds of Busia's sausage," I whispered.

Without saying a word, Fred walked over, took a big key off a hook on the wall, and unlocked the cell.

While the bishop was gathering up his coat and briefcase, the P.R. man came up to me. "Take us to our hotel - right away."

"I'm sorry, Mr. – er – "

"Custer."

"Custer, but we have you staying in a private home."

"A private home!" He hit his forehead. Then he came closer to me and lowered his voice. "The bishop is having – er - plumbing problems. He really should be put up in a hotel."

"That's too bad, but I really don't think he would like our only hotel. It's pretty noisy because of the cafe and bar and bowling alley, but on the other hand the private home is very nice. In fact, it's the biggest house in town, and it has plenty of bathrooms. Unless you rather stay here?"

"No, I guess that will have to do. Come on, bish., get your gear and let's get out of here."

When we got outside, the bishop got into the back seat of the big Chrysler. The P.R. man grabbed my arm. "Don't let this out. If word of this ever got back to the Council of Bishops …"

I shook my head.

"You'll have to drive," Custer said. "The sheriff took away our licenses until we leave town."

After we pulled up to the Bird Sisters' huge Victorian house, resting in the midst of its overgrown bushes and trees, I noticed the bishop shudder. I grabbed a couple of suitcases and led my two honored guests toward the old wooden steps. As we went up the steps, the front door swung open, and there were the Bird Sisters twittering excitedly.

"Bishop Shears, may I present to you the Bir - the McConnell sisters. This is Rose." I pointed to the larger of the two. "And this is Emily."

The bishop bowed to the occasion. "I am charmed to be staying with such attractive ladies."

The ninety-year-old women giggled, their frail, bony hands fluttering. The two of them together probably weighed less than my 150 pounds.

Emily, the sprier sister, led the bishop up to his room, while the P.R. man tried to explain to the giggling Rose about the bishop's personal needs.

I spent a restless night, with recurring dreams about the bishop behind bars. In my dreams I was unable to persuade Fred to let him out. Fred kept saying, "There's not enough sausage in the whole world." The Coffee Gang ran tours to see "the only bishop in captivity,"

In the morning, I stumbled out of bed and doped myself up with a cup of coffee. There would be plenty of food later on in the day, but now it was time for me to rush to the airport.

After I went out the front door and got into the Buick, I heard a whining crunch, followed by a beep, and suddenly Ron was at my window. "Hey, Dave, trying to sneak out of town?"

"Ron, you're just in time. Come on out to the airport with me to meet Vic and Miriam."

"I hope he's not flying his old balsa wood fighter."

"No, he has a brand new Cessna now."

Ron came around and got in the car. "Well, I bet you're pretty excited about having Pontius Pilate here."

I started the engine and drove off. "Ron, I'm in real trouble. The bishop was thrown in jail last night."

"No kidding!" Ron whistled. "Tell me all about it."

We were sitting on the fenders of the Buick when we spotted a far-off speck. Miriam and Vic flew in shortly before eight - just as he had said. Victor let Miriam out, and she hurried over and hugged us both. Then he taxied up to the hanger and talked to the airport manager, who also was the mechanic, the grass cutter, and even the person who darned the wind sock. After some money changed hands, he came striding over to us.

"Just look at how trim Victor looks," Miriam said proudly. "He's lost forty pounds, and he's gained back some of his old romance. We owe it all to you boys."

Victor gave us an affectionate pummeling. "You two rascals turned my life completely around, but the change hasn't been all good. Miriam, tell them about the quarterly conference at Hampden."

Miriam laughed. "Well, you see how much weight Victor has lost. When he got to the Hampden church, he asked where he could plug in his slide projector. Several people pointed up at the light fixture. He was feeling pretty frisky after his weight loss, so he stood up on the table. However, as he reached up, his baggy trousers came down - "

Victor broke in. "Some of the folks said they had seen a whole new side to the D.S."

"That's when I decided that Victor needed a brand new wardrobe."

"How do you like this tweed? I got it at the Hudson Bay Company in Winnipeg. They have great woolens at reasonable prices."

"Wow," said Ron, "you'll knock 'em dead!"

I turned to Miriam. "Are you sure this is the same guy who used to ride around in hearses and dive out of rowboats?"

"No, he isn't." Miriam put her arms around her husband, and they smiled into each other's eyes.

"Say, you lovebirds, we better hurry if we're going to catch breakfast with Ben and Birdie before the service."

We piled into the Buick, much to Sylvester's dislike. He had to move from the seat onto the rear ledge.

The church was packed, but I looked around for the one person who really counted. She wasn't there, so I went over and whispered to Mrs. Olson: "Where's Arlene?"

"Oh, Arlene had to work this weekend."

I hadn't seen her since the day I had fallen off the pedestal. Would she ever come back?

I hurried down to the basement where the bishop, Vic, Lars, and Ron were all robed and ready. Why hadn't I bought a robe for this important occasion? I felt so conspicuous in my suit, but I soon forgot my uniqueness as I watched the P.R. man rushing around, bossing our local editor, and popping flashbulbs at the proud-looking bishop. The bishop seemed to have forgotten all about his prison term and was basking in the warmth of the flashbulbs.

I asked the bishop to lead us pastors in prayer before we went upstairs to begin the service. That was another mistake, for never have I heard the deity offered such full and complete instructions. But this prayer didn't last the bishop very long, for no sooner were we upstairs than he was on his knees by the pulpit chair. What a humble man!

Miss Osgood entered and groped her way down to the organ. She turned on a switch, and the organ wheezed into life.

I had gotten to the point where the regular Sunday service held no more terrors for me, but now that we had special guests and a church full, I felt nervous. My throat kept clouding up, but I labored through my portions of the service, calling upon the principals in turn.

Mayor Lysne came to the pulpit. "I'd like to present the key to the city to Bishop Shears."

The bishop frowned. Perhaps he was thinking that he could have used it last night to get out of jail.

Lars Olson read the scripture, Ron led the responsive reading, and Victor offered prayer.

After I introduced the bishop, he came to the pulpit. "Thank you Brother Knecht. It is a pleasure to be here in Fairmount, South Dakota."

He had my name wrong, the town wrong, and the state wrong. Hope was reborn - maybe he would not associate me with his time in the pen.

The bishop moved into his message. "I take as my text 'The Parable of the Ten Virgins' in the twenty-fifth chapter of Matthew." He then spent forty minutes retelling the story of the ten virgins going to meet the bridegroom: The five wise ones took extra containers of oil for their lamps, but the five foolish ones didn't. When the bridegroom was delayed and the lamps of the foolish ones were beginning to go out, they asked the wise virgins for some of their oil. "No," they replied, "for then there wouldn't be enough for us." So the foolish virgins had to go find an oil merchant who was open that late. While they were gone, the bridegroom came, and the wise virgins went with him into the wedding hall. By the time the foolish girls got there, they were denied admittance because they hadn't been ready at the right time.

At last the bishop tried to drive home the moral with a question: "And where would you rather be? Inside the wedding hall with the wise virgins, or out in the dark with the foolish virgins?"

I didn't dare look at Ron or Vic or anyone else. The safest place seemed to be the octopus chandelier. Ron poked me and whispered, "The bishop's done."

I jumped up and went to the pulpit. "I am sure that we are all grateful to the bishop for his ... er ... challenging words."

Finally we came to the high point of the service, the dedication of the memorial to Brother Berdahl, the walking circuit rider. I led the bishop, Victor, Ron, and Lars down from the platform over to the glass case that Ben had built.

The Bishop again pontificated: "We are fortunate to have a fitting memorial to that great pioneer preacher who walked all over this territory spreading the gospel. His descendants have preserved a pair of the great man's socks, which have been bronzed in his memory." The bishop opened the glass case to lift up the holy relic, but suddenly staggered back. Incredibly, even though they were bronzed, they still stunk. For a moment there was an aerial battle between the cedar and the socks - with the socks winning.

I leaped forward and slammed the lid shut. Though the bishop's eyes were watering, he struggled on. "There will never be another - gasp - Brother Berdahl," the bishop spoke through his handkerchief. "He is absolutely unique in the annals of Christian history. Although he is dead, his memory - whew - lingers on. We therefore dedicate these socks as a perpet - choo - al memorial."

After I quickly pronounced the benediction, everyone rushed out of the church; no one lingered inside to visit; no one seemed interested in the luncheon that was laid out in the basement.

Outside, the P.R. man collared me. "The bishop has to get back to his room right away."

"Oh, that's right, for the church consecration at Fargo."

I didn't want to be alone with the two convicts so I called out to Vic and Ron. "Why don't you come with us?"

Ron piled into the front seat, forcing the P.R. man over toward me as I slipped into the driver's seat. That left Victor to hobnob with the bishop, who was still wiping his eyes.

When we arrived at the Bird Sisters' home, the bishop and the P.R. man went hurriedly upstairs to pack, while the rest of us visited with the two old ladies.

I happened to glance in the birdcage. There in the bottom was a copy of the *Webber Wolfcall*, with Bishop Shears' picture looking up at the business ends of two busy parakeets. It was the second time that weekend that he had been behind bars. When I heard our episcopal leader coming down the stairs, I quickly interposed my body between him and the birdcage.

The bishop was in high spirits. "Well, dear ladies, we must be off, but first I must say goodbye to your delightful parakeets. All God's animals are pure, but there is nothing more angelic than birds. Brother Knecht, would you mind stepping aside?"

"But, bishop, I don't think they should be disturbed just now."

"Nonsense, my boy. Just step aside. Goodbye, my little angels. Thank you for your joyous - what?" For a moment he looked in horror at his splattered picture in the bottom of the birdcage. Then he turned and stormed past the Bird Sisters and out the door. "Never have I been so humiliated - never have I been so ... smeared!"

The P.R. man walked over and stared into the birdcage. All we could see was his back trembling as we waited for the volcanic eruption. He turned around, his lips twitching, and pointed back at the cage. "That - that's not good P.R." He exploded in a series of sneezing guffaws, dabbing at his eyes and nose. "Unfortunately I can't print it, but 'Truly, I say to you, wherever the gospel is preached in the whole world, what they have done will be told in memory of them'." (Matthew 26:13) He saluted the bewildered Bird Sisters and left.

"O.K., Ben, can you top this?" Ron Wright

18 Oh, the Preacher and the Laymen Should Be Friends

After the P.R. man left, Ron said, "He didn't turn out to be such a bad guy after all."

Rose and Emily were blinking in bewilderment as they nested for security in each other's arms. Victor spoke to them soothingly. "The bishop gets these spells sometimes - too much pressure, you know."

I again took up my post in front of the birdcage. "Now why don't you ladies take these gentlemen on a tour of your lovely old house, while I sit here and meditate?"

Ron picked up on my suggestion. "Yes, I'd like to see your home." The Bird Sisters brightened and started preening themselves.

"Be sure and show them all your treasures in the attic," I suggested.

"Oh, we will," chirped Emily.

Victor gallantly offered Emily his arm, and Ron followed suit with Rose.

As soon as I heard their steps on the stairs, I opened the bottom of the cage and slid out the 'desolating sacrilege'. What could I do with it? Then I spotted a pile of papers in the corner, grabbed the top one, and rolled the Bishop's picture up inside. To the garbage can for the whole mess. When I got back into the house, I took another paper from the stack and slid it into the cage.

When they came back, they found me reading the *Post*.

Ben and Victor thanked the Bird Sisters for the tour, and I thanked them for putting up with the bishop.

By the time we walked back to the church, Ben had caulked the lid of the memorial case and had set up a couple of window fans.

"Thanks for clearing the air, Ben."

"You're welcome, Rev'rend."

"Now I suppose we'll have a hard time getting the folks to come inside."

"I don't think so. Yon, call 'em in for the food."

From the mouth of Yon Yonson came the most awful sound, something like "SUEE, SUEE, SUEEEEEE."

"What in the world?"

"That's his pig call. We're gonna make pigs of ourselves, ain't we?"

Everyone seemed to know what it meant, for they started filing in to the biggest orgy ever held in a Methodist Church. The food! Ummm. Now that Brother Berdahl's socks had been hermetically sealed, we could smell baked turkey, Swiss steak, pork roasts, and myriad vegetables and baked goods. Every woman had prepared her best - in at least triplicate. Mrs. Grundy, alone, had brought in four turkeys and five pans of double-frosted brownies. Ten dozen hot rolls and six mincemeat pies were Birdie s contribution. Hannah had made some lutefisk and lefse. The former was a pickled fish, and the latter was a flat pastry that looked somewhat like a dishcloth but with plenty of butter and jam tasted all right. It was a love-cooked meal and a love-served meal. The ladies served their mouth-watering dishes with plenty of hugs and kisses. No wonder we were able to eat so much!

Ron mumbled through a mouthful of dumplings, "Mpff-um-lish-slurp-yum!"

"Well said. Have you noticed that in the Judeo-Christian tradition all women are Jewish Mothers?"

Ron gulped a few times and wiped his mouth. "Yes, and their main text - or pretext - was given at the foot of Mount Sinai by the mother of Moses. It was known as the First Dietary Law: 'The way to a man's heart is through his stomach'."

"How true!" I responded. "Long ago they invented the stomach by-pass - everything right to the heart."

Ron nodded. "Their motto is: 'Eat this and you'll love me'."

"Then when you're stuffed, they lament, 'If you really loved me, you'd try to eat this'."

Just then Birdie appeared at my elbow with a bowl of mashed potatoes. "How 'bout some more, Rev'rend?"

"No thanks, Birdie. I couldn't." But when I saw her smile curve downward into basset-hound sadness, I said, "O.K., just a spoonful." Out shot a ladle the size of the Big Dipper.

It was a no-lose situation - for the cooks.

Miriam tugged at my sleeve. "Dave, could you get Victor out of here before he gains back the forty pounds."

"He isn't the only one in mortal danger. We all better go."

I rounded up Ron and Ben, and together with the Hansons, we walked out into the fresh air.

Ron moaned. "I'll never eat again - until possibly suppertime."
We all groaned.

I opened the doors of the Buick, and they eased their way in. Ron was teasing Victor. "Do you think you can get the plane off the ground now?"

"Maybe four or five feet. We'll have to fly under the power lines."

When we got out of the car, Victor put his arm around my shoulders. "Dave, don't worry about the bishop. He'll forget it in a week - he forgets everything in a week. The P.R. man keeps the poor bishop going at such a pace that he is completely disoriented in time and space."

"Don't sign him on as navigator," Ron cautioned.

"Not a chance in the world. Besides I'm pretty happy with my own navigator." Victor put his arm around Miriam. There was more hugging and kissing. Ben, Ron, and I were included, too.

Vic and Miriam climbed into their Cessna, and he called out, "Try to stay out of trouble, you two. Don't merge with the Lutherans or form a new denomination until I get back."

We laughed and waved as the little plane raced across the field and took to the air, bearing these dear friends of ours on their second honeymoon.

"Nice folks," Ben remarked. "And that's su'prisin' considerin' the way he was ravin' after his plane crash. I've known Reverend Hanson for years around' the Conference, and he's always bin a purty cold fish."

"Oh," Ron said breezily, "that was B.C."

"You don't mean *Before Christ?*" Ben asked.

"No, *Before Camp*," Ron replied.

"Hmm, just what did happen at that camp?"

"Nothing much. Someday we'll tell you a story about it."

"Well, now," said Ben, "I've found that those 'someday' stories seldom git told, so why don'tcha come over to my place right now and tell it."

"Birdie, we got company," Ben called out. There was no answer, so he went into the kitchen and then upstairs. He came down, having exchanged his suit coat for a bathrobe and slippers. "Birdie must be hung up at the church - prob'ly won't be home for hours. Meanwhile, why don'tcha 'men of the cloth' take off some of that cloth and git comfortable."

"Good idea, Ben." Ron and I. removed our suit coats and ties and proceeded to get comfortable. Ron took the big chair next to the fireplace, and I sat at the end of the davenport, slipped off my shoes, and put up my feet.

Ben settled in his rocker and said, "And now for the story."

Both Ron and I started talking at once about "The Endless Line of Squalor". Then we stopped, and Ron pointed at me. "You start, Dave. You were the dean."

"Correction: co-dean."

"Careful, co-dean can become habit-forming," Ron quipped.

Ben looked puzzled. "Codeine?"

"Ben," I said, "remember after the D.S.'s plane crash ..."

"Ya, ya."

"He made me dean of the camp."

"Ya, ya."

"Well, I asked Arlene to be co-dean of the camp?"

"Oh, co-dean. O.K., now I gotcha."

"Unfortunately, the D.S. had volunteered to be the 'inspirational speaker'."

Ron groaned. "He was about as inspirational as wet putty."

"Ben, can you guess how Victor came to camp?" I asked.

"Flew, I s'pose."

"No," I said, "he came in a hearse."

"Yes," added Ron, "stretched out in the back like a corpse - scared the kids to death."

"And then," I explained, "he roped Ron and me into helping him set up the stage sets he had stored in the barn since The Flood."

"Helped him - we did everything!"

"In fact," I added, "we were his only audience. The kids slept through the services, but we had to stay awake to handle the lighting and special effects."

"I handled the last special effect myself," Ron declared proudly.

"Ben, this crazy guy poured a bucket of prune juice into a cow - "

"With spectacular results!"

"Yes," I said, "that ended the D.S.'s indoor services. Unfortunately the D.S. continued them outside. Ben, picture yourself sitting on a hillside overlooking the lake. All is tranquil, peaceful, quiet."

"When all of a sudden your ear drums break." Ron clapped his hands sharply.

"The D.S. is coming in a rowboat and playing a trumpet,"

"And then he stands up in the boat to preach," said Ron.

"Really ?" Ben asked.

"Briefly." I looked at Ben. "The boat overturned."

"And the lifeguard pulled him out."

"What?" asked Ben. "You mean a D.S. can't walk on water?"

"That's what did it," Ron declared.

"He's been a changed man ever since his near drowning."

"Well, well, well." Ben rocked for a few minutes. "I always say there's more than one way to tip a camel's hump. You boys sure got some unusual methods of spreadin' the gospel."

"Well, that's the story," I said.

We sat back, luxuriating in our camaraderie.

Ron started chuckling. "Do you know what my finance chairman said to me last night? It was right before board meeting, and he whispered to me, 'What's a tithe?'"

"I'll bite - what is it?" I asked.

Ron ignored me. "Boy, laymen are so dumb - present company excepted."

Ben rocked back and looked up at the ceiling before drawling, "Well, now, I think your story 'bout camp shows that preachers is purty dumb - present company included."

I laughed. "You've got us cold, Ben."

"Now wait just a minute." Ron bristled. "Let me tell you about some more dumb laymen."

"Go ahead, young fella," said Ben, "and I'll come up with two dumb preachers for every dumb layman."

"Now take it easy, fellows. Keep it friendly."

"Oh, we're friendly, all right." Ron picked up a poker and slapped it against his palm. "But I'll hang onto this just in case."

Ben laughed, and Ron couldn't keep from grinning. "O.K., Ben, can you top this? One time I went to a prayer meeting over at the Assembly of God. Joe Williams, the druggist, got up and gave his testimony: 'I bin suffering' for years from a spastic colon, but since I met Jesus I bin goin' all the time'."

"Just like our cow at camp," I said.

"That's purty good, Ron, but would you swear to that on a stack of Bibles?"

"Well, not a stack, but maybe one modern translation."

"Now it's your turn, Ben," I said.

"Lemme see … it's hard to know where to start … there's so many…. First lemme tell you 'bout the preacher we had before Dave. One Sunday he was preachin' about the church as the body of Christ and gittin' all warmed up to the climax when he yelled out – 'The church is a livin' orgasm!'"

"Is there another meaning to that?" I asked.

"That's what the preacher was prayin' for all the way home to his dictionary, but there ain't," declared Ben.

"That isn't being dumb," Ron said. "That's just a slip of the tongue - like a spoonerism."

"What's that?" asked Ben.

"I'll give you an example," said Ron. "That's like the preacher who was going to bury a woman whose only claim to fame was a slender volume called *Campfire Verses*. At the funeral the preacher said, 'And we will not soon forget her *Vampire Curses*.'"

"Just which side of the fence are you on, Ron?" I asked.

"I heard one of them spoonerisms at the last Conference," said Ben. "One of the preachers did that to *'fiery darts* of the wicked.'"

"Hmm, you're sure it was a preacher?" Ron inquired.

"Ya, ya."

"O.K., back to dumb layman," said Ron. "I invited a lady to attend our services, but she never came because she was hooked on radio preachers. In fact, she was telling me about a four-Sunday series on Methuselah's last years. Have you heard of anything more irrelevant than that?"

"Sounds relevant to me," Ben said. "Have you ever heard of Arson the Parson? No, well he was the pastor of a big old city church. One night somebody broke into the church, tore up the pulpit Bible, and set the place on fire. However, somebody turned in the alarm, and the fire department caught it 'fore it burned the place down. The pastor thought that this'd be a great opportunity to relocate and build a new church, but the board took the insurance money and used it to fix up the old church rather than build a new one.

"I was commiseratin' with the pastor at Conference. 'That's too bad - I suppose you're lookin' for the man that started the fire.' 'No, no,' he replied sadly, 'I'm lookin' for the man that turned in the alarm.'"

"He was probably just trying to pour oil on troubled waters when 'whoof' - spontaneous combustion." At any rate, my analysis sounded good to me.

"O.K., you doubters," said Ron, "here's one last story. Once I - " Ben interrupted. "You forgot to say, 'Once upon a time'."

Ron gave Ben a mock frown and cleared his throat. "Once upon a time I was invited to speak to the Woman's Society at a neighboring church. I got there early, but the church was locked, so I stood around for about a half hour. Finally the president came and rummaged through her handbag for the keys. No luck - she had left them at home. When she got back, she started the meeting and ran through the usual line of trivia, like what color tickets to have for the bazaar. That took an hour, and I still hadn't gotten to speak. Then she called out right from the podium, 'Effie, would you be a dear and go put on the coffee?' Dear Effie went out and started banging around the kitchen. The next thing I knew, Effie stuck her head out of the kitchen door and yelled, 'I can't find it.' The president yelled back, 'Look in the cupboard next to the refrigerator for the coffee pot, and the coffee is in the pantry near the switch.' The president sighed and turned to me. 'The devil sure doesn't want this meeting to go over.'"

"Let's give credit where credit is due," I said.

"Well, all I can say is that Ron here reminds me of old Brother Miller. When he'd preach, the tears would trickle down the old watercourses and join the saliva dribblin' over his chin. Ya, he was all wet, too."

Ron grimaced. "Hmm, well, I'm leaving it up to David to decide who's dumber.

"C'mon, David," said Ben. Who do you think the church would be better off without - preachers or laymen?"

"Well, Ron, you made a pretty good case against laymen ..."

Ron stood up and took a bow.

"But I feel that Ben did equally well against preachers, so - "

"So?"

"So?"

"So, I'm forced to conclude that the church would be better off without both preachers and laymen."

"Strange how at weddings friends act like fiends." David Rowe

19 A Marriage Not Made in Heaven

November came in like a lion with the first blizzard of the year. Suddenly everyone looked like Eskimos. Now I was glad that Ken and the ladies at Penney's had outfitted me for winter as I waded through the drifts to the post office. I felt warm except where the wind bit my exposed cheeks, though I wondered if a person could get frostbitten in one block.

After picking up my mail, I stayed in the P.O. long enough to thaw out. On my way home, I happened to glance at the Red Owl. The window was covered with ice and steam, but as I watched it, a small circle was rubbed clear, and I saw Frank's face peering out. I waved and continued on my way.

"Hey, Rev'rend, can you come in for a minute?"

I looked back to see Frank leaning out the door, his white apron flapping in the icy wind. "Sure, Frank." I walked carefully over the slippery sidewalk to the entrance. Frank had spread some sand just outside the door because it was too cold for salt to do any good.

After I stepped inside, I saw the history of the water cycle being reenacted in his store: snow fell off boots, turned into slush, formed puddles of water, and eventually rose in steam to gather on the ceiling and drip down in indoor rain.

There was a young couple standing next to Frank. The girl had blonde hair and features like him. The young man reminded me strongly of someone in Webber, but I couldn't remember whom.

"Rev'rend, this's my daughter Judy and Curt Winter's boy, Joe. Kids meet Rev'rend Rowe."

Strange that he called them kids, because they looked about my age. Joe extended a work-hardened hand. His eyes passed shyly past mine, and he mumbled something that sounded friendly. Like his father, he had a short frame, but he was stocky rather than roly-poly.

Judy was the same height as Joe but only about half of his width. (I don't know why women as tall as men always look taller.)

"Oh, Rev'rend, Daddy's told me so much about you." She flashed light blue eyes like beacons. "I think it was just hilarious the way Daddy and Ben slopped up the communion for you and how your cat cleaned up on all of Schroeder's tough dogs. And Brother Berdahl's smelly socks - did they really almost overcome the bishop?"

"Yes, and everyone else."

Frank was grinning. "I t'ink the kids got sumpthin' to ask you."

I looked from one to the other. Judy waited for Joe to speak, but he was looking at the frozen window. Judy sighed. "Well, Rev'rend, we were wondering if you would marry us. Isn't that right, Joe?" Joe shuffled his feet and nodded.

"Yes, I'd be glad to. Have you set a date?"

"Next Saturday. You see, I'm home just a week before I have to go back to nursing school."

"That's fine with me. Why don't you two drop over this evening, so we can discuss arrangements."

Around 8:00 the door opened and Judy blew in.

"Hi, Judy. Where's Joe?"

"Oh, he got hung up at the farm. He'll be in later."

"I see. Here, let me take your coat." She came out of her fur coat like a butterfly out of a cocoon, beautiful and fluttery as she shook her long blonde hair over her shoulders.

"I'm - I'm afraid the furniture isn't very comfortable," I stammered.

She bent over and examined the davenport and chairs. "Hey, this looks like our old front room set." I turned red in embarrassment. "That's O.K., Rev'rend. I won't report you." She had disconcerting blue eyes - almost like X-rays.

As she settled onto the davenport, I perched on the uneasy chair and rubbed my hands together. "Uh, you said you were going to nursing school."

"Yes, over in the Twin Cities. This is my last year. When I came home for vacation, Joe just swept me off my feet."

"Swept you off your feet?"

"Yes, with his father's 2,000 acres." I frowned. "Don't go holy on me, Rev'rend. I've knocked around long enough - two years of college, a stewardess for seventeen months till I was grounded, a model for awhile, and now nurse's training. I'm ready to settle down and be supported by someone else, but I'll finish nursing school – just in case."

"Hmm."

"Unless you have a better idea, David. You don't mind if I call you David?" Her voice grew very low and husky. "Unless you are interested yourself?"

I was used to a snail's pace, and now I had just been blitzed by light speed.

"I - " The outside door opened, sending a welcomed icy draft through the house. I heard the stamping of heavy boots. "Joe." I hurried to the door. "Thank God you've come - I mean, I'm glad you made it. Here, let me take your parka. You go sit next to Judy. There, now, have you given any thought to - uh - special, music?"

Joe looked blankly at me; Judy appeared to be gritting her teeth. They were silent so I swept on. "Well, I think it's always nice to have 'The Lord's Prayer' sung, and 'Because' is always good. If you think of anything else later, just call Miss Osgood."

"The Blind Woman." Judy gave a half-sneer as she drew her legs up under her.

"Now, do you want a small affair - er, ceremony - in the parsonage, or will it be a big church wedding?"

"Rev'rend Rowe, I want people to talk about this wedding for a long time to come." Judy burned me with her intensity.

"Oh ... O.K. What time do you want the service?"

Joe looked at Judy.

"We're having it at two o'clock."

"Let me backtrack a bit. Now if Judy goes back to nursing school, then you won't have a honeymoon. Is that right?"

"Not right away, not until I finish school next June. You'll want to go away then, won't you, Joe?" He turned crimson and looked down at the floor.

"Maybe it might be a good idea to postpone the wedding till June." Judy shot me a deadly look. "No? Well, it was just an idea." Silence filled the room, a contrast to the shrieking wind outside. "Where are you two going to live?"

Joe started shuffling his feet and working his mouth. I think he was testing his unused P.A. system. "Uh, Dad'll move inta the little house and let us have the big one." This appeared to be the big speech of his life, but with Judy around, what need had he to ever talk again? I didn't like it, but what could I do? She had made up their minds and wasn't about to change them.

The big day came, my first all-out church wedding. I had borrowed Ron's robe and was as nervous as the groom, pacing, checking my watch, and running up from the kitchen to peek through the sanctuary door. The soloist, Colonel Robert Frank, a professional mourner or rejoicer - depending on whether the guest of honor was horizontal or vertical - was late as usual. I ran down to the kitchen, to the six men waiting like pallbearers. "The soloist isn't here yet."

The cigarette in Joe's hand was shaking. His husky young friends appeared as ill at ease as he did, possibly because they rarely darkened (or even lit up) the inside of a church.

And then we heard the unmistakable nasal tones of Colonel Frank. Just how did he get to be the community soloist? He was rending his special version of "Because."

I beckoned to the pallbearers to follow me and rustled up the steps in my long robe. At the top I tripped and grabbed the doorknob. I peeked again. Judy's mother was just being escorted down the aisle to the first pew. I opened the door and walked to the front of the platform. The pallbearers followed me and went to their assigned places. We looked expectantly at the bridesmaids; the bridesmaids looked expectantly at Miss Osgood; Miss Osgood looked dreamily into space. I nodded at her, but then realized that she couldn't see me. Finally, I crossed the platform and whispered, "We're ready for the processional."

"WHAT?"

"PROCESSIONAL!"

"OH!" She began adjusting the rubber bands on the old stops before she began pumping and music started pouring out of the old relic. As I went back to my place, the first bridesmaid began her long, hesitating journey to the front of the church, to be followed by number two, number three, number four, number five, and the maid-of-honor. Judy had really whipped up a big wedding in one week. Even the huge doors to the overflow room had been raised to accommodate the crowd. The marriage of two of the children of Coffee Gang members practically made attendance compulsory. It was a royal wedding for Webber.

Finally the complete wedding party was in. Each groomsman had a different colored bridesmaid. There was even a flower girl and a ring bearer who couldn't stand still. The rest of us not only had to stand still but also stand near the central floor register. The heat wasn't getting to the people in the pews - they still had on their winter coats - but it was getting to the wedding party, especially to the bride, the groom, and me. Sweat was pouring down in rivers from Joe's face, but then he had been sweating in the cool basement. Judy was lovely, though moist and pale. I was probably the warmest one of the three, since I was up on the platform. I thought back to my first trip to the coalbin. Was this another part of my warm reception to Webber, or was this a foretaste of the afterlife?

As I began the ritual, I noticed Judy swaying, so I kept glancing at her. She definitely was getting paler and paler and swaying more and more - until she pitched forward. I dropped the book of ritual and caught her. "Frank! Joe!" They stood there daydreaming about what? Maybe Frank was wondering how to pay the bills, especially for that big shopping trip to Minneapolis to outfit the wedding party. Joe may have been thinking about a woman entering his bachelor existence. Judy may have been trying to escape from thinking at all.

"Frank! Frank!" Finally he noticed his daughter slumped against me. He started forward, circled around her hoops, and looked for a proper handhold. Finally he put his arms around her waist and carried her out vertically.

I walked down to the rest of the Coffee Gang. "Ben, please shut off the furnace, unless you want to see us dropping like flies. Either Joe or I are next. Carl and Alf, please open up some windows."

When we got back together, I noticed that someone had put a small oscillating fan next to me, to blow on the now pink-cheeked bride. I began the ritual again and proceeded through it to the ring ceremony. "The rings please." The best man lifted the ring bearer up onto the platform. I reached down to pick up the rings, but found they were pinned to the pillow. Setting my book down, I opened the safety pin and was rewarded with a stuck thumb. Wincing, I took the rings, read the blessing, and started to hand the rings to the bride and groom.

"Hold it!" came a voice over my shoulder. I turned to see a photographer standing on my pulpit chair. "Hold the rings a little higher, Rev. There, that's good." Blinded by the flash, I dropped the rings. They rolled toward the register, stopping on the edge. Joe leaned over to pick them up, but the little ring squirted out of his thick fingers into the depths of the red-hot furnace, soon to be followed by the larger ring. The adding machine in her father's head rang up more dollars.

I must have moved too close to the fan, for it caught the end of my borrowed robe and wrapped it around the shaft. I stood there tugging Ron's robe out of the fan. Finally it came out in shreds and tatters. This was the social event of the year all right. Another flash confirmed that the photographer was catching it all.

I think I completed the ceremony; I hope they were legally married.

Because of the weather, we had the receiving line downstairs. People came single file down the narrow stairway, went through the receiving line, and picked up some punch-less punch. From there they went to sit along the wall or to stand around in chattering clusters.

Two people didn't come down the narrow stairs: Mrs. Grundy and Mr. Yonson. Mrs. Grundy's girth would have barely passed through, but then she would not have been able to take Grampa Yonson's arm. The two of them went out the front door and walked around to the side door, which led directly into the basement.

Mrs. Grundy then took over in the kitchen, the room she was most capable of handling next to a schoolroom or a library. In just a few minutes she had the ladies organized.

I lingered in the sanctuary, putting out the candles and visiting. Suddenly there was the noise of several cars pulling up fast on the gravel. I went to the door and saw about a dozen young men pile out of the cars. A couple of them went over to Joe's car, probably to pull some prank. Strange how at weddings friends act like fiends. The rest came running up the steps.

"Afraid you missed the wedding, fellas, but you can still catch the reception downstairs."

They brushed by me without speaking and went downstairs. They seemed strangely grim, but I supposed they were disappointed to miss the wedding.

The sheriff grabbed my arm. "Rev rend, that's the Rock Creek Gang. We're in for trouble. When Judy was a cheerleader back in high school, she usta be purty popular with the Rock Creek crowd. We better git downstairs fast. You go the inside way, and I'll go around back."

I hurried down the steps just in time to see a guy throw Judy over his shoulder. As he scuttled for the back door, his friends ran interference. One threw open the back door, and the rest poured through. All the wedding guests were frozen until they heard the sound of cars racing away.

"C'mon," Frank shouted out. "What're you guys waitin' for? Let's go to Rock Creek." The men woke up and started moving for their cars.

Ben rushed up to me. "Dave, you better come along to try to prevent bloodshed."

I hurried out, my tattered robe flapping, and saw the sheriff lying on the ground. Ben and I helped him up. "Boy, just wait'll I git my badge on." He reached a skinned hand into his pocket and pulled out his badge.

"Over here!" someone called. Fred, Ben, and I stumbled over to a door held open by Curt Winter and piled into the back seat. Curt jumped into the front seat next to his son, the groom, and we raced after the lead car driven by Frank. Four or five other cars followed.

Before we even got out of Webber, the car was filled with a terrible odor. Each one looked suspiciously at his neighbor. Ben sniffed. "Somebody sick?"

"Smells like limburger to me." The sheriff was the ultimate authority on food.

Then I remembered two of the gang who had been poking around Joe's car. "I think they smeared limburger cheese on the motor."

"Thank goodness," cried Curt. "I thought the motor was burnin' up."

Joe wasn't going to stop for anything. He raced on. The rest of us rolled down the windows to try to get fresh air.

"This reminds me," gasped Ben, "of the time we stole the county seat back from Rock Creek."

"We really didn't steal it, Rev'rend," Curt explained. "We won the election fair and square, but Rock Creek wouldn't give up the county records."

Ben laughed. "We went over - that was just after we got back from the war - and took the records. Old Man Yonson lifted the safe onta the truck all by hisself."

"Ya," said Fred, "always bin a rivalry 'tween the two towns, sports and everything, but kidnapping's too much."

"I see 'em." Joe stared ahead. We were closing the gap.

"They're prob'ly headin' for Crist's Bar," Fred said. "That's where they hang out. Crist is the father of the gang leader and as strong as a bull moose. He's the best arm rassler in the county."

Soon after that the Rock Creek Gang did turn into the bar, an old building at the back of a large parking lot, bordered by huge piles of snow. It was a shock for me to see *Christ's* name on the sign, for Fred had been giving the name its Scandinavian pronunciation. Joe turned into the lot after the Rock Creek Gang, and even before we stopped, Ben was out of the car and running pretty fast for his fifty-five years. When Frank and Joe and the others came up, he blocked the door.

"Now just cool off, you guys. 'Remember, the Rock Creek Gang's thirty years younger than most of us. Now, Joe, just take it easy and let the Rev'rend do the talking."

All the moisture went from my mouth to the palms of my hands as I tried to walk resolutely into my first bar. It was dark, and I couldn't see anything but the glow of a mirror, so I walked toward it. Two guys at the bar grabbed their drinks and scooted fearfully toward some distant sanctuary, alarmed either by my tattered black robe or the angry-looking Webber men at my back.

I looked over the scratched and stained bar to the rows of bottles beneath the mirror. This must be where Christ serves communion to his disciples, I thought. A big, heavy-jowled man behind the bar scowled at us. Then I noticed a sign on the mirror: "Any guy who can beat me in arm rassling gits free drinks. Losers pay double."

"Whadda you want?" Christ snarled.

"Free drinks," I said.

"O.K., kid." He put his great arm on the bar.

"No, not me. We're all going to take you on, starting with the weakest. You first, Mr. – er - Smith." I used an assumed name for Grampa Yonson, just in case Christ had heard of his prowess.

"WHAT'S THAT, REV'REND?"

"ARM WRESTLING - WITH HIM." I pointed to the bartender.

Grampa Yonson nodded and stood his frail-looking arm next to the bartender's mighty tree.

"Take it easy on Grampa," Ben pleaded.

"Don't worry," the big man sneered. "It'll be a nice clean break."

The two closed hands, and Grandpa's thin arm was almost surrounded by the excess flesh of the bartender. I hoped I had done the right thing. If he broke Grandpa's arm, I would never forgive myself. I wouldn't blame the Webber men if they never forgave me either.

"Goodbye, Gramps," said the bartender, tensing the huge muscles beneath the flab, but nothing happened. Grandpa's arm was unmoved. The bartender looked surprised and shifted his grip. He applied more pressure. Still Grampa's arm was as unmoved as an oak post driven into the ground.

"O.K., you old geezer. I ain't gonna baby you no more." The bartender heaved all his weight and muscle against Grandpa's arm, which stood as unmoving as a steel rod set in concrete.

"Cheat! This guy must be wearin' a metal brace!"

"TAKE HIM NOW, FODDER," Yon said in his normal roar.

"O.K., SON." As Grampa's thin arm began to move forward like a locomotive piston, shock hit the bartender's face. Then Christ dug in his heels and grunted till his pudgy face turned red, but even this "Battle of the Bulge" could not stop the slow, inexorable movement of Grampa's arm. Without visible effort, Grandpa forced Christ's knuckles down, down, down, onto the bar.

When Grandpa released the bartender, Christ cupped his elbow in his good hand and stepped back.

Ben set his scrawny arm on the bar. "I'm next."

"No, no!" cried the bartender. He turned and called out to his assistant. "Pete, free drinks for all these guys."

"No," I held up my hand. "We didn't come for drinks - we came for the bride."

"Ya, sir! Right away, sir!" He walked toward a door at the end of the bar, still cupping his sore elbow.

"I wouldn't trust 'im," Frank said. "Do you have your gun, Fred?"

"Don't worry, Frank. I t'ink the Rev'rend and Grampa put the fear of God inta him."

We heard voices arguing in the back room. Slap! Silence. The door opened, and Judy rushed into Joe's arms. Joe turned red under the smiles of all of us. "Gee, Judy, can't you wait till later?"

We roared. Carl Lysne poked Joe. "You're gonna hafta marry her now, Joe."

The Webber men went out relaxed and joking, quite a contrast to the avenging vigilantes that had come in.

I turned in the doorway. "One more favor. We'd appreciate your changing the name of your bar."

"Ya, sir!"

After we piled into the cars, I found myself sitting next to the Yonsons. Up front were Ben, Carl Lysne, and Frank, the driver.

Frank called back over his shoulder. "T'anks, Rev'rend, for gittin' Judy back - without a fight, and thanks to you, Grampa, for takin' on the bartender."

I knew Grampa couldn't hear, so I hollered in one ear while Yon hollered in the other.

"NO NEED TO YELL," yelled Grampa. "I LIKE TO BEND AN ELBOW NOW AND THEN."

"You can shear a sheep a hunerd times, but you can skin him only once."
Eldon Chance, church treasurer

20 Treasurers and Other Con-Artists

When our caravan rounded the dairy corner, we saw the women, looking anxiously toward us, in front of the church. We pulled up under their worried looks. Hannah came rushing up to our car and peered in at me. "Did you git Judy back?"

"Oh, yes." I pointed to Joe's car.

Judy and Joe got out, and her mother ran to her. Inside of a minute there was a big huddle of the Webber women around Judy. Gradually it peeled away like the layers of an onion till only Judy and her mother were left.

Hannah, followed by Mrs. Grundy in all deliberate speed, came back to me, "Are you alright, Rev'rend?" Hannah asked.

"Yes, I'm O.K. Thanks."

Mrs. Grundy inquired if there had been any fighting.

"Just some arm wrestling. Grampa Yonson beat Christ the bartender."

The two ladies turned toward the old man. Mrs. Grundy embarrassed him mightily by drawing him to her queenly bosom. Hannah slipped up and gave him a dry peck on the cheek.

"TARNATION! GIT THESE WIMMEN OFF ME!"

No one made a move except Judy, who gave him a moist and grateful kiss on his wrinkled brow. Grampa Yonson turned turkey red, but I think he really enjoyed it. He had already proved that he wasn't as old as he looked.

When I got back to the parsonage, I took off the borrowed robe and made an inventory of the damage. The lower right front panel was tattered and greasy up to about knee level from its tangle with the fan. Two of the little hooks, along with pieces of cloth, had been pulled out of the front. And, to top it off (or really to bottom it out), I must have sat on one of the sheriff's marshmallow candy bars. How could I break it to Ron?

I lifted up the phone. "Tillie, please get me Ron Wright over at Rock Creek."

"Do you think you oughta be callin' Rock Creek – after what you done to 'em?"

"Now, Tillie, all I did was – "

"No need to tell me! I heard it all from Mad Ole, who had it straight from Alf Langdon, how you tore apart Christ's Bar and beat up the bartender and even ripped down the sign and dropped it on his chest. Well, I better put you through before you git violent and tear the phone out of the wall."

"Tillie, Tillie," I called to her over the rings. "Wait a minute, Tillie."

"No, this isn't Tillie; this is Ron Wright."

"Oh, Ron - this's David. I wish I knew how to tell you about your robe." I looked at the remains of it lying over the back of one of the rickety dining room chairs.

"Oh, what about my robe?"

"Dottie told me how your home church had given it to you - "

"What about it?"

"As an ordination gift."

"David, for heaven's sake, tell me!"

"It got caught in a fan."

"In November?"

"Well, you see, the bride fainted - "

"Fainted?"

"Because she was standing over the furnace."

"What in the world?"

"Remember how the floor register is right in front of the platform. Well, the wedding party was standing right next to the register."

"Now you're starting to make sense."

"Good, I'm glad you understand." I lifted up the robe. "Sorry about the holes in the front."

"From the fan?"

"No, the fan tore just the bottom."

"Well, what tore the front?"

"I guess the hooks got pulled out when we jumped into the car … after the bride was kidnapped."

"Kidnapped?"

"Yes, a gang of young guys ran off with the bride, so we followed. That must have been when I sat on the marshmallow bar."

"Oh, no!"

"I didn't do it on purpose, Ron. It must have fallen out of the sheriff's pocket."

"Was he in on it, too?"

"Yes, in fact, a lot of the men at the reception jumped into their cars."

"Oh," said Ron, "a regular posse."

"Yes, and we followed the gang to Christ's Bar."

"Ah, ha! Now that crazy rumor makes sense. I heard about an angry mob led by a mad minister in a tattered robe - my robe! - that stormed into Christ's Bar and beat up the bartender and roughed up his son."

"No, Ron. I don't know if you'll believe this, but the only violence was a 91-year-old man beating Christ in arm wrestling."

"You don't expect me to believe that?"

"But - "

"Somehow I believe you, David."

"Good, but I'm sorry about your robe - I know it was an ordination gift. Of course, the marshmallow and the grease can be removed, but I doubt if it can be mended, so I'll just buy you a new one."

"Don't worry, David. I haven't worn that robe in years - except for your 75th anniversary service. In a moment of weakness I put it on to impress the bishop."

"You aren't just saying that - "

"No, I mean it. I think that clerical garb should have gone out with the bustle. As Prof. Kolbe used to say: 'If the plural of bag is baggage, then the plural of garb should be garbage.'"

"I still feel bad about it, though, and I was wondering if you and Dottie would be my guests at our 'Man in the Moon' Banquet next Friday night."

"Sounds good, but what is it?"

"Oh, we're planning a surprise banquet for our church treasurer. He's served twenty-five years."

"Twenty-five years! I can't keep a treasurer more than six months ... O.K., we'll come - providing you forget about the robe. Let Sylvester sleep on it, or use it for the cat's pajamas."

On the day of the banquet, I made half a dozen trips over to the church basement, which was a mistake, because I got roped into a dozen odd jobs: "Rev'rend, would you tack the moon on the wall? ... Rev'rend, would you hang the crepe paper? ... Rev'rend, would you dump the trash?" Sometimes it's not good to be the youngest person present.

I slipped away as soon as I could because I wanted to polish up my speech. I was one of the roasters and pretty nervous about it. My attempts at humor had fallen flat in my high school variety show and in the Northwestern Follies. Also, I hate to admit it, but there was a gulf between me and the treasurer. Whenever I came into the back room where Eldon Chance and his buddies were counting the collection, they all clammed up until I left. Ben said that the treasurer was quite a storyteller and that some of his stories weren't quite fitting for church. Somehow Eldon had gotten it into his head that all preachers were sobersides.

Because of this he attended church seldom, but always came in afterward to handle the money. This left me feeling somewhat left out of the group of "moneychangers in the temple."

Suddenly I heard the whine of Ron's VW bus over the crunch of the gravel. I put my note cards in my inside pocket and hurried to the door. Ron was coming around the front of the bus. "Hey, Dave!" He came toward me, shaking my hand and squeezing my arm. My, he was a powerful guy.

I looked over at Dottie, still sitting in the bus. "Ron, I think you forgot something."

"Sorry, baby." Ron swept over to the bus and opened the door with a flourish of verbal trumpets: "Ta, taa, ta, ta, ta, taaa - presenting the Queen!"

Dottie slipped down and came rustling in a long blue gown.

I bowed. "Welcome, your Majesty. Ron, you're fortunate to have such a cute little wife."

"Cute!" Ron snorted. "Are you blind? She's the most gorgeous woman I've ever seen!"

I straightened up. "I have the feeling I'm being quoted to myself."

Dottie was looking back and forth between the two of us. "What's going on?"

"I said that once to Ron about Arlene."

"Oh," said Dottie, "how is Arlene?"

"I don't know - I'm afraid I ruined my chances with her."

"It ain't necessarily so," Ron sang in a clear tenor. "I told you that you had to fall off the pedestal. How did you do it?"

"I - I grabbed her and kissed her."

"I bet she didn't know what hit her."

I nodded … then hung my head. Ron put his arms around me and Dottie.

"Well, Dottie and I didn't have that problem - she never had me up on a pedestal."

She laughed up at her husband. "You were too down-to-earth."

Ron squeezed my shoulder. "Don't worry, Dave. It'll come out all right."

"Thanks, Ron …" I tried to brighten things up. "Say, why don't you come in and sit down for awhile? We have some time before the banquet."

"O.K.," said Ron, "just so you don't show Dottie those five bedrooms - I don't know if I could ever get her home."

"Silly." She punched him playfully.

"Bong!" I called. "All right, go to your corners - and sit, if you dare." Instead they sat close together on the nohair sofa.

"Dottie, I like your dress. It goes well with your blue eyes. Only one problem - you don't look like a poor minister's wife."

She laughed. "I had been wondering all week what to wear, and then - just this morning - Ron came back from the post office with a big box of rummage from his home church. I'm so lucky."

She looked so radiantly happy that I marveled at her. Here she was: living on a low income with five kids in a tiny parsonage that didn't even have a bathroom. I wondered if Arlene were made of material like that. And then my thoughts came back to the occasion for the occasion.

"Ron, I'm sorry about that robe."

"No robe talk, remember?"

"O.K., but I've messed up so many things. Maybe I'm just not cut out to be a minister. I spilled communion wine and dropped the wedding rings in the furnace and even knocked my sermon notes under a casket."

"That's nothing," said Dottie. "You should hear Ron's great baptism experience."

"Do I have to tell him?"

"Go on, honey. It may cheer David up."

"All right. Well, back when I was in my first church, I came to my first mass baptism. The Pokagon church had saved up all the kids for baptism on Palm Sunday. I said the usual words, 'Suffer the little children to come unto me ...' Well, they came squalling, and I started to suffer." Ron clasped Dottie's hand. "And this little dickens was laughing the whole time."

"It was so funny!" Dottie whooped.

"Not to me. I was scared, but there was someone who was more scared than I was, a little fellow about three who was named ... Tommy Lewis. He ran and dived under the first pew, and his father had to reach under for him. There was a brief, unequal struggle, and Tommy was dragged out kicking and screaming. I was tempted to try 'the laying on of hands'."

"Ron talks tough, but he has the world's tenderest heart."

"Quiet, woman, or I'll flatten you."

"Yes, monster."

"Well, I must admit I did feel sorry for the little tyke. After I put water on Tommy's head, I whispered, 'There, now, that didn't hurt, did it?'"

"'IT DID TOO!' his voice echoed through the church."

"'Out of the mouth of babes." I grinned.

"Don't forget the dog," said Dottie.

"How could I? It was a warm Sunday, and the doors were wide open. Just as I started my sermon, a big German shepherd came padding down the aisle, circled around behind me, and went for my leg. At any moment I expected to feel sharp fangs ... but I was saved by a pretty little girl who dragged the dog back up the aisle. What a day! I should have 'stood in bed,' as they say over in that region."

"Thanks, Ron. I feel better already."

"But now I feel depressed."

"Oh, poor baby." Dottie drew Ron to her.

"Now I feel better. Just one favor, Dave. Don't tell that story to Ben. I don't want to be added to his Dumb Preacher Collection."

"I won't, Ron. Well, we had better be getting over to the church."

We let Sylvester out and walked next door. The snow had melted on the walks, but still covered the lawn. Dottie held up her long skirt as she went down the slushy walk, so I caught a glimpse of her worn loafers.

As we went down the steps to the basement, Ron grabbed my arm. "Be sure to introduce me to your ancient arm wrestler."

I paused on the last step and looked over the heads of the crowd. "There's his son."

I led Ron and Dottie through the crowd to the Jolly Blue Giant. "Yon Yonson, meet Ron Wright, the pastor at Rock Creek."

"WASN'T YOU OVER TO OUR SEVENTY-FIFTH?"

"Yes, I was, and I nearly passed out from Brother Berdahl's socks. By the way, you fellows might be glad to know that Christ's Bar has a new sign. Now it's Swenson's."

"That's good," I said, "but a rose by any other name ..."

"True, but Christ himself has started coming to church. Who knows? Maybe it will lead to something. Mr. Yonson, I understand your father was the one who beat Christ."

"YA, YA."

"I'd sure like to meet him."

He turned and spoke in his conversational bellow, "FODDER, C'MON OVER HERE." His voice easily drowned out all the other sounds in the room. The crowd parted, and the remarkable old man shuffled over.

"FODDER, THIS HERE'S REV'REND WRIGHT FROM OVER TO ROCK CREEK."

As Ron shook hands with Grampa Yonson, I could see Ron gradually bearing down, testing the old man's strength. Suddenly Ron's eyes opened wide and he cried, "Uncle, uncle!" When Grampa let up on the pressure, Ron quickly withdrew his hand and pried apart his crushed fingers. "Now I'm a believer. You've got the strongest grip I've ever come across."

"OH, FODDER USTA BE STRONG WHEN HE WAS YOUNG."

"Rev'rend Rowe, Rev'rend Rowe," Ben called out, "come on up here and give the blessing'."

The room quieted down as I led Ron and Dottie up to the head table where Ben and the Lysnes were waiting: After I gave the prayer, Ben announced. "'Fore you set down, I got sumpthin' to say 'bout our Man in the Moon Banquet. Just the other day Eldon asked me why it was called that, and tonight I can tell 'im. Eldon, you're the Man in the Moon, and tonight we're gonna honor you for being' our church treasurer for the last twenty-five years. C'mon up here, Mr. Man in the Moon, and bring your lovely bride."

As Ben was speaking, the red was creeping up the back of Eldon Chance's neck and now ringed his ears.

"I wanna thank everyone for keepin' it a secert," Ben continued. "They said it couldn't be done, but we done it." Ben shook Eldon's numbed hand, kissed Effie's check, and pulled out their chairs for them.

Eldon kept shaking his head. "I just don't know what to say."

"Then shut up and eat."

The food started coming: platters of roast beef, bowls of buttered potatoes, green beans, creamed corn, and baskets of hot rolls. Those Webber cooks couldn't be beat. Birdie spent most of the evening in the kitchen along with Mrs. Grundy, Hannah, and half a dozen other super cooks.

After dinner, Ben stood up - with some effort.

"Everybody git enough?" There were mingled groans and cheers. "Good, but lemme tell you, things was nip and tuck here at the head table. Somebody made the mistake of settin' the meat platter right in fronta Eldon. He thought it was all for himself and ate every last scrap. We were so hungry we almost roasted Eldon before the meal, but we decided to save 'im for dessert. Hannah kept us from starvin', though. She went down to the cafe and got seven carry outs."

Laughter is hard on full stomachs, but we laughed as hard as we could. "Well, Eldon Chance's bin cracking jokes 'bout us and stealin' our money for the last twenty-five years. Now's our chance to git back at 'im. First off, I'm gonna call on Carl Lysne to tell us more 'bout our guest of honor."

A chair scraped back. At the far end of the head table, Carl stood up. "Tonight I wanna tell you 'bout Eldon's actin' career. Prob'ly a lotta you have forgot or tried to forgit Eldon's first and last Christmas pageant."

The guest of honor covered his face.

"We was a little short of actors that year, so we drafted Eldon to play the three wise men. He come down the aisle dressed in his bathrobe and carryin' a gold brick. As he started climbin' up the steps, he stepped on the bottom of his robe and walked completely around the inside of his robe and back down the steps and out the door. Since that time, he ain't known whether he was comin' or goin', but he was smart enough to hang onta the gold brick."

As Carl pounded Eldon on the back, all the folks burst into applause. I fidgeted, wondering how I could follow an act like that. Fortunately, I didn't have to, for Ben called upon George Olson next.

George laid down *Rustler* magazine and came up to the speaker's stand. "Eldon Chance taught me everything he knew 'bout money – that's why I'm goin' broke. When I got to be thirteen, Eldon asked me to be a usher, so I watched him real close. When he got the collection plate from the preacher, he done a fast shuffle back up the aisle, so I shuffled my feet all the way up the aisle carpet just like he done. (I thought it was some kinda religious walk.) But when I handed the plate to the sheriff, a six-inch spark jumped from the plate to his hand and jarred him wide awake. I guess that's why our members is always shocked when we talk 'bout money."

Warm laughter greeted this sally. Fred was heard to say, "I thought the young punk done it on purpose."

"Is that why you watch George's store so careful?" Ben asked.

Ron rose to his feet. "I hope you don't mind if I say a few words. First, I'm jealous that you have a treasurer who has served for twenty-five years. I haven't been able to keep one for as long as one year. I've had treasurers who - well, let me tell you about two of them. My first treasurer didn't believe in banks. I had to go down to his barbershop to collect my salary. I felt like a welfare case each time he pulled a bag out of his safe and counted the money into my hand in front of all the big blabbermouths of the community."

Many shook their heads in sympathy, especially Eldon.

"I thought my next treasurer would be good, because he worked in a bank, but after a few months I noticed that we were starting to get second and third billings. No explanation from the treasurer - he never came to board meetings and never made reports. After six months of this, the Finance Committee decided to drop in on the treasurer."

Ron paused to drink some water.

"The treasurer was very friendly and invited us in. The Finance Chairman hemmed and hawed around and finally said, 'Well, John, we've been talking it over and have decided that maybe the treasurer's job is a little too much for you besides your bank duties.'"

"No trouble at all, Ed.'"

"'Well, we'd like to pick up the books to audit them.'"

"'Sure, Ed, but I'll need a couple of weeks to get them up-to-date.'"

"'We'd like them *now*.'"

"At that the treasurer's smile faded. He got up and began searching his house. 'I don't know where all the junk is.'"

"Gradually a pile grew at our feet of old bills, offering envelopes, loose change, and assorted papers and ledgers. We walked out of that house with three full shopping bags. Now you can see why I'm jealous of you folks."

Ron got a good hand, and then it was my turn. I got up nervously and began: "Since Mrs. Grundy is our church historian, I asked her to do a little checking into Eldon Chance's background." Out in the kitchen, Mrs. G. pulled her plump arms out of the dishwater and dried them as she came up to the serving window. "Little did I realize to what lengths she would go. She searched old church records, went to the Smithsonian, and even hopped a jet to Israel. Last Saturday she called me collect from Jerusalem. She sounded very excited as she said, 'I've just been examining the Dead Sea Scrolls with ultraviolet light and have found some marginal notes no one else has ever seen! Guess what - I've found that the Scriptures contain last names!' Well, here is the story that Mrs. Grundy was able to piece together.

"In the beginning God created Adam and Eve Graves." I looked down at Ben and then toward the kitchen, where Birdie was standing next to Mrs. Grundy. "After God placed them in the Garden of Eden, Adam said to Eve, 'You know, I've been wondering about who should be officers of our Garden Club, and I've decided that I should be Chairman since I am not only first-created but also male. Eve, since you're a woman, you have to be secretary. But don't expect me to do the treasurer's job, too. I'm just falling behind in all the book work - counting all the trees and fruits and flowers and animals. I need someone to help me.' So God gave Adam First Chance to take care of the books."

Here I received the first tentative laughter.

"Things went along pretty well until God audited the books and came up with one apple short. Then it was to the salt mines for the whole crew. That was the first eviction proceedings.

"The next one we hear about in the Scripture was Random Chance and his wife Fruitful. She gave him Chance after Chance. And then we move into a black period, a period of slavery, when people were selling Chances.

"God decided these wicked people should be punished so He told Noah Lysne (I glanced over at Carl) to build an ark. Here was this crazy old coot building a ship right in the middle of the desert, 100 miles from the nearest creek. The Chance clan had a field day taking bets - 5 to 1 it will never rain, 100 to 1 it will never float. And then it started to rain. Noah Lysne went aboard … and he took no Chances. But the Chance family had made enough money on the bets to charter another ark. I guess survival is a chancy business.

"The next chapter of our story takes place in Egypt. There was a man by the name of Joseph Schwartz (my eyes caught the sheriff), who was thrown into jail for some indiscretion - I think stealing sausage from Pharaoh's kitchen. While he was there, Pharaoh asked him to interpret the dream of the seven lean cows eating up the seven fat ones. Joseph wiggled his toes in the sand while he thought about that for awhile. 'That means we're going to have seven years of plenty followed by seven years of poverty, but I don't know what to do about it.'

"Now in that same cell were two brothers, Fat Chance and Slim Chance. Fat Chance spoke right up: 'Listen, Pal, use it while you got it. There's a strong chance you won't live more than seven years anyhow.'

"'Don't listen to him,' cried Slim Chance. 'As long as there is even a slight chance, we should take it. Save up food during the seven fat years so we have enough during the seven lean years. So Joseph sold Pharaoh on Slim Chance's plan, and Pharaoh made Joseph Schwartz Secretary of Agriculture of all Egypt. Right away Joseph set up a surplus commodities program and began giving out food stamps. The Chance clan made their usual ten percent on each transaction.

"We don't hear of the Chance family for many years until Nehemiah Winter (I looked around till I spotted Curt Winter) is allowed to return home from Exile to rebuild the Temple. Nehemiah came and stood in front of the Temple ruins with his old buddy, Rams Horn (sort of a blowhard). 'Just look at the Temple,' said Nehemiah. 'It's been reduced to rubble by the Edomites, the Jebusites, and the Termites. And the finances are even in worse shape. There's plenty of money, but it's all designated for candlesticks and urns and other furnishings. There's nothing for building. We're designation-poor.'

"Rams Horn spoke up. 'There's a local fellow here who is pretty good with figures. Why don't you give him a chance?' So Nehemiah Winter got Juggler Chance to balance the books. Frozen assets melted -

you never saw money move so fast. In no time the Temple was rebuilt, and refurnished, too.

"By the way, that explains another mystery. That's why the area around the altar - where Juggler Chance counted the collection - is called the Chancel.

"Even outside of the Bible there were famous Chances. The man who invented the carnival game with three walnut shells and a pea was named No Chance. And the first bookie called himself Better-Than-Even Chance.

"And now we come to Eldon whom I sometimes call ... Last Chance. All the traits of his ancestors have come to full flower in Eldon." (I saw that Eldon was as caught up in the story as the others.) "Those of you who have attended Official Board have heard him give his reports - which I am sure that the great P. T. Barnum would have envied. Eldon carries up a stack of three collection plates, one of which contains one bundle of $1000. 'Look, nothing in my hands - nothing up my sleeves. Now see if you can see where the money goes ... Mr. Graves, we have $1000 in the Current Expense Fund (he does a fast shuffle with the collection plates) and $1000 in the Building Fund (shuffle, shuffle) and $1000 in the Missions Fund.'

"And after the report, Ben Graves always leans over and whispers to the sheriff, 'Is that legal?' And the sheriff always answers, 'No, but it works!'

"A lot of people have wondered how Eldon has been able to raise so much money in Webber. I stumbled on the answer to that question the other day when I went by to get my salary. I knocked at his door, but no one came. Since I was a little short of cash that week, I went around to the back. It was then that I heard the noise of heavy machinery coming from his basement, so I peeked in the window. There was Eldon at a printing press, and the money was rolling off.

"Eldon, for your twenty-five years as treasurer, the Government would like to award you twenty-five years of free room and board." I pointed at Eldon. "There will never be another Chance like this."

I was surprised at all the applause. Clapping, Ben was on his feet, and everyone else rose except Eldon Chance. He seemed overwhelmed.

"Alright, Eldon," said Ben, "what do you have to say to that?" Eldon rose slowly and came up to the stand.

"I - I'm speechless."

"Hooray!" cried out Alf Langdon. "Then sit down."

Eldon shook his head. "Rev'rend, I usta think I was a purty good storyteller, but I admit I can't hold a candle to you. In fact, I'm gonna make you honorary chairman of our After Church Story Club. I promise we'll clean up our language when you're around. Also I wanna say thanks to Carl, George, Ben, and Rev'rend Wright. and a special thanks to all the ladies in the kitchen and to all of you for comin' and su'prisin' me with the best-kept secret in Webber's history." Tears glistened in his eyes and started rolling down his plump cheeks. "I'll never forgit tonight."

"... be jubilant my feet ..." Julia Ward Howe (from the "Battle Hymn of the Republic")

21 The Correct Emphasis

With the 75th anniversary, wedding, and treasurer's banquet over, things were settling down to the normal range of pastoral duties: shoveling the sidewalk, stoking the furnace, and sweeping out the church.

I tried to keep busy, because I didn't want to think about being an unmarried pastor - especially in a world that contained Arlene. Depressing - Arlene didn't even come home on weekends anymore. I was moping along past her house on my morning walk through the snow to the post office when I heard: "Yoo-hoo, Rev'ren' Rowe." I looked back to see the pink, motherly face of Mrs. Olson. "Rev'ren', I wonder if you'd mind picking up my mail this mornin'. I got some kuchen 'bout ready to come outa the oven."

"No, Mrs. Olson, I wouldn't mind a bit, providing I could trade-it for a piece of warm kuchen."

"Oh, Rev'ren' Rowe, always thinkin' of your stomach."

And my broken heart.

I stepped into the warm lobby of the post office and shook the snow off my boots. The lobby was filled with townsfolk and farmers chatting leisurely amidst the odors of tobacco and damp clothes. I stood in line, exchanging greetings with a lot of my parishioners.

When I got up to the window, I asked for the Olson mail, but the postmaster felt obligated to give me his official speech: "I ain't supposed to do that. This here's a gov'ment installation, and mail's supposed to go to the proper person - not just to any parson." He chuckled as he emptied the Olson box as well as my own. "Now here's everything' you asked for plus sumpthin' you didn't ask for - we're mighty generous 'round here." He slid a big package toward me. "That's the best-wrapped package I ever seen. It's from your folks. Who's the wrapper in your fam'ly?"

"My father."

The postmaster pointed with an ink-stained finger. "Notice all the string on that package, and at every place two strings cross he's tied little strings 'round the big strings. That package is a work of art. I'd like to meet your father."

"I'm afraid he doesn't travel much anymore. To meet him, you'd have to take a trip to Chicago and buy a burglar kit for breaking and entering."

"Maybe I will, Rev'ren'; maybe I will." Then he turned and called out: "NEXT."

There was a man who loved his job.

I strode out the door and back to Mrs. Olson's. She had the inner door open. The warm, moist air from the kitchen had condensed on the glass of the storm door and was already freezing into patterns of crystal forms and branches. I opened the door and stepped into the delicious aroma of hot kuchen. "Here's your mail, Mrs. Olson."

"C'mon out inta the kitchen. I've cut you a piece of kuchen, and I'll pour you some coffee." I slipped off my galoshes and hung my coat on the hall tree. Then I went into the kitchen, laid the mail on the table, and sat down. Mrs. Olson's more than ample figure rolled over to the table with a cup of coffee. "Do you use cream and sugar?"

"Guilty on both counts."

She giggled and went first to the cupboard and then to the refrigerator. "I hope you don't mind takin' your cream right out of the cow." She set down a bottle of milk along with a sugar bowl. Then she wiped her hands on her apron, sat down, and picked up the mail. "Oh, here's a letter from Arlene." She slit it open, her lips moving as she read. I dug into the kuchen, a German coffee cake, and waited for news of my beloved.

Mrs. Olson squealed in delight. "Arlene's bin elected Queen of the Winter Carnival. That ends up with a big formal, and she's already got two invitations to the dance. One's from Eric the Red - he's captain of the hockey team. and the other's from … the senior class president … Why, what's the matter, Rev'ren'? Is there sumpthin' wrong with the kuchen?"

"No, it's fine, but please excuse me, Mrs. Olson - I have to take care of some funeral arrangements." I didn't tell her it was my own.

When I stepped outside, the frigid air revived me. By the time I got to the parsonage, my dizziness had passed. That did it. I wasn't even going to think about Arlene any more.

I walked out to the kitchen and got a tablespoon out of the drawer. The handle, I've always found, is the weapon of choice to open the mail. I was young; I was lonely; I read everything - even the junk mail. There was a post card from my father- he's the only person I've ever known who reinforces his post cards with Scotch tape. "Dear Hijo de mi Alma," which I think means 'son of my soul'. "Package coming under separate cover. Call collect if you don't get it. It is insured. Love, Padre."

Nice of Padre, but it was going to take a power saw and a crowbar to open it. Then I remembered the sharp linoleum knife I had bought when I was browsing around Olson's Hardware. I ran down the steps into the basement and got it out of my tool chest. While I was down there, I checked the furnace. I didn't mind being fireman, but it was rough on white shirts. I often had two or three rings around the collar.

Upstairs again, I began working on the package that made the Gordian knot seem pretty simple. Fortunately I didn't have to untie it - just slice my way through. Then I tore off the paper and opened the cardboard box. There was my old stamp book, *Stamps of the World*. Oh, the hours and pennies I had spent on that. And underneath it, my coin collection. Tears came to my eyes, and I almost didn't see the note. "Between Indian attacks you may need something to do. Maybe you can purchase some wampum from the trading post." I guess a lot of city people don't know what life is like in North Dakota.

Back to the mail. Ah, here was something that looked official as well as personal.

UNIVERSITY OF NORTH DAKOTA
Grand Forks, North Dakota
Office of the President

The Reverend David Rowe
Webber United Methodist Church
Webber, North Dakota

My Dear Mr. Rowe:

On behalf of the All-Campus Religious Council, I would like to invite you to be the keynote speaker at Religious Emphasis Week, December 17-20. Essentially we are asking you to present four messages. Each will be followed by a discussion period, chaired by a student leader.

Please glance over the enclosed draft of the program. We will make whatever adjustments you deem fit.

We regret this short notice, but your Bishop just gave us a last-minute cancellation along with the most glowing recommendation of you.

Please reply as soon as possible.

Thanking you in advance, I am

Yours Sincerely,
Edward Starch
President

I was jubilant - I might bump into Arlene. I was confused - did the bishop have me mixed up with someone else? It didn't matter - I was definitely going.

Before I hit the sack on December 15, I plugged in the headbolt heater to keep my car radiator warm overnight in the subzero temperature. I wanted to make sure that my old Buick would start for my trip to Arlene's college.

On December 16, I woke up thinking that something beautiful was going to happen. What was it? Not Cat Week or Advent but Religious Emphasis Week! Divine Institution. As I shaved I thought my hair looked a little long, so after breakfast I went up to Mad Ole's.

"Hi, Rev'rend. Be with you in a minute."

I took off my coat and hung it on the rack.

In the chair, he had a mummy, its face wrapped in hot towels. Ole picked up his ax, stropped it on a piece of leather, and approached the mummy. A chill went up and down my spine and lingered near the region of my neck. Ole whipped off the towels to disclose Ben, sound asleep. As Mad Ole brought the ax blade closer and closer to Ben's neck, I watched in mute and horrified fascination, powerless to stop him.

The ax touched Ben's neck, miraculously cutting only the hair. After a few moments he shook Ben awake. "All done now."

"Thanks, Ole. Here's $1.00. Keep the change." Ben stretched. "Best sleep I've had in a long time. Hi, Dave. How you doin'?"

"Fine, Ben. I'm leaving town today, but I'll be back before Sunday."

"Where you goin'?"

"To the University of North Dakota."

"Well, say hello to Arlene if you git a chance." He winked.

"Yes, sir."

"Want me to check the furnace while you're gone?"

"Thanks, Ben."

When I got into the chair, Mad Ole asked: "What do you want, Rev'rend? Haircut or shave?"

"Uh, just a haircut." I didn't have Ben's faith, and I didn't dare go to sleep in Mad Ole's chair. After all, he might try to give me a free shave.

When I got home, I picked up Sylvester and carried him across the street to Mrs. Larson's. "Hannah, would you please take care of Sylvester. I'm going to be out of town till Saturday."

"Of course, Rev'rend."

"And would you keep an eye on the parsonage."

"Oh, thank you, Rev'rend." The all-seeing eyes filled up.

Everything was in good hands now.

As I was packing, the phone rang and Ben said, "Just bin listenin' to the forecast. 'Fraid you're due for a bit of weather. Why don'tcha stop over here, and I'll fix you up with some snow tires?"

Ben was a prince.

Before I got away from Ben, I had snow tires, chains in the trunk, more antifreeze in the radiator, and a full tank of gas. Ben even threw a couple of blankets and a box of Hershey bars into the back seat in case I had to spend the night in a ditch. I guess he knew that nothing was going to keep me from starting out.

North Dakota threw everything she had at me. The wind whipped up, and the snow started blowing across the road. Sudden gusts wrapped me in a white shroud. I found myself drifting till I hit the shoulder, and then I angled back, judging where the road was by glimpses of telephone poles and fences.

The wind increased in rate and pitch, carrying with it "snirt," composed of snow and dirt from the plowed fields. A black blizzard. I slowed but still kept going. To Grand Forks. To Arlene.

Traction was good, so I let the speedometer creep up to thirty-five, but then I hit ice. Suddenly I was hurtling sideways. I spun the wheel. The car hit the shoulder and ricocheted back to the other side. Back and forth I went until I finally straightened out at five miles an hour. I stopped until I stopped shaking.

My next skid wasn't so lucky. The Buick wound up nose down in a ditch full of blackened snow. I tried my door, but it was wedged shut. Just as I was reaching across to try the other front door, I heard a tapping at my window. When I wound the window down, I saw it was my old trucker friend.

"I t'ink you need help this time, ya?"

"You're right!"

"Then I hook up chain and pull you out."

"Sounds great."

I heard the clanking of the chain as it was being wrapped around my axle. A few moments later the truck motor roared, and the Buick was slowly pulled out of the ditch.

I opened my door and walked around to the back of the car.

"Thanks a million." I began digging in my pocket for money.

"No need to pay me, young feller. Just help someone else if you gits a chance."

I watched him drive away. He had a good philosophy … and I still had forgotten to ask his name.

An older, wiser pastor would have turned back, but I made it through the blizzard and over the ice to Grand Forks.

When I walked into President Starch's outer office, I saw a slender young secretary with her back to me, machine-gunning a typewriter. She whipped out a page and turned around.

"Ar - Ar - Arlene!"

She gave me a business-like smile, flipped the intercom, and announced: "President Starch, Reverend Rowe is here to see you."

"Arlene, I was hoping to bump into you. I wanted - "

"Come in, come in, Reverend," boomed a hearty voice behind me. I spun around to see President Starch. He put his arm around my shoulders and walked me into his office. "So nice of you to help out at the last minute like this." He pulled a chair closer to his desk. "Sit down, Reverend. Here is the final program - oh, yes, would you care for a cigar?"

"No thanks, I don't smoke." Flustered by his heartiness and Arlene's nearness, I handed him back the program and stuck the cigar in my pocket.

He looked puzzled for a moment, but passed it off as smoothly as a politician, which was what a college president had to be. "Usually we secure the services of an older clergyman, but this time I believe your Bishop has made a good recommendation. It's time we had a younger man someone who could get closer to the student body."

That sounded like a good strategy to me. As if reading my mind, he flipped on the intercom. "Miss Olson, would you please come in now." The door opened, and in walked Arlene, looking very business-like and professional and beautiful. "Reverend Rowe, this is Miss Olson. She is not only my secretary but also chairman of the All-Campus Religious Council. She will conduct you to your room and guide you around campus for the rest of the week - sort of shepherding the shepherd, you might say."

Incredible! I had come to the campus hoping to catch just a glimpse of my beloved, and now it looked as if we were going to be together all the time.

"And now, Reverend, I leave you in the lovely and capable hands of Miss Olson. And don't forget to vote for Proposition 13, Increased Tax Support for State Colleges and Universities."

I nodded dumbly and followed Arlene in a daze. She took her purse out of a drawer and got her coat and boots out of the closet. Was this businesswoman the same kid that had run around camp in shorts? And now that I was with her, what could I say? I followed her out of the office and down the corridor of Old Main. She looked so cool and unapproachable.

"Arlene, I'm - I'm sorry about how I behaved that day."

A couple of students walking with a professor turned and stared at us, and Arlene put her finger to her lips. Silence grew between us till we got outside.

"Where did you park your car, Reverend Rowe?"

"Over there." I pointed down the road toward my old Buick parked in front of the library.

As we came up to my car, I saw a yellow ticket on the windshield. Arlene pulled it off. "I'll take care of that for you. Here, you better put this Visitor's Parking Permit inside your windshield."

She opened the car door and slipped inside. I glimpsed only a minimum of slender calves, but it was enough to make me weak.

After I got into the car, our conversation continued in the same impersonal vein as we drove to the Student Union and as we went up the stairs of the glassy new building. "We have you booked in one of the suites for the visiting dignitaries, number three." She took out a key and unlocked the door. I followed her into the room - I would have followed her into a fiery furnace. And it was almost that: the VIP suite was decorated in Hawaiian Sunburst. She pulled open the drapes to disclose a lovely view of the campus covered by a fresh snow. "This is where President Starch puts those he hopes will come through with a big endowment."

She gave a slight smile as she crossed to sit in a plastic chair. I sat, too. "Now, Reverend Rowe, do you wish to go over the arrangements for Religious Emphasis Week, or would you prefer to rest for awhile?"

"Neither, Miss Olson."

Her eyebrows shot up. "Why are you Miss Olson-ing me?"

"Why are you "Rev-ing me?"

Her cool mask slipped down. "David, why didn't you write?"

"You wanted me to write - after what I did?"

She nodded.

"But when you didn't come home, I thought you didn't want to see me again."

"I've been working two jobs - didn't mother tell you?"

"No, just that you were working the weekend of the seventy-fifth anniversary."

"David, I work every day and every weekend, too. I'm putting myself through school."

"And I was eating my heart out thinking of you enjoying the social life at college. Boy, it sure is lucky this Religious Emphasis Week came up."

"Dear, dense David, who do you think engineered it all?"

"You? You? You!"

"Yes."

At last my body caught up with my mind. I leaped out of the chair and raced toward her. She met me halfway, and we threw our arms around each other.

"Don't you want to hear how I did it?"

"No, all I want to do is kiss you again." This time when she lifted up her face, she didn't look startled. She looked as radiant as she had at the closing campfire. Our lips met in a lingering kiss, a kiss that was a wedding of tears and laughter.

"Arlene, it's been so long." I hugged her and swung her gently from side to side.

"Three months and eleven days."

"It won't happen again, darling. We'll have Religious Emphasis Weeks all year long."

"She stood there, the Queen of Winter and every man's dream ... "
David Rowe

22 Winter Queen (An Engaging Conversation)

Arlene was sitting in an orange plastic chair with her feet tucked up under her like a kitten. "I really didn't know how to get you here until I bumped into the D.S. on campus. Victor is grandfather to Eric the Red and has become quite a hockey buff in his A.D. period."

"A.D.?"

"Yes, After David. All time is marked by your advent."

"Wow!" I started out of my chair, but she held her hand up.

"Please let me finish the story, darling." She looked so beseechingly at me that I collapsed back in my chair with laughter. "Victor is such a kindly man that I asked for his help. He told me that the bishop has the six superintendents take turns running his office while he is out on the road. When it was Victor's turn, he wrote a cancellation for the bishop and a recommendation for you."

"I wondered if the bishop had me confused with someone else."

"Victor's letter - on top of my arguments - persuaded President Starch to ask you. The president runs everything on campus."

"I was beginning to think that you did, cute stuff."

"Just following the Bible - 'to be wise as serpents and innocent as doves.'" (Matthew 10:16)

"Fly over here, dove." She came and sat in my lap.

"David, I have a favor to ask you."

"What do you want me to do? Vote for Proposition 13 or remember the college in my will?"

"No business." She nuzzled her nose against mine. "No, I need a date for the Winter Formal tonight."

"You need a date? How about Eric the Red? How about the senior class president?"

She stiffened. "You want me to go with someone else?"

I pulled her closer. "Never, darling."

"I didn't think so. That's why I put a size 38 dinner jacket in your closet."

I laughed. "You were pretty sure about me, weren't you?" I nibbled her ear.

"Ever since that unexpected kiss. In a way, ever since the first Sunday you came to Webber. You looked so new and lost and helpless."

"I needed a guardian angel - and you came to my rescue."

"And the way that you looked at me!"

That seemed to be a good place to stop for some nonverbal communication, but even kissing can't last forever without breathing. When we paused for a moment of inspiration, she asked, "Then you'll take me to the dance?"

"I think you may consider that last kiss equivalent to a 'yes'."

Arlene jumped up and spun around a few times. "Then I'm off - I have to go make myself beautiful for you."

"That should take no time at all."

"Flatterer."

"Ministers never lie - at least not that time."

"Will you drive me to the dorm?"

"Gladly, sweetheart." I jumped up and did a few dance steps of my own.

"Are you happy, David?"

"Happy? That's too mild a word for it I would say 'jubilant', going on 'ecstatic'."

Reverend Rowe and Miss Olson had come formally up to the room, but a couple of kids skipped out.

When I got back to my room it was 4:30 - not much time left. I grabbed the phone. "Operator, I want to place a collect call to Ben Graves in Webber, North Dakota, number 14-J. I'm calling from 6-W in Grand Forks."

The impersonal voice asked, "Your name, please?"

"David Rowe."

"Thank you."

Almost 180 miles away the phone started ringing and Ben's wonderful Scandinavian-tinged voice came on the line. "Hello, Graves' Service."

"Will you accept a collect call from David Rowe?"

"Ya, of course." He raised his voice. "Dave, are you O.K.? Did you have any trouble with the Buick?"

"No, no trouble. Sorry to call you collect, but I'm broke. In fact, that's why I'm calling you, Ben. Would you do me a big favor?"

At 8:00 that evening I pulled the newly-washed Buick as close as I could to Johnstone Hall. I joined the throng of college boys arriving to pick up their dates. From my vantage point of twenty-five, they looked very young. On the other hand, they must have thought I looked awfully old, because two of them even held the double doors open for me.

A couple of cute coeds manned (really womanned) the telephone desk. One looked up from the list of residents and said, "Do you have some business with the housemother, sir?"

"No." I frowned. It must have been my infernal gray hair, which I started to get when I was sixteen. "I came to pick up Arlene Olson."

The girl blinked and fumbled through her papers in embarrassed confusion, but finally buzzed Arlene's room. "If you'd like to sit down, sir, you can have my chair."

"No thanks, miss. I'm wearing my geriatric shoes and support hose tonight."

Then I noticed a flash of white at the top of the stairs. I looked more closely and so did all the boys. It was Arlene, and she came floating down the stairs in a white cloud.

"You are my angel!" I grabbed the railing to steady myself. Maybe I should have taken that chair.

The boys whistled, sighed, or moaned - their dates forgotten.

I feasted my eyes upon her. She was pure white except for the brown of her hair and eyes and the red of her inviting lips. "Arlene, I didn't see how you could be any more beautiful, but you are!"

She came right up to me, smiling radiantly, and put her finger tips to my lips. "No kisses now, darling. I have to remain somewhat presentable for the coronation. Do you mind, darling?"

"Terribly - you'll have to make it up to me later on."

The girls at the telephone desk were leaning forward, their ears straining and their eyes bulging.

Arlene stepped back. "David, you look so handsome in your white dinner jacket."

"I'm a quick change artist. I can go from black to white, from Sinister Minister to Knight in Shining Armor in seconds."

She laughed. I loved to hear her laugh and to watch her laugh.

We walked to the front door, and she gave me her white lace shawl "Would you please cover my shoulders?"

I eyed her creamy shoulders rising out of her strapless gown. The texts from the Song of Solomon were true. "Yes – but reluctantly."

Then she looked at the slush in front of the dorm and started to extend a thin slipper, but I scooped her up into my arms. "Oh, David, I'm not too heavy for you, am I?"

"Do you even crack 100 pounds?"

"By quite a bit."

"As many as two or three?"

"Seven."

"Obese, I'll probably get a hernia and have to wear a truss for the rest of my life."

"My mother told me never to truss a man." I shook with laughter. "Don't drop me!" she shrieked.

"I think I'll just dump you in that snowdrift over there." She clung more tightly and I melted. "I wish I hadn't promised to postpone kissing."

"Don't worry. Later all you have to do is 'ask and you will receive'." (John 16:24)

"A Biblically sound approach ... and I can think of a good Biblical number."

"What's that?"

"Seventy times seven." (Matthew 18:22)

After I carried her over to my old car, she opened the door, and I set her down on the worn seat. Then I went around and got behind the wheel. "You know, it's a shame to give a rich-looking doll like you a ride in this old clunker. You should be in a Rolls Royce."

"Dave, remember, I'm just a poor country girl, but tonight we can pretend we're rich."

"Why should we pretend when we really are rich? I reached out my hand for hers.

Neither of us realized how rich we were to feel.

The dance was over at my place, that is, the first floor of the Student Union. I drove up the circle drive, let Arlene off, and parked the car. As I walked toward the building, I could see her looking eagerly for me, even though a lot of the college boys were stopping and trying to talk to her. When she spotted me, her smile went on like a beacon, and I smiled back. When I came up to her, she took my arm in a pleasantly possessive way, and we walked into the Union.

There were girls in red dresses and black sheaths and blue gowns, but none to match Arlene, which was why she was going to be crowned Winter Queen. We walked past the check room. "Darling, shall I check your shawl?" I could afford that much.

"No, I better keep it. I feel a little chilly. Besides, if we check it, we'll get caught in a long line at the end."

She had been two jumps ahead of me so far, but maybe tonight I would be able to catch up.

As we walked into the ballroom, a tall, arrogant boy came up and took hold of Arlene's arm.

"I've got to talk to you, Queenie Baby."

She disengaged his arm smoothly and turned to me. "David, this is Rick Bradhurst. He's the M.C. for tonight. Rick, this is David Rowe."

Rick looked at me in a not-too-friendly way and then concentrated on Arlene, but he didn't try to take her arm again. "At 10:00 I want you to come forward for your solo - you can work out the piece with Bob Crosby. Right after that we'll have last year's queen turn her crown over to Eric, and he'll crown you - got that?" She nodded. Then Rick glanced at me. "Nice meeting you, Old Man." As he spun quickly around and started toward the bandstand, other students fell back out of his way.

Feeling a little blue, I said, "Who was that - one of your old flames?"

"Don't be jealous, darling. He can't hold a candle to you."

The music starred a good band out of Minneapolis, directed by special guest Bob Crosby. I'm not a good dancer, but Arlene was so light and supple in my arms, and I was feeling so high that I'm not sure we even touched ground. "Dave," she whispered against my shoulder, "you dance divinely."

I laughed, and she looked up at me curiously. "Remember the first Sunday," I said, "when Miss Osgood came in wearing the terrible turban with the pink sequins? Well, she looked like the mirrored globe at the Stardust Ballroom in Chicago. That's where I learned to totter around the floor a little."

"Umm, I think we're floating, and I don't want to do anything else except dance with you."

Gradually I became aware that everyone was looking at us. "Sweetheart," I whispered."

"Umm," she murmured dreamily as we kept twirling and floating.

"I hate to tell you this, but the music has stopped."

"Oh," she opened her eyes, embarrassment bringing a soft pink to her cameo features. "Well, now that I'm back on earth, I suppose I should go see Mr. Crosby about the solo. Would you excuse me, darling?"

"Sure, but come back soon." She nodded and rustled her way toward the bandstand. I took the opportunity to dart into the men's room and was in one of the little confessional booths when I overheard some fellows talking.

"Did you see the old guy Arlene Olson was with?"

"Yeah, if I'd known she liked gray hair, I would have dyed mine."

I smiled to myself. I had always hated my gray hair, but maybe it wasn't so bad after all. As I walked out of the booth, I said, "Good evening, boys. Isn't it past your bedtime?" I whipped out my comb and ran it through my gray hair while I watched their red faces in the mirror. One of life's little triumphs.

Back on the floor, I could see Arlene talking to Bob Crosby until something like a wall blocked my view of her. I looked up at a pair of broad shoulders topped by a freckled head with a shock of red hair. I knew immediately who it was. "Eric the Red."

"Ya, and you must be The Silver Fox." A pair of powerful arms grabbed me and lifted me from the floor. I was helpless in the clutches of another angry flame. When I despaired of ever seeing Arlene again, Eric let go of me, and I tottered weakly on unsteady legs. "It's good to meet you, Rev'ren'. Grampa's told me all about you. You've caused quite a change in 'im." Luckily this Viking was friendly, for I had no desire to enter Valhalla yet.

"Oh, ya," Eric said, "I was real mad at first, but who could stay mad at Arlene and the Rev'ren' that saved Grampa?" He pounded me on the back like a friendly bear.

I tried to dodge the blows. "Eric, my big friend, I have a favor to ask you. First, would you please stop dislocating my spine, and, second, would you ..."

When I had finished talking to Eric, I saw Arlene making her way toward me. "Oh, David, now that I have business out of the way, we can dance till 10:00." She came into my arms again and we floated away.

I don't know where that hour went, but suddenly we heard the commanding tones of Rick Bradhurst, the M.C. "All right, roosters, put those slick chicks down and gather round for some music by the most beautiful girl on campus, none other than our own Arlene Olson."

Arlene and I slipped through the crowd to the bandstand. Rick offered Arlene his hand to help her up on the platform, but Arlene seemed not to notice it as she stepped lightly up. She stood there, the Queen of Winter and every man's dream, as fresh and pure as the new snow covering the campus. Then the soft strains of the melody began as Arlene introduced the song: "Here it is midwinter and we're cold, especially we girls in our thin gowns, so let's turn our thoughts for a moment to ... (she started singing) 'Summertime and the livin' is easy; Fish are jumpin' and the cotton is high.'"[5] Her melodious voice filled the ballroom, and her humor made everyone warm on that winter night, especially the one who knew she wasn't all ice.

Bob Crosby moved over to the mike. "Thank you, Miss Olson. I've never felt so warm and so cold as I have tonight. If you ever want to take your lovely voice out on the road, just let me know."

Even the M.C. seemed to have been softened a bit by Arlene, for his voice now lacked some of his barker loudness. "Will Miss Lila Larson, the reigning Winter Queen, please come forward." A big Valkyrie jumped clumsily up on the platform: "And now, I call upon the captain of the hockey team to perform his traditional duty."

Eric jumped up beside Miss Larson - the Valkyrie and the Viking looked like a good match. Eric then removed the silver tiara from his date, and put it on Arlene's delicate head. The crowd cheered as the M.C. announced, "Now I present this year's Winter Queen, Arlene Olson." The predominant timbre to the cheers was baritone - none louder than mine. Arlene smiled directly into my eyes and then came down from the platform right into my arms.

"Darling, I'm back."

"Congratulations, Arlene. I've never danced with a Queen before. Now you are both Queen and Angel."

"Don't put me back up on a pedestal, David. Would you rather worship me from afar or have me up close like this?"

"There's no comparison, sweetheart." I held her even closer. "Let's go somewhere where we can ... talk."

"O.K., darling, now is the 'later' I promised."

As we tried to dance off the floor, couples kept blocking our way and congratulating Arlene. Finally we reached our destination, the doors to the balcony, but blocking the doors was the complete hockey team, a defensive line that no one had been able to score against for the last two seasons. Eric the Red stepped forward, and Arlene trembled. He tried to lower his bull voice to a whisper, which was probably heard only on the nearer parking lots. "I held the balcony for you, Rev'ren', and here's the bag that just come. I had the team watchin' all the doors just like you wanted." He looked at me as eager to please as a puppy. "Did I do O.K.?"

"Well done, good and faithful servant. If you ever want someone to tie a free knot, just call on me."

"Thanks, Rev'ren'." He beamed as he opened the doors for us. Then he turned to the hockey team. "They're prob'ly gonna talk 'bout Religious Em - Empha - oh, nuts - Religious Week." I heard no laughter from the team - he had them under complete control.

As we stepped onto the balcony, the chill Dakota wind whipped snow around the corner of the building into our faces. Arlene shivered and drew her shawl around her bare shoulders. "I'm cold, David. Put your warm arms around me."

I needed no second invitation. She felt so soft and nubile. "May I kiss the Queen?"

"Permission gladly granted."

Our lips joined in the freshness of newly-found love, in a kiss that was both promise and fulfillment. Her lips were soft and sweet, and they responded to my yearning with their own unspoken message. Love was the theme of our unsung song.

"David, does this give you any ideas?"

"Unministerial ideas."

"I mean *permanent* ideas."

"You mean like - like being yoked together? Like - like being co-laborers in God's vineyard?"

"You're babbling again, Reverend. Don't you think I'd make a good minister's wife?"

"Yes, but the problem would be to find a good minister."

"I think I've found one."

"Thanks, Sweet. I thought you might think that way, so I want to give you this." I handed her the brown bag. "I haven't seen it yet myself - it just came from Webber."

"Whatever could this be?" She opened the bag with her graceful hands and took out a little package wrapped in silver. After she gave me a look composed of curiosity and disbelief, her quick hands soon had the paper off to disclose a tiny box. When she opened the lid, there was a flash of cold fire. She gasped as she looked at the diamond ring.

"I thought the Winter Queen might like a piece of ice."

"David, I don't know what to say."

"Just say 'yes'."

She threw her arms around my neck. "Oh, yes, darling David, yes, a thousand times yes." And then she drew back. "But you haven't told me yet that you loved me."

"I thought my lips had been saying that all day. Yes, I do love you, and I have loved you, and I will love you - forever."

She came back into my arms. "David, I love you - you'll never know how much."

I was filled with the scent of her and the sound of her and the sight of her and the feel of her and the taste of her. "I think I know. Here, let me slip the ring on your finger."

"That's the only reason that will make me let go of you."

She handed me the tiny box, and I picked up the ring, which reflected the light from the ballroom, the moon, and a million of God's stars. "Now hold out your left hand." I slid the ring on her slender finger. It fit perfectly, but then it had come from Olson Jewelry, her uncle's store. "Now we are engaged, Angel."

"Yippee!" she cried.

"That's a very unqueenly thing to say."

"I don't care - I'm so happy; I couldn't be happier."

"I couldn't either."

But we were both wrong.

When I took her hand, the tiny box dropped in the snow, and as I bent over to pick it up, I saw a small piece of paper. "Look, Angel, there's a note." We read it in the light that filtered through the ballroom curtains.

"Dear Arlene and David, don't worry about paying for this ring - it's all taken care of. Please accept it as a gift from people who love you very much. Love, Ben and Birdie."

I was surprised and touched. "Angel, I called Ben this afternoon and asked him to go to the jeweler's and arrange for something modest on time payments. I never dreamed -"

"Modest! You could work all your life and never afford a ring like that."

"What do you think, Angel? Should we accept it?"

"I think we should, darling. I think it would make Ben and Birdie very happy - almost as happy as we are."

"My prayer for a warm reception must have finally worked its way up through rank upon rank of angels clear to the Almighty's desk." David Rowe

23 Blest Be the Tie That Binds

I woke up in a dazzle of Hawaiian Sunburst, closed my eyes again, and tried to remember where I was: University ... Arlene ... Religious Emphasis Week ... Arlene ... Arlene ... Arlene. The phone rang me out of my second dream. I fumbled for the receiver.

"Hello?" I mumbled.

"Good morning, darling." Her words poured through the wires like a warm fragrance and flowed up my aural nerve into my brain. "Sorry to wake you up, David," said a delicious alto, "but you're due to give your first message in an hour."

"Arlene! Did yesterday really happen?"

I heard her throaty chuckle. "Yes, David, I'm looking at the biggest, most beautiful diamond that has ever appeared on this campus. Thank you, darling."

"Oh, good! For a moment I thought it was all a dream."

"It is a dream, Dave. Can you meet me in the coffee shop downstairs in half an hour?"

"Yes, I'll be there; I can hardly wait to see you. Goodbye, my fiancée."

"It feels good to be called that - see you soon."

Usually I'm pretty slow in the morning, but that morning I shaved and dressed in minutes and was in the coffee shop when she walked in. She was dressed in a brown sweater and skirt, and she was beauty in motion. Her smile was incandescent as she came into my arms and gave me a warm kiss.

"Are you ever a knockout!" I said. "But did I notice you dragging your left arm?"

"Oh, yes, darling, from the weight. Just look at that sparkler."

I looked; the bus boys looked; all the students in the coffee shop looked; and even the cooks came out of the kitchen. The consensus was that it was a gorgeous ring. I agreed, but had to tell the truth: "It's nothing compared to your smile."

That made her smile even brighter. "Thank you, my fiancé."

Suddenly President Starch's head poked in between us. He whipped out his reading glasses and examined the ring.

"Reverend, you certainly did get close to the student body - and very quickly, too. That's quite a rock you have there. Hmm, the rural pastorate must be paying more these days. Why don't you stop by the office so we can discuss an endowment program?"

Arlene glanced at her watch. "Excuse us, President Starch, but we had better be going into the ballroom. It's almost time to start."

We had a glorious four days. The hockey team with their girlfriends and Arlene's dorm with their boyfriends formed a nucleus which grew every day. Word spread to come and see "The Silver Fox who trapped our Winter Queen." Those who came were caught up in our happiness; they stayed to share our joy.

President Starch was so pleased with the attendance and the response of the students that he gave Arlene the weekend off. On Saturday we left for Webber, the first time Arlene had been home since early September.

Just before we left Grand Forks, we saw a Highway Patrol car blocking the turn onto Highway 2. The patrolman came up to my window. "Good morning, folks. The highway is clear of snow and ice all the way to Williston, so you'll have to remove your chains. There's a crew of University students who will help you. Just pull over to the side."

We pulled over and Eric the Red came up to the window. "Hi, Rev'rend Rowe. Hi, Queen Arlene. Just let me borrow your trunk key and we'll have your chains off in no time."

"I'll jack up the car for you," I said.

"No, just set still, Rev'rend. We don't need no jack. We just lift the car." He pointed to the hockey team.

In five minutes, the hockey team removed the chains, threw them into the trunk, and waved us good-bye.

Arlene slept all the way on my shoulder, tired out from the exciting week. It felt very good to have her there.

It was a beautiful day in December; the snow had started melting and the air felt as balmy as spring. Mile after mile of the wonderful open prairie rolled by, and I was getting sleepy myself - when suddenly I was brought fully awake by a siren. Arlene sat up abruptly as I brought the old Buick to a halt. Behind us a police car was flashing its lights. Through the mirror I saw the door open and a huge shape come lumbering toward us. I turned to Arlene, "It's the sheriff."

"What happened, Dave? Were you speeding?"

"No, I don't know what's the matter."

The sheriff came up to our window. "Morning, Rev'rend. Mornin', Arlene. Sure glad I caught you."

I was puzzled. "What's up, Fred? Why did you stop us?" Arlene leaned toward me and the sheriff. "Yes, why?"

"Well, now, I can't rightly say. I just have my orders to hold you here for a little while." He turned, waddled back to his car, and got back in. We could hear the loud static of the police radio: "Checkpoint Able calling Checkpoint Charlie. I've got 'em and I'll hold 'em till you git here. Ten-four."

"What in the world is going on?" Arlene asked.

"Beat's me, Hon. I guess we'll just have to wait and see."

In a few minutes a car appeared on the horizon. It was unusual looking, a foreign car, and it had two occupants. When the car stopped on the other side of the highway, I could see the nameplate, Rolls Royce. A woman in a calico dress and a head scarf got out of the car and started toward us. "Why, it's Aunt Ellie!" I opened the door and hopped out.

Aunt Ellie threw her arms around me and cried, "Davy-boy, how are you?"

"Just great - when did you get back?"

"The day before yesterday, but I'll tell you all about our trip later. First I have to meet your fiancée."

"How did you know about that?"

"Don't you know it's a capital offense to keep a secret in Webber?"

"Arlene, come over here and meet my wackiest relative."

Arlene came uncertainly around the car. "Arlene, this is my Aunt Eleanor."

Aunt Ellie engulfed her in a warm embrace. "You have all my sympathy, wanting to marry into our crazy clan." And then Ellie pointed to the driver of the Rolls Royce, improbably dressed in bib overalls. "Arlene, you know Charles, of course."

Arlene's eyes grew large. "Mr. Barrett?"

Charles got out of the Rolls Royce, bowed, and kissed her hand. "May I extend to you all my felicitations upon your engagement? Now

I will attempt to counteract the bad publicity you have been hearing recently. It is indeed a very good clan to join."

"Why thank you, Chubby Hubby. Davy, how do you like Charles's bib overalls? They're custom-made by Huntsman's of London, the only pair they ever made."

"Amazing!"

"But she hasn't completely reformed me." Charles unbuttoned his expensive work shirt to disclose the orange and black of his old Princeton tie.

"Yes," said Aunt Ellie, "the rascal *always* wears that tie - no matter what he's doing."

"Tut, tut, my dear." Charles held his finger to his lips. "They are not married yet, you know."

"Charles's highest virtue is discretion."

"Quite right, my dear. Now we would be most appreciative if you young people would give us a ride to town."

"You would rather ride in my old Buick than your Rolls Royce?" I asked him.

"Wouldn't anyone?"

I turned and called back to the sheriff. "Fred, may we go now?" He nodded. As we piled into the Buick, I saw Alf Langdon get out of Fred's car and get into the Rolls. Things were getting curiouser and curiouser.

"What's going on, Charles?"

"You need no longer call me Charles. Now that we are almost related you may call me 'Chuck'."

"Ch – Ch - Chuck?"

"Yes, David, you must learn to drop that ministerial dignity and unbend a little."

I rolled my eyes at Arlene. "O.K., Chuck, we're off."

The police car and the Rolls Royce fell in behind us, making a strange procession, which looked like the history of transportation.

I looked at Aunt Eleanor in the rear view mirror. "Ellie, I didn't know you had freckles."

"I thought that if Charles was going country, so would I. You can't imagine how long it took for me to put these on."

"Oh, look!" said Arlene. "Webber is already decorated for Christmas."

First we saw the greenery which had been wound around the telephone poles and strung across the street, and then we saw two big white banners: WELCOME BACK CHARLES AND ELEANOR followed by CONGRATULATIONS ARLENE AND DAVID. When we looked down, we were surprised to see that the street was lined with people. They were all beaming and waving to us. The Yonsons, the entire clan of towheads including the ninety-one-year-old patriarch with his foul pipe, were standing on the back of their truck. Martha and Lars Olson, the retired pastor and his wife, called out, "Welcome back, dear ones." The Bird Sisters were twittering with excitement. The two doctors stood together, the tiny white man and the black giant. And, as a backdrop to the entire populace of Webber, the store windows were plastered with signs: ROWE DAY SPECIALS, BARRETT BARGAINS, and OLSON GIVE-AWAYS.

What a contrast to my advent six months before. I had come like a pioneer to Webber with only a cat for company, and now - I reached out and squeezed Arlene's hand. My prayer for a warm reception must have finally worked its way up through rank upon rank of angels clear to the Almighty's desk.

The sheriff's car pulled ahead of us and stopped, so I had to stop behind him. Then the crowd opened up, and from a side street came the high school band led by the blind Miss Osgood in pink top, pink tights, pink boots, and, of course, the pink turban - the oldest drum majorette in the world. She marched into the Buick, backed off, bumped into the police car, and groped her way around it. The band, apparently used to the unsteady movement of their blind-guide, followed behind, as did the three cars. Every now and then Miss Osgood would blunder into the crowd, but someone would point her in the right direction, and off she would go again. Arlene was waving out the window to the pleased onlookers when Ellie asked, "How did Ben get ahold of the Hope Diamond?"

Arlene looked back at Ellie. "It's a lovely ring from a lovely man."

"Hey," I said, "don't I count too?"

"I meant you, David." Arlene slid over and kissed me, and the crowd cheered.

Charles spoke: "I've never seen the inhabitants so warm. By Jove, you've defrosted God's frozen people!"

"Well, perhaps I did have a hand in weaning you away from bachelorhood and suits, but I think that the credit should go to Ellie."

"Davy, I never would have come to Webber if you hadn't been here."

"Yes," said Charles, "and you would have missed the thrill of your sheltered life."

In the mirror I saw Ellie slide over to Charles. "You're right, Snookums." Charles turned red under the eyes of the crowd.

I was still musing. "Well, maybe I did help bring Hannah Larson out of seclusion ..."

The editor came up to the window and handed Arlene a paper. Arlene gasped. "And according to this, you saved me from a fate worse than death." She held up the newspaper. There, in seventy-two-point Roman, was the headline: OLD MAID SNARES PREACHER. She took the paper back. "That's something for my scrapbook. And, look, at the bottom of the column the editor has thrown in one of his slogans: 'Watch Webber Grow'."

"I'll hold you to that, Angel."

Instead of turning by the dairy corner, we continued into the next block past Mad Ole's shop, Busia Kowalski's grocery, and the fire hall. Busia pushed her way through the crowd and handed Arlene a grease-stained package. "For you and the Father." Her old eyes blinked. The prospect of a "priest" getting married seemed to put a severe strain on her theology.

I glanced across the street at Ben's station, but it was deserted. Where was Ben?

The parade bumped over the railroad tracks, made a U-turn around Seter's Elevator, and came back down Main Street. I could hear Ellie telling Arlene what a great gourmet Charles was. "Why, Charles eats everything: frog's legs, chocolate-covered grasshoppers, whale steak - even squid."

My heart sank as I saw the Rowlands. They took up almost the entire block, and each one was holding a glass jar. I was afraid I knew the destination of all those jars. As the Rowlands started toward my car, I received another inspiration. "Thanks, Rowlands. Just put them in the Rolls Royce, the next car back."

"What?" asked Charles?

"Arlene and I have the sausage, so it's only fair that we share some food with you."

"Ulp - not their infamous Small Game Preserves!"

"But, Charles," Ellie laughed, "I thought you weren't afraid to eat anything."

We were laughing as we turned the corner by the dairy and came in sight of the Lutheran parsonage. Rolf and Debbie (who was noticeably rounder) were standing on their little porch. They waved and pointed to their outdoor bulletin board: MARTIN LUTHER SENDS HIS GREETINGS.

And across the street, someone had changed our Methodist bulletin board to read: BROTHER BERDAHL SENDS HIS GREETINGS TOO.

Now we were going by the parsonage, and I looked over at Mrs. Larson's, the cat sitter. She was standing in her doorway and holding Sylvester. When I started whistling "Chicago," Sylvester streaked out of her arms to the Buick, jumped on the hood, and made an eighteen-claw landing on the roof of the car. Another roar went up from the crowd, who had been following our leisurely progress.

Hannah came up to the car, and waved a bunch of newspapers. "Welcome back, Rev'ren'. I bought a bunch of 'em."

I thought back to our passage down Main Street. A lot of people had been holding similar-looking papers.

"All right, Charles. What's going on?"

"Well ..." He cleared his throat.

"Go ahead and tell him, Chubby Hubby."

"Please, Mr. Barrett." Arlene looked at him with beseeching dark eyes that would have melted a snowman.

"Um, I guess that it would be all right to tell them now. Yesterday I was in Mad Ole's shop - do you realize that he gives the best shaves in the world? It must be the weight of the ax that - "

I squeezed the steering wheel. "The story, Charles. The story.

"Oh, yes. Well, I was in the chair with a hot towel on my face so I suppose they didn't know it was me."

"It was I," Ellie corrected.

"When I'm wearing bib overalls, I speak the vernacular."

"Oh, Charles!" exclaimed Ellie.

"David, it seems that after you called Ben about the ring he went right to work and called an emergency meeting of the Coffee Gang at the cafe. They considered various schemes to raise money for the ring. Sitting as the Volunteer Fire Department, they voted to raise the rent on the Library. Sitting as the Library Board, they voted to have two fund-raising events a year, comparable in magnitude to the grand opening. Lastly, sitting as the Town Council, they voted to raise the city's debt limit and to put out a special bond issue called The Bonds of Matrimony."

I tried to say something but my throat tightened up.

As we were approaching the courthouse, Arlene cried, "Look!" The lawn was covered with trestle tables, and the tables were covered with food. On each table was a steaming coffee urn. Some ladies straightened up and turned toward us: Arlene's mother, Birdie, and Mrs. Grundy.

My attention was caught by a group on the speaker's stand. It was the rest of the Coffee Gang: Ben, Frank, Carl, Curt, and Mad Ole. Fred and Alf slipped out of their cars and headed toward the other members of the gang. Also on the speaker's stand stood Victor and Miriam, beaming proudly. Next to them was the person I was going to ask to be my best man, Ron Wright. "Arlene, do you see what I see?"

"I think so - I see some members of our wedding party. I would like Ben to give me away – he's been like a father to me since dad died, and I suppose you'll want Victor to perform the ceremony and Ron to be best man."

"Right, darling."

"You're quite a catalyst, David." Charles gulped and clapped me on the shoulder. "In six months you have transformed an entire community."

From somewhere came a torrent of rain completely obscuring the windshield. I turned to Arlene but couldn't see her either.

"Does anyone have a spare handkerchief or some Kleenex?"

There were muffed sobs from the other occupants of the car. Charles was handing me something and muttering, "'Greater love hath no man than this' - here." (John 15:13 KJV)

I grabbed what he gave me and started wiping my eyes and blowing my nose. Then I noticed that the cloth was orange and black. "Thank you, Chuck. This must be the tie that binds our hearts in Christian love!"

"Therefore a man leaves his father and mother and cleaves to his wife, and they become one flesh." Genesis 2:24

24 The Wedding

The next six months were busy with snow storms, church events, and frequent visits to see Arlene at the university. And then the day came for our wedding on the courthouse lawn, there being no church in Webber big enough to hold the wedding and reception.

I arose early – excited about my wedding day – and walked over to the bandstand around 6:00 a.m. on June 15. Clad only in jeans and a short-sleeved shirt, I looked out at the courthouse grounds. Rows of folding chairs had been set up already, with a few pews from the courtroom in front. Back behind the chairs were empty trestle tables. Everything was supposed to be ready by 2:00 p.m.

A bicycle swished by, powered by a girl in shorts with unmistakable legs. I let out a wolf whistle, and she slammed on her brakes and pedaled back.

"You're up pretty early?" I said.

"I'm excited – today's my wedding day!"

"That's a coincidence; it's mine, too. Are you happy?"

"Delirious!" Arlene leaned her bike against the bandstand, ran up the steps, and kissed me. "I shouldn't have done that. It's bad luck for the groom to see the bride before the wedding."

"That's an old superstition from the days of arranged marriages. If the groom saw the bride – for the first time - before the ceremony, he might jump on a fast camel and head out of town."

"But I'd catch you on my bike." We kissed again. "David, this is an arranged marriage – arranged by me."

"Arranged by us."

That called for some serious kissing – until we were interrupted by the blast of a car horn.

Arlene looked over at the street. "What is that strange looking car?"

"It's my parents in their Duesenberg Phaeton!"

I grabbed Arlene's hand and we ran over to the road. "Welcome to Webber, dad and mom. May I present my bride-to-be, Arlene Olson?"

"I'm so glad to meet you," said mother as she got out of the car and hugged Arlene. Mother was dressed in a simple flowered housedress and father was dressed in his torn bathrobe.

"It's wonderful to finally meet you, Mrs. Rowe and Professor Rowe.

"I am pleased to meet you, Miss Olson," said my father, "but I am astounded by your youth. What is the minimum age for marriage in this frontier state – about 16?"

Both Arlene and I laughed, and she said: "Thank you, Professor, for a compliment, but – according to the newspaper - I'm an old maid of 21."

"Yes, dad, she just graduated from the University of North Dakota."

"You mean there is a university out here on the frontier."

"Yes," replied Arlene, with a twinkle in her eye, "since 1883."

"Zounds! Will wonders never cease? Your university is almost as old as Northwestern."

"Mother, you surprised me. I thought that you were coming by train."

"That's what I would have preferred, but your father insisted that we take the old Duesenberg out for this great occasion, and he drove every inch of the way."

"I'm amazed at you, father!"

"You're my beloved son, with whom I am well pleased." (Matthew 3:17)

"That calls for a hug."

He shuffled backwards. "No, you'll raise dust out of the bathrobe, not to mention millions of germs."

I sighed. "Same old dad."

Arlene covered the embarrassing moment. "That's a beauty of a car you have there and it's such a lovely red."

"My father left this to me as his sole legacy. It's a 1935 Duesenberg Model SJ La Grande Dual Cowl Phaeton or Duesy, for short."

"Wow! You've taken very good care of it," said Arlene.

"Before I forget it," said mother, "your brother sends his regrets. He's tied up with so many tax return problems."

"Mom and dad, let's go over to the parsonage while Arlene makes herself beautiful."

My father bowed to the fair Arlene. "That should take her no more than five minutes."

"Thank you, Professor, but it's going to take much longer than that."

"Just so you're back by 2:00 p.m.," I said with mock severity. "Don't race out of town on your bike."

****

It took several hours for my folks to have breakfast and change their clothes. Mother put on a long blue gown and father was forced into a new suit. After a quick lunch, I slipped into my tuxedo, packed my folks into my car, and returned to the courthouse grounds. I directed my folks over to the last row of chairs and introduced them to some of the near-by residents, including Lars and Martha Olson, the couple who had served my church during the Great Depression. "Wait here – one of the ushers will seat you in front just before the ceremony."

Then I went into the band shell and looked over the crowd. Everyone in Webber was there - except for the wedding party! I glanced at my watch - it was now 1:47. How could we get everything ready for a 2:00 p.m. wedding?

And then things started to happen.

A VW bus raced up and disgorged Ron Wright, my best man, and his wife Dottie. Ron carried his oldest girl up to me. "Beth is so sad that she broke her leg and can't serve as flower girl."

"Alf," I called to our fire chief. "See what you can do to help this poor flower girl."

"O.K., Rev, I'm on it." He picked up Beth. "How'd you like to ride in the fire truck?" She squealed as he carried her toward the truck. I lost sight of them in the melee.

Ron and Dottie joined me up in the band shell.

Next to arrive were Victor Hanson, our District Superintendent, and his wife Miriam. Mad Ole had met them at the airport and driven them to the courthouse. They hurried over to the band shell, and Mad Ole rushed back to his car. I turned to my friends and said. "I don't think that everything will come together by two o'clock."

"Don't worry, Dave. It'll happen when it happens," said Victor.

Just then I spied my dear Lutheran friends. "Rolf and Deborah, can you come up here?" They joined us in the band shell. After introducing them to the Wrights and the Hansons, I apologized to Rolf.

"I meant to ask you before, but would you please read the scripture today."

"I'd love to," said Rolf. Then he turned to the Wrights and the Hansons. "David saved my marriage."

"Our marriage," added Deborah, clutching Rolf's arm.

Victor said, "David saved my life, my ministry, and my marriage."

"Amen!" said Miriam Hanson.

We wound up in a group hug until Mrs. Hanson suggested that all the ladies go down and find a place to sit together.

Ben, in a new Ford, drove up with Arlene, her mother, and her brothers, George and Teddy. They stayed in the car, awaiting the processional music. I waved to them and Arlene waved back.

Charles Barrett drove up in his Rolls Royce and parked behind Ben's car. He and Aunt Ellie also stayed in their car.

Mr. Yonson and his father had carried the old pump organ out of our church, put it in their truck, and driven over to the band shell. Now they carried the organ into the band shell. Then the elder Yonson led Miss Osgood to the organ. As she began playing a prelude, the citizens of Webber surged forward to find suitable chairs.

I beckoned to the people in Ben's and Charles's cars to get in their places. Victor, Ron, and Rolf were in the band shell with me. Fortunately the low railing provided the audience with a good view of the ceremony.

Arlene's mother was ushered to her seat by Mayor Lysne, and Curt Winter ushered my parents to the opposite pew.

Arlene and Aunt Ellie (her matron of honor) were now standing at the back of the crowd as Miss Osgood swung into the processional. There was a delay, while they looked up into a tree. Suddenly the flower girl swung from the trees in a basket - thanks to Alf's ingenuity - and dropped flower petals down the center aisle. Then Aunt Ellie started down the aisle, followed by my lovely bride on Ben's arm.

Victor led us smoothly through the wedding ceremony until he came to the sentence: "If anyone has any reason why Arlene and David should not be joined together in the holy estate of matrimony, may he speak now or forever hold his peace."

The tall, distinguished principal of the consolidated school stood up and said: "I speak for all the men and boys in this community who secretly have wanted to marry Arlene Olson. We have seen her blossom like a beautiful flower."

"Hear ye, hear ye!" chorused a rumble of masculine voices.

"Nevertheless," continued the principal, "if Arlene wants to marry someone else, we're glad it's Rev'rend Rowe."

"Amen, amen!" chorused the men.

Arlene bowed her head as red suffused her creamy complexion.

The rest of the service went without incident until Victor came to the questions for Arlene. "Wilt thou have this man to be thy wedded husband, to live together in the holy estate of matrimony? Wilt thou love him, comfort him, honor and keep him, in sickness and in health; and forsaking all others keep thee only to him, so long as ye both shall live?"

"No," replied Arlene, a frown creasing her unlined forehead.

"No?" I looked puzzledly at her.

"No?" Victor lowered the hymnal.

"No" echoed throughout the crowd.

"NO!" shouted Mr. Yonson.

His father looked up at him. "YOU MEAN I WASHED MY OVERALLS FOR NOTHING'."

"I'm sorry, David," said Arlene. "I just didn't have time to tell you. Victor, can we change that last line from 'so long as ye both shall live' to 'forever'"?

"Why, certainly you can - if it's all right with David," said Victor.

"I second the motion," I replied, grinning at Arlene.

"Then I say a definite yes!" said Arlene.

"Make that a forever yes for me, too," I added.

The crowd gave a collective sigh of relief.

The rest of the ceremony flew by until Victor pronounced us husband and wife and I got to kiss my bride. Then the audience stood and clapped as we made our way down the aisle to form a reception line behind the chairs.

When Charles Barrett came through the line, I asked him, "Don't you think that Arlene is the most beautiful bride you have ever seen?"

"Well, David, I would have to say that Arlene is the second most beautiful bride." Charles took Ellie's arm. "Your aunt is the most beautiful bride."

"Why, Charles, you old flatterer," said Eleanor. "I'll give you a double portion of dog food tonight."

"In that case, I had better load up with the finest cooking in Webber."

My folks came through the reception line, my father keeping his hands clasped behind his back for fear of germs. "Mom and dad, I know that you always wanted a daughter, so now I have given you one."

Arlene hugged my mother and gave my father a kiss on the cheek.

I glanced at my father in alarm, but he said, "It's all right, son - I can gargle with Listerine." He pulled out a bottle from his pocket and took a swallow. Then he pulled me aside and whispered, "I see that your car is all painted up – please take the Duesenberg on your honeymoon - see I went to the parsonage and drove it over. Mother and I can stay in the parsonage while you are gone, and I can study the frontier dialect."

"Thank you, father."

I whispered to Arlene: "Dad is lending us the Duesy for our honeymoon."

"Oh, good, that will take the spotlight off me."

After people passed through the reception line, they walked over to the trestle tables, which were loaded with even more food than in December. Mrs. Grundy, Hannah Larson, and Birdie led an army of Jewish Mothers who had outdone themselves. No finger food today but stick-to-your-ribs fare: turkeys, chickens, beef, and pork - even a table laden with Small Game Preserves, which was manned proudly by Mr. and Mrs. Rowland. Next to them stood a freezer full of B.K.P.S. and a grill where Busia Kowalski could cook her famous sausage.

Then we got down to some serious eating, a mid-west orgy of food and non-alcoholic drink, although I did see the Coffee Gang passing around a bottle in a brown paper bag. I didn't need that to get high.

Everyone wanted to talk to us and give gifts to us and hug us, so we were trapped there for hours and hours. I was getting more and more frustrated. "Arlene," I whispered, "let's get going."

"In a minute, dear."

Another dozen people came up to wish us well.

"Arlene, let's go."

"Soon, dear."

Finally I picked her up and ran toward the Duesenberg.

"Someone's kidnapping the bride!"

"No cause for alarm," called out Ben. "It's just the Rev'rend hurrying his bride off on their honeymoon."

I carried Arlene to dad's car and put her gently down on the front seat. "Now I've finally got you to myself."

"And I have you…forever."

Epilogue

Arlene snuggled against me in our queen-sized bed. "Wake up, dear. It's our anniversary."

"Is it our tenth?" I asked. We always go through this pleasant ritual on our decade anniversaries.

"No, that's when we had our last child.

"Is it our twentieth?" I asked.

"No, that's when we moved to Baltimore."

"Is it our thirtieth?"

"No, that's when our first grandchild was born."

"Is it our fortieth?"

"No, that's when we went to Bermuda."

"Is it our fiftieth?"

"No, that's when our first great-grandchild was born and when we took the whole family to Willow Valley Resort."

"Is it our sixtieth?"

"Yes, and grandson # 1 will come to take us to the celebration."

"Well, I better get up and get ready," I said.

"No rush - let's just snuggle for awhile," said Arlene.

"Sounds good to me."

End Notes

[1] "Popcorn Blizzard" appeared on page 628 in *A Treasury of American Folklore,* edited by B. A. Botkin, New York: American Legacy Press, copyright 1944 (See notes on page 626 of the above book for earlier sources of the story.)

[2] "May the Lord go with you—down the side aisles," written by Robert Hale; copyright 1969 by The Methodist Publishing House. First published in the August 1969 issue of *Together.*

[3] "I finally got tired of these rocks," copyright 1972 by Robert Hale (Robert Lathrop Hale, Sr.); first published in the April 30, 1972 issue of *Sunday Digest.*

[4] "Five Fighting Fingers," copyright 1973 by Robert Hale (Robert Lathrop Hale, Sr.). First Published in the September-October 1973 issue of *Alive Now,* a publication of the United Methodist Publishing House. (At a summer camp, an Asian student told this story, which I revised for *Alive Now* and again for my book, *Jesus and His Friends.* The original story probably comes from one of the Eastern religions.)

[5] "Summertime" lyrics by DuBose Heyward and Ira Gershwin, music by George Gershwin, from *Porgy and Bess,* Gershwin Publishing Corporation, 1935